LORD LANSBURY'S CHRISTMAS WEDDING

Helen Dickson

MILLS & BOON

First published in Great Britain 2015
By Mills & Boon, an imprint of HarperCollins*Publishers*
1 London Bridge Street, London, SE1 9GF

Large Print edition 2016

ISBN: 978-0-263-26289-6

Our policy is to use papers that are natural, renewable and recyclable products and made from wood grown in sustainable forests. The logging and manufacturing processes conform to the legal environmental regulations of the country of origin.

Printed and bound in Great Britain
by CPI Antony Rowe, Chippenham, Wiltshire

Suddenly the train lurched, propelling Jane out of her seat and across the distance that separated her from Lord Lansbury, sending her crashing into his steely warm chest.

Christopher's eyes captured Jane's with some considerable surprise, while Jane looked into his face and for a long moment could not look away again, held by something she was unable to name but which her female body instantly recognised. His eyes had narrowed in sudden concentration and he looked faintly surprised at something *his* body was telling *him*.

Unprepared for the sheer force of the feelings that swept through her, she knew, with a sort of panic, that she was in grave danger—not from him but from herself—and was aware that she must, absolutely *must* pull back. But she was too inexperienced and affected by him to do that.

Her eyes became fixed on his finely sculpted mouth as he came closer still, and she knew he was going to kiss her.

Author Note

I've always enjoyed reading stories that blend history and romance, featuring handsome, enigmatic heroes and audacious heroines.

In Christopher Chalfont, Earl of Lansbury, I hope I have captured such a hero. Having been betrayed by a woman in his past, and just managing to hold on to the ancestral home his deceased father very nearly gambled away, he is prepared to wed an American heiress, thinking she will be the answer to his prayers. Until Jane Mortimer comes along and throws his whole life and his ideas about marriage into confusion.

Before long Jane falls in love with the handsome Earl and becomes more and more wrapped up in a world so different from the one she left behind. She has the ability to reach into the darkness of Christopher's mind and heal his injured heart.

Helen Dickson was born and still lives in South Yorkshire, with her retired farm manager husband. Having moved out of the busy farmhouse where she raised their two sons, she has more time to indulge in her favourite pastimes. She enjoys being outdoors, travelling, reading and music. An incurable romantic, she writes for pleasure. It was a love of history that drove her to writing historical fiction.

Books by Helen Dickson

Mills & Boon Historical Romance

Seducing Miss Lockwood
Marrying Miss Monkton
Diamonds, Deception and the Debutante
The Bride Wore Scandal
Destitute on His Doorstep
Beauty in Breeches
Miss Cameron's Fall from Grace
When Marrying a Duke...
The Devil Claims a Wife
The Master of Stonegrave Hall
Mishap Marriage
A Traitor's Touch
Caught in Scandal's Storm
Lucy Lane and the Lieutenant
Lord Lansbury's Christmas Wedding

M&B *Castonbury Park* Regency mini-series

The Housemaid's Scandalous Secret

Mills & Boon Historical *Undone!* eBook

One Reckless Night

Visit the Author Profile page
at millsandboon.co.uk for more titles.

Chapter One

1875

A light rain had settled over the sea, mottling the surface of the choppy water into a dull blackish grey. Jane leaned against the railing of the steamship, letting her eyes skim over the vast expanse of water as it carried her closer to Dover. It was carrying her further away from the wild and mystical beauty and the heat of the Far East, of India and the countries around the Mediterranean, into a new phase of her life.

Tears came to blur her vision when she thought of the circumstances that had brought her to this day, of the anguish that had beset her, almost drowning her in a sea of despair when her beloved father had died in Egypt two months earlier, leaving her bereft.

This morning she had risen before dawn in Paris

to catch the boat train to Calais, where she had boarded the ship. She hoped to arrive at her aunt's London home with something akin to dignity, but her appearance was far from being at its best. The dark-blue bonnet and black woollen cloak served to protect her from the cold, damp wind even if it lent nothing to a stately grace.

There were a great many passengers aboard. Most of them had sought the comforts below for the journey, but Jane preferred to remain on deck. A girl's laughter drew her attention and she turned to look at her. She was dressed in a warm red woollen cloak with a fur muff and bonnet over her fair curls and clutching a small Pekinese dog. Perhaps eight or nine years old, slightly built with luminous blue eyes, she was such a pretty, dainty little creature with a pale small-featured face that Jane could only gaze at her in wonder.

She was with a fashionably attired woman Jane assumed to be her mother. She noted there was another plain-clad woman beside her. This, she realised, must be her maid, which told her the child's mother must belong to the gentry. They were accompanied by a tall man in a sleeved cloak and wide-brimmed, low-crowned hat. Several yards away from where they sat and close to Jane, with his back to them, he stood at the rail, his head turned to look at the ship's wake. He withdrew a thin cheroot from his jacket pocket which he lit, bending his head and cupping his hands over the flame.

The tobacco smoke drifted her way. Closing her eyes, she breathed deeply, inhaling the familiar smell which evoked so many memories. Her father had always enjoyed smoking a cigar, and suddenly she was swept back in time to the nights when he would sit outside his tent after a gratifying day's work, sipping his favourite brandy and smoking a cigar. Moving closer, she expelled the breath she hadn't realised she'd been holding. The tiny sound made the gentleman glance at her. His eyes narrowed, in surprise or displeasure, she wasn't certain. Caught in the act of staring at him, she blurted out the first thing that came to mind.

'I'm so sorry. I didn't wish to disturb you.'

His dark brows lifted a fraction in bland enquiry. 'Do you mind?' he asked, holding out the cheroot.

Several things hit Jane at once—his piercing grey eyes and his voice, which was richly textured and deep, and the fact that he was tall, several inches taller than she was. He was clean-shaven, his skin dark, slashed with eyebrows more accustomed to frowning than smiling, which he was doing now. His mouth was hard, the chin beneath it doing its best to curb its tense, arrogant thrust. It was a face which said its owner cared nothing for fools, and in his darkly lashed grey eyes, silver flecks stirred dangerously like small warning lights. Hidden deep in them was a cynicism, watchful, mocking, as though he found the world a dubious place to be.

'Mind?' she repeated stupidly.

'The cigar.'

'Oh—no—no, of course I don't mind,' she hastily assured him, stepping away.

He looked away at the same moment that the little girl got up to cross to him. A sudden gust of cold wind swept across the deck, causing passengers to reach out and cling to the rail. The little girl stumbled, falling to her knees, and when she reached out to grasp her mother's hand, she let go of her dog. Jane's heart dipped frantically in her chest as the child missed her mother's hand, bringing those about her to a horrified standstill.

The deck was wet and slippery, a threat to those who did not walk with care. The child got to her feet. Her sudden anxiety had become dismayed terror as her adored pet scampered to the far end of the deck. With no other thought than reaching her pet, the child went after her.

Alarmed, the woman got to her feet. 'Octavia, do come back this instant!'

Jane's mouth opened on an appalled shout to warn the child to be careful of the wet deck, but it was too late. Losing her footing, the child stumbled and fell and rolled across the deck. Jane thought she heard the woman cry out, but there was nothing in her mind but the frantic necessity of grabbing the little girl before she slipped through a gap in the lower rails and into the sea.

The other passengers not as close to the girl as Jane stood frozen to the deck, watching in horror, women with their hands to their mouths, men ready to dash forward to save the child who was sliding ever closer to the abyss, but on seeing Jane scamper after her they did not move.

Without thought for her own safety, Jane threw herself forward, grabbing the child and landing half on top of her just in time, her larger frame preventing them from slipping through the rails.

Women had begun to scream and the man who stood smoking a cheroot, white faced with shock, seeing what was happening threw his cheroot into the sea and strode quickly towards the young girl.

By the time he reached her she was lying on the deck with her rescuer. Picking up the weeping child, after making sure she was unharmed and handing her over to the older woman to be comforted, he went down on one knee and raised Jane up, lifting her in his arms.

She leaned against him in a dizzy, helpless silence, aware of nothing but the power of his arm and the muscular chest beneath his cloak as he balanced her against him, the fine aroma of cigars and brandy on his breath which fanned her cheek. Even in her dazed state she was shaken to the core by the bewildering sensations she felt. A hot wave of pure visceral attraction rushed through her. Fighting to maintain her wits, shaken and pale, she moved away from him a little unsteadily, standing a moment to compose herself. She brushed down her skirts before looking up at the gentleman, her eyes enormous with passionate gratitude on seeing his concern.

'Are you all right?' he asked. 'You didn't hurt yourself when you fell?'

He spoke in the well-modulated voice of the perfect English gentleman, with that faint arrogance and authority of his class. There was a nonchalance about him that Jane liked immediately.

'No—no, thank you, I am quite unhurt,' she answered, speaking in a soft, well-bred voice that displayed no discernible personal feeling. Her mouth was tinder-dry with shock, her heart pounding in her throat, but she made efforts to compose herself. She still felt a bit wobbly, but was determined not to show it.

Staring at him, she was utterly taken aback by the raw masculinity that radiated from him. The most curious thing happened, for suddenly everything around her faded into the background and there was only this man. His face was strong and exceptionally attractive, the expression cool and compelling. His magnetism was unmistakable. The long, tapering trousers he wore seemed to emphasise the muscular length of his legs. As her thoughts raced, once again she looked into the startling intensity of his eyes. Her heart seemed to suddenly leap into her throat in a ridiculous, choking way and she chided herself for being so foolish. This gentleman was, after all, a stranger to her. She dropped her gaze in shock as he took a step closer.

'I can't thank you enough for what you did. Your quick thinking saved my sister's life. I am indeed grateful, Miss...?'

'Mortimer,' Jane provided. 'In all truth, when I

saw her slip and begin to roll towards the rails, I didn't think. I just knew I had to stop her.'

'I am grateful, Miss Mortimer. She could easily have fallen through the gap, small though it is, into the water.'

The amazing eyes still focused on her as she drew a deep breath. 'She is a child and children do impulsive things all the time.' There was a deep blush on her cheekbones, as much to her gathering annoyance she found herself actually enjoying his presence.

'Unfortunately my sister seems to make a habit of it.'

'I am relieved she is unharmed—and see,' Jane said, indicating a man who approached the child and placed a fluffy white bundle in her outstretched hands, 'her dog is being returned to her.'

'Thank goodness. Octavia would be devastated if anything happened to that dog. It is so precious to her.' His gaze returned to her face. He gave her a long slow look, a twist of humour around his beautifully moulded lips. The smile building about his mouth creased the clear hardness of his jaw and made him appear at that moment the most handsome man in the world.

Then, suddenly, his direct, masculine assurance

disconcerted her. She was vividly conscious of his proximity to her. She felt the mad, unfamiliar rush of blood singing through her veins, which she had never experienced before. He had made too much of an impact on her and she was afraid that if he looked at her much longer he would read her thoughts with those brilliant eyes of his. She was relieved when the child's mother got up and came to her. Tears of gratitude swam in her eyes.

'Thank you, my dear, for your brave intervention. You have my heartfelt thanks and gratitude.'

'I'm glad I was able to help.'

'Is there anything we can do to repay you...?'

The colour rushed to Jane's face once more, embarrassed that she should be offered payment for helping a child. 'No—of course not. I only did what anyone else would have done.' She stepped back. 'Excuse me. We are approaching Dover. I must go and locate my baggage.'

'Of course,' the woman said. 'Are you going far?'

'To London.'

'So you will be taking the train.'

'Yes.' She smiled. 'Please excuse me.'

Turning from them, Jane went to retrieve her bags as more passengers began to appear on deck.

* * *

Christopher Chalfont went to check on Octavia. Thankfully she seemed no worse for her ordeal. He glanced over his shoulder to take another look at the young woman who had rushed to help his sister with a complete lack of concern for her own safety, but she was nowhere to be seen, having been swallowed up in the passengers as they gathered to disembark.

Something stirred within him that he was at a loss to identify—neither pity nor compassion, but a glimmer of something more complex and disturbing. Instinct told him he'd be better served not to look for her. He was quite bewildered by his own interest in this girl who was thin, plain and nondescript.

True, some might be attracted by her, but she was not to his taste. He disliked her generous mouth, the black abundance of her lashes and particularly her eyes that had stared at him too intently. They were too large and a peculiar shade of violet with flecks of grey. They were clear and sharp as glass and they had met his with a steady challenge, studying him carefully as though she was trying to make up her mind about something.

For an instant he knew that someone else, someone with similar violet eyes, had stared at him like that long ago and there had been faithlessness and betrayal and he had known suffering so great it was not to be borne. Something that had been darkly, beautifully perfect had been bruised and broken, and he had suffered aching bitterness and a pain so deep it was ready to destroy him.

And then the impression vanished, leaving only sharp resentment and a memory he could not shut from his mind, a memory that was alive and tactile, and because it had been so, the betrayal of the woman who had done this to him had become a profanation of the integrity of love itself. He had continued to live, to eat and sleep and exist the only way he knew how, but he vowed that never again would he allow himself to be so weakened by a woman's body and a pair of darkly seductive eyes.

Frowning thoughtfully, for the short time left to them on board, Christopher concerned himself with seeing to the comforts of his mother and sister, and when he left the ship he forgot all about the young woman with the violet eyes.

As Jane sat on the train taking her to London, she relived every moment of her meeting with the gentleman whose sister she had rushed to help; the gentleman who had made a deep impression on her like no other ever had. Who was he? she asked herself, realising that he had infiltrated every part of her body and mind and yet she didn't know the first thing about him. That was the power he had, the magnetic force that had attracted her to him. What was it about him that made her feel things she had never felt before? She had never met anyone like him. Just thinking of him was enough to bring his image, tenacious and encroaching, into her mind.

Gazing out of the window at the passing scenery, she breathed a sigh of regret. It was a hopeless situation for it was most unlikely they would meet again. Swallowing her disappointment, she knew there was nothing for it but to put him from her thoughts, only to find over the coming days that it was no easy matter.

Jane's father had been an academic and writer on Asian and European history and antiquities. When he had died she was fortunate to have a generous-hearted paternal widowed aunt to take her in. Jane had seen her just twice in her life when her father's work had brought him to London.

Aunt Caroline gave what she called 'soirées' at

her small but elegant house in a fashionable part of London. It was decorated and furnished in the latest aesthetic fashion, with the walls festooned with peacocks and pomegranates and several pieces of Japanese porcelain.

Her guests were mainly invited through her charities—she worked on several committees—but there were sometimes politicians and a sprinkling of what she called 'the Bohemians': artists, musicians and writers and such like. Sometimes she would engage a violinist or a pianist to perform—those were her musical evenings—then there were card evenings and some supper parties. She enjoyed entertaining, but her charities were always at the forefront of her mind and the money that could be raised from these occasions.

Today she was hosting one of her charity events attended by several of her fellow patrons. A gentle, caring soul, Caroline Standish was a very worthy lady who took her work seriously. The destitution and brutish conditions in some parts of the capital touched her deeply and she worked hard to alleviate the suffering in any way she could.

Jane watched ladies sip the very best tea from Assam and Ceylon out of her aunt's best china cups and eat cucumber sandwiches and cakes off china plates, her eyes coming to rest on one before moving on to the next.

They were a mixed collection of ladies. Most of them led privileged lives. Their husbands were gentlemen and some titled. The younger ladies were quite beautiful and Jane wondered that such beauty could exist. As an unmarried woman of limited importance and at least three inches taller than what was considered fashionable, it was with wry amusement that she also wondered why nature had seen fit to bless so many with the gift of so much beauty, of face and figure, affording herself nothing more than a tenacity of spirit and a wry amusement that up until now had allowed her to transcend her own shortcomings.

As far as husbands were concerned, Jane didn't suppose it would happen to her. Even if she did meet someone, she would rather die a spinster than submit herself to a man she did not love—a man who did not love her. All her life she had been aware and deeply moved by the quiet dignity and deep, voiceless love her parents had borne for each other and by their example she would settle for nothing less in her own marriage. With a mind of her own, she possessed a will to live her life as she saw fit and would not submit to mere circumstance.

In her opinion she was nothing out of the ordinary, her looks being unconventional. Being neither stylish nor dashing, she couldn't blame anyone for not favouring her with a second glance.

'Too thin,' an elderly lady had once said. 'Too tall,' said another. 'Too plain,' someone else had commented.

But as Jane looked at her reflection in the mirror, she doubted a glimpse of her face would frighten anyone. Some men might actually like cheekbones that were too high, a mouth that was too wide and eyes that were a peculiar shade of violet touched with grey. Her hair was the bane of her life. It was long and thick and so rich a brown to be almost red. The weight of it was brushed back severely from her brow in an attempt to subdue its defiant inclination to curl. Most of the time it was kept confined in an unflattering tight knot at the nape of her neck.

Jane knew she didn't make the best of herself. But if anyone had been inclined to look deeper they would have found that behind the unprepossessing appearance there was a veritable treasure trove. Twenty-one years of age and formidably intelligent, she had a distinct and memorable personality, and could hold the most fascinating conversations on most subjects. She had a genuinely kind heart, wasn't boastful and rarely offended anybody. She was also unselfish and willing to take on the troubles of others.

Aunt Caroline had told her she was expecting Lady Lansbury—the Countess of Lansbury—and her young daughter at her gathering.

'They have been in America—New York, I believe,' she explained, 'and have spent some time in Paris before returning to England. They have a house in town, but I understand they will shortly be leaving for their estate in Oxfordshire.'

'How did you meet Lady Lansbury?'

'She came to one of my Tuesdays. Such a caring soul. She likes to be involved and gives of her time unsparingly, but donations cannot be relied upon. The poor woman was left quite destitute when her husband died. Her son inherited the Chalfont estate in Oxfordshire—at least what was left of it. The old earl left them near bankrupt. But that was twelve years ago and the present earl has worked hard and managed to keep his head above water. But rumour has it that unless he can find a way to inject some money into the place, he might have to let it go.'

'What a worry it must be for them.'

'I'm sure it is. I believe Lord Lansbury is considering selling the London house to raise some capital. It is rumoured that he might even resort to marrying an heiress—an American heiress—and why not? He won't be the first impoverished nobleman to marry for money and he won't be the last.'

'That seems rather drastic.'

'To you, having lived almost all your life abroad, I suppose it does. In English society, marrying for money is considered a perfectly acceptable undertaking. However, pride is a dominant Chalfont trait and the Earl of Lansbury will find it extremely distasteful having to resort to such extreme measures. But that does not concern us. Young Lady Octavia is a charming girl, although she gave Lady Lansbury a hard time when she came along. Born early, she was pronounced delicate. She has—difficulties, but she's of a gentle, loving disposition. You will love her.'

Aunt Caroline was right. Lady Lansbury, a regal lady, arrived with her daughter in a carriage with a resplendent coachman and a little page at the back to leap down and open doors.

Jane could not believe her eyes when she saw Lady Lansbury—she was the woman she had met on the ship and the child Octavia was just as she remembered. She was touched that Lady Lansbury should remember her.

'Why, Miss Mortimer! I am so pleased to see you again. Allow me to thank you once again for what you did for Octavia. Your niece was extremely brave, Mrs Standish,' she said to Jane's aunt. 'She risked her life to save Octavia when she fell on the deck of the ship when we were crossing the Channel and was in danger of sliding into the sea. I was journeying from Paris accompanied by my son, Lord Lansbury. We were indeed grateful that Miss Mortimer acted so quickly.'

Mrs Standish looked at her niece with some degree of surprise. 'Really? You never mentioned it, Jane.'

'I had no reason to. We were not introduced so I had no idea the two of you are acquainted. When the child slipped and fell I did what anyone else would have done. At the time I was close to her.'

'You are too modest, my dear,' Lady Lansbury said. 'Your prompt action saved her life.'

'I was glad I was able to help.' Jane longed to ask after Lady Lansbury's son, but thought better of it. After all it was unlikely they would meet again. Lord Lansbury had made a large impression on her virgin heart. When she was least expecting it thoughts of him would fill her mind so that she was unable to think of anything else which totally confused her. No man had ever had this effect on her before. But he was an earl, the Earl of Lansbury, way above her station in life and all she could do was admire him from afar. She looked at the child, who, it was clear, didn't remember her. 'Lady Octavia is such a lovely child.'

Jane's wonder increased when Octavia, clutching her beloved Pekinese in the crook of one arm, danced up to her and said, 'I like your dress. It's very pretty.'

'Thank you,' Jane said, responding warmly to the compliment, even though she disagreed with her. It was much worn and certainly not fashionable. But the colours were bright, the pattern bold, and she was in no doubt that it was this that had drawn Octavia's attention.

Octavia sat beside her on the striped sofa, placing her dog between them. The dog lifted its paw, cocked its head and peered up at Jane with yellow eyes, as if to fathom the spirit of this new person.

'She wants you to shake hands with her,' Octavia informed her.

Jane took the proffered paw and a pink tongue

lolled out the side of the jaws almost in a smile. 'Does your dog have a name?'

'Poppy. She's called Poppy.'

'That's a nice name. She is safe, isn't she?' Jane questioned with a teasing light in her eyes. 'I mean—she doesn't eat people, does she?'

Octavia tilted her head to one side and looked at her curiously, amazed that this lady should think her precious dog might bite. 'No, of course she doesn't. She likes you. I can tell. I like you, too. You are a very nice lady. Will you be my friend? I don't have any.' There was no hint of sadness in her remark. It was a matter-of-fact comment. That was the way it was.

Jane laughed and said she would like that very much. Stroking the ears of the Pekinese she studied the young girl. With silver-blonde hair and eyes a shining bright blue, her features piquant, she was a lively and restless girl with an independent spirit and full of energies she was unable to repress. For the time the visit lasted Octavia never left Jane's side. Jane realised that Lady Lansbury was closely following their exchange and watching them attentively, speculatively. She did not withhold comment.

'I can see Octavia has found a friend in you, Miss

Mortimer. You are fortunate. She doesn't take to people easily.'

From the small table beside her Jane took a painted tin of bonbons she had bought earlier and held them out to the girl. 'I don't think I can eat all these, Lady Octavia. Would you mind keeping the tin for me and helping me along with them?'

Octavia blinked her large eyes and looked enquiringly at her mother as if seeking her guidance. Lady Lansbury nodded and smiled her approval, and hesitantly Octavia's gaze came back to Jane. Accepting the tin, she immediately opened it and selected a bonbon, popping the sugary confection into her mouth and beaming her delight at the taste.

London was an exciting and fascinating place to be. Jane loved it. Aunt Caroline accompanied her on her excursions, pointing out to her buildings and places of note. They strolled in the parks and Jane was thrilled to see all the bright and beautiful flowers in borders and beds. Having spent most of her life surrounded by hot and arid landscapes, she found it truly amazing to see so much colour in one place.

At other times she was trying to sort out her father's affairs and considering her future. She gave little thought to her meeting with Lady Lansbury, so she was surprised when she called on the off chance one week later, hoping to find her at home.

Thinking her visit had something to do with one of the charities they supported, Aunt Caroline ushered her into the drawing room. Over tea they chatted about trivial matters. Jane listened, saying very little. Beneath a tiny jacket Lady Lansbury had on a beautiful gown in a silky material which shone where the light touched it. It was in a colour that reminded her of the sun when it was sinking at dusk, a sort of mixture between brown and gold and warm pink. The skirt was full and on her head was a pretty straw hat decorated with flowers to match her dress.

Jane was conscious of Lady Lansbury's eyes studying her, not critically, nor with the kind of morbid fascination with which many of her class would gaze at her unfashionable attire and plain looks. Rather it was with an assessing frankness, a frankness and even an admiration one woman directs at another when she sincerely believes that woman is worthy of it.

'How is Lady Octavia?' Jane found herself asking. 'It was a pleasure to meet her. She is such a charming, sweet girl.'

'Yes, she is—but then she is my daughter and I love her dearly.' Lady Lansbury placed her cup and saucer down. Her face, which had been firm with some inner resolve, softened imperceptibly. 'Of course I am so glad you think so, Miss Mortimer, because my visit concerns Octavia. When we were here last week I could not help noticing that you seem to have a way with her—and she has talked of nothing else but you since. I have come here today to ask for your help.'

'Oh!' Jane uttered, slightly taken aback, for she could not for the life of her think how she could possibly be of help to the Countess of Lansbury.

'When I spoke to your aunt, I seem to recall her mentioning that you have returned to England after spending many years travelling abroad with your father.'

'That is so,' Jane confirmed quietly. 'Sadly my father died when we were in Egypt, which is why I have come to stay with Aunt Caroline while his affairs are put in order and I consider my future.'

'Do you like children, Miss Mortimer?'

'Why—I—yes, of course, although I confess that being an only child and constantly on the move, I have no experience of them.'

'You appeared to get on with Octavia well

enough. I wondered if you would consider helping me take care of her. She can be difficult on occasion. All the young ladies I have employed in the past do not make it past the first month before they are heading for the door.'

'I—I don't know…'

'Miss Mortimer, please, I beg you, let me finish. I want to offer you permanent, full-time employment. We will be leaving London for our family home—Chalfont House in Oxfordshire—within the week. Octavia has developed a slight cough. I believe the country air is so much better for her than this London smog. I can't tell you how happy it would make me if you were to come with us.'

'Lady Lansbury—I don't know what to say. I freely admit you've taken me by surprise.'

'I hope you will say yes. I will not pretend that it will be easy taking care of Octavia. As you have seen she is not—not quite—like other girls of her age. She is twelve years old but looks and behaves much younger. She is fragile and needs tender care. She finds it difficult to tell people what she needs and how she feels—she also finds it difficult to understand what other people think and how they feel. She finds it hard to meet people—and to make friends—but she seems to like you. I do love her so very much, but I have grown weary and I often despair of what will become of her…'

For a moment Jane thought Lady Lansbury was about to break down. She bent her head, placing the back of her immaculately gloved hand to her head, swallowing painfully. Jane stood up, ready to go to her, to kneel and place her own soothing hand on hers, wanting to comfort, but recollecting herself when Lady Lansbury raised her head staunchly.

Jane smiled, a compassionate warmth lighting her eyes. She could almost feel the tension inside this regal lady splitting the air. Jane didn't take any persuading to accept her offer of employment. Through his work her father had told her that on his death she would be a wealthy woman, but until his lawyer had sorted out his affairs and the will was read she had no idea of her worth, although she knew it would be considerable. Never being one for crowded places, getting out of London into the English countryside for a while appealed to her.

There was also another reason that added weight to her decision—Lady Lansbury's son, the Earl of Lansbury. The temptation to see him again was too great for her to resist. She had not believed their paths would cross again and for the first time in her life she acted on impulse.

'I am sorry to hear that, Lady Lansbury, and I will help if I can.'

As she spoke a kindly light appeared in Jane's eyes. Her interest and feeling towards the girl were obviously sincere. Octavia was unpredictable, dainty and fragile as gossamer. She reminded Jane of a fluff of swansdown blown along on the breeze and may blossom that showed its beauty so profusely in spring. The blossom, flushed with pink, was no more delicately lovely than this child who had latched on to her from the first.

'I accept your offer, Lady Lansbury. I will return with you to Chalfont House—although I cannot commit myself indefinitely. But for the time being I would dearly like to be Lady Octavia's companion and I promise I will be patient with her.'

Lady Lansbury's eyes were bright with tears of gratitude. Miss Mortimer's acceptance of the post lightened her spirits, as though a great weight had been lifted from her shoulders. 'Thank you, Miss Mortimer. I can't tell you what a relief that is to me.'

'There is one thing I must ask of you, Lady Lansbury. When my father died a good deal of his work was not completed. It meant a great deal to him—and to his publisher and other antiquarians he worked with. I was his assistant and I am doing what I can to finish his work.'

'Of course you must. I quite understand. You will not be caring for Octavia all the time. We have a perfectly good library at Chalfont. It is a quiet room. I am sure you will find it the perfect place for your work.'

'Thank you. I would appreciate that.'

'Nonsense. It is I who am grateful to you.' She looked at Jane's aunt, who had listened to their exchange closely. 'What do you say, Mrs Standish? I do so hope you approve of Jane's acceptance to my proposal. I am certain she will be a great help to me—and to Octavia.'

'It is not for me to approve or disapprove, Lady Lansbury,' Mrs Standish said, choosing her words with care. 'At twenty-one my niece is old enough and sensible enough to decide her own future. But since you ask my opinion I will say that I am—concerned about the position she will hold in your household and how it will be seen by the others who work at Chalfont House. In age Jane will be on a par with your maids in the kitchen and...'

'Please, say no more, Mrs Standish. Jane will

never be on a par in any way with the maids in the kitchen. I know that she is the daughter of an academic, a highly intelligent man, an acclaimed writer, whose own father held a high-ranking position in the army. Her mother is from good stock, the Grants of Derbyshire. They were not a wealthy family, but they were of the class.'

'But—how do you know this, Lady Lansbury?' Jane asked.

'When I saw how taken Octavia was with you, I—made a few enquiries. I ask nothing more of you, Jane, than that you be my daughter's companion—her friend. Octavia has never reached out to anyone the way she has to you.'

'I will do my best to make her happy.' Knowing how concerned her aunt was about her, Jane tried to put her at ease with the situation. Looking after Octavia would be a demanding position but a pleasurable one for the girl aroused a protective fondness in her. 'Please—do not worry about me, Aunt,' she said gently. 'Ever since I returned to England I've been undecided as to what to do with my future, which path to take. As you know my mother died when I was very young. Having spent almost my entire life with my father, helping him with his work and wandering from place to place like nomads, I don't know what I'm cut out for.'

'You don't have to do anything, Jane,' her aunt said quietly. 'And didn't you mention that one of your father's colleagues is to come to London shortly?'

'Yes. Phineas Waverley. He is to set up an exhibition of artefacts and photographs and the like. No doubt he'll write to me when he knows more himself. In the meantime I have to do something. I'm not cut out for a life of idleness. I need to be busy. Chalfont House is within easy reach of London so I'll not be far away.'

On returning to Lansbury House, Lady Lansbury broached the matter with her son of Miss Mortimer accompanying them to Chalfont to help take care of Octavia. She found him unexpectedly obdurate and impatient.

'Why this girl? How can you be so certain about her on such short acquaintance? Of course Octavia took to her. It is what she does when anyone shows her kindness.'

'You dislike Miss Mortimer?' Lady Lansbury was puzzled by his vehemence. 'I find her quite charming.'

In a voice that was matter of fact rather than critical, he continued, 'I cannot be accused of being either uncharitable or unaccommodating in this instance. And contrary to what you might think, I have formed no opinion of her whatsoever. It's just that…' He faltered, avoiding eye contact with his mother. 'I don't dislike Miss Mortimer. Why should I?'

Lady Lansbury eyed her son closely. Why should he, indeed? For the first time in years she thought of the girl—Lily, her name was—Christopher had fallen for and how it had almost destroyed him when she had left him. Could it be that in Jane Mortimer he saw similarities to Lily? Perhaps that was it, but apart from the colour of her eyes, in her opinion there the similarities ended. Jane was not in the least like Lily.

'I am glad to hear it. Has it not entered that arrogant, stubborn head of yours that you might even like her? You may be pleasantly surprised.'

'Even for an arrogant, stubborn man like me it is not beyond the realms of possibility,' Christopher conceded.

'My fear is that when she is faced with your formidable manner—a daunting prospect for any girl—it will alienate her from the start.'

'What I dislike is wasting time on such a trivial matter when Octavia is perfectly happy as she is. Actually, there are one or two minor problems associated with your plan,' he said drily, but he couldn't bring himself to dampen his mother's enthusiasm completely. 'Miss Mortimer will be the latest in a long line of young ladies we have employed to care for Octavia in the past. Not one of them lasted more than a month and each time they left Octavia was distressed. I doubt Miss Mortimer will be any different. Why don't you give the entire project some careful thought and we'll discuss the various aspects of it when we reach Chalfont?'

'No, Christopher. I have made up my mind. Octavia's care is my concern and it would help me a great deal knowing that when I have to I can leave her with someone I can trust.'

Christopher sighed. He was not completely heartless. Looking after Octavia, worrying about her, wearied his mother. Finding the right person to care for her had proved a problem in the past. 'I'm sorry, Mother. Of course you must do as you see fit. Go ahead and employ Miss Mortimer if it makes you happy.'

'More importantly, Christopher, is that she makes Octavia happy.'

* * *

Chalfont House was the Lansbury seat in the heart of Oxfordshire. Jane was irrevocably touched by its timeless splendour. A wide stretch of stone steps led up to the colonnaded front door, while on either side two great wings stretched out to portray, in perfect proportions, the great arched dome which surmounted the centre of the building. Inside, the pomp and grandeur, which the countess took for granted, left her breathless.

As soon as she entered the house she was greeted with unaffected warmth. She felt this was a house where courtesy and mutual affection ruled in perfect harmony.

A maid appeared and whisked a tired Octavia to her room, leaving Jane with Lady Lansbury. She stood in the hall, looking about her with interest. And then, as if she was seeing a dream awaken before her, Lord Lansbury appeared from one of the many rooms leading off from the hall and strode toward them.

It was strange, but it was as if she had first seen him only yesterday. He had made such an impression on her on the ship and it had remained, only now it was stronger. He had a look she saw rarely—the complete indifference of inherited position. It was something that could not be acquired or even reproduced. It had to develop over time. Attired in a dark-green jacket and pristine neck linen, tall, lithe, his features strong and darkly, incredibly attractive, he moved with the confident ease of a man well assured of his place in the world and completely unconcerned about the world's perception of him.

Accustomed all her life to foreigners and older men of her father's acquaintance, men who gave thought of nothing other than their work and gave no thought to their appearance, she had never seen anything like Lord Lansbury. Unable to tear her eyes away from him, she was bowled over anew by that same dark, delicious magnetism she remembered vividly from her first glimpse of him on the ship.

His hair was thick and dark brown, as shiny as silk brushed back from his brow, his glorious grey eyes the colour of smoke. He had a long aquiline nose and his eyelids were heavy, drooping low, giving him a lazy, sleepy look. At over six foot tall, he was built like one of those Greek athletes she had read so much about, lean and muscular, all supple grace, and when he spoke his voice was deep and throaty, reminding her of thick honey and making her think of bodies, of bedrooms and the erotic engravings she had seen on her travels through the far east and Europe with her father.

Lord Lansbury had travelled to Chalfont ahead of Lady Lansbury. When Lady Lansbury introduced her, he looked at her, inclining his head courteously. But he did not see her, not really, and she hadn't expected him to. He did not look at her in the way a man would look at an attractive woman. His eyes were startling and distracting, not so much for their silver-grey colour or the size, which was substantial. What gave them their unique power seemed to be the fact that the centre of his eyes filled the clear white from top to bottom and the thick lashes both obscured and revealed his gaze, depending on his whim.

'Miss Mortimer is here to take care of Octavia, Christopher. You will remember that she was the young lady who saved Octavia's life on the ship. I informed you she would be coming today.'

'Yes, so you did.' He fixed Jane with a cool gaze. 'We are in your debt, Miss Mortimer, for what you did that day. But your work will not be easy. Getting Octavia to do anything she doesn't like is like piloting a ship into the harbour. It needs a steady hand on the tiller.'

Jane laughed, suddenly nervous. She felt Lord Lansbury was only being polite and sensed he was uncomfortable and wishful to escape. A sense of disappointment rippled through her. How she wished he would look at her differently, that he would find her attractive.

'Please don't be concerned. My navigational skills are quite exceptional.'

'I'm glad to hear it. Your father was a well-known writer and antiquarian, I believe.'

'He was Matthew Mortimer, a knowledgeable writer on many things—Roman and Greek history and antiquities were his passion.'

'He must have been an interesting man. My mother tells me you have spent a great deal of your time abroad.'

'Yes. Together we travelled to many countries—Europe and beyond. We lived in India for five years.'

'Really?' Jane felt and saw his interest quicken. 'You must find life here very different indeed from that hot clime.'

'Very different,' she said, trying not to let herself sound too regretful.

'And dull.'

She laughed. 'I'm afraid I haven't had time to find out.'

'You appear to be a sensible young woman, Miss Mortimer. I am sure you will adjust. I hope you won't find the English winters too cold and miserable.'

'I'm sure I will,' she said with a wry smile. 'I'm also sure that I'll survive.'

'You must miss your father.'

'Yes,' she replied, struggling to conceal the sadness she always felt when speaking of her father. She still felt his loss deeply. 'Not only was I his daughter, but his assistant. When he died I'm afraid much of his work was unfinished so I have a lot of loose ends to tie up for his publisher. Lady Lansbury has kindly offered me the use of your library—when I'm not looking after Lady Octavia, that is.'

'Of course. Feel free to use it any time. I am sure you will do an excellent job taking care of Octavia. I hope you will enjoy your time here.'

Jane's heart skipped a beat as his beautiful grey eyes met hers. Pleasure washed over her. 'I'm sure I will, Lord Lansbury.' She swallowed hard, unable to think of anything else to say until he had turned his back on her and walked away. 'Thank you,' she finally managed to call out, but he must not have heard her words, for he did not turn to look at her again.

'Oh, dear! My son is hasty sometimes,' Lady Lansbury said, noting Jane's dismay. 'He has grave matters to worry him and he is always so busy. But come, my dear. I'll take you to Octavia's rooms.' She looked at Jane who was somewhat flushed. 'Are you all right, my dear?'

'Yes—perfectly.'

A cloud shifted across Jane's face and her eyelids lowered. The expression in them was unreadable, which was just as well, for she loved Christopher Chalfont from that moment. How else could these feelings that consumed her be explained—she, who had no experience of men in the romantic sense? She told herself that she should doubt her reactions to Lord Lansbury, the first man she had ever been attracted to. She was unable to understand why this should be.

The day she had left France and climbed aboard the boat bound for Dover would live with her for ever, because that was the day she had met him, the day he had entered her mind so that she was unable to think of anything else. Because the differences between them were too vast, she did not fool herself into believing it could ever be any different and that he would ever return her love.

Nothing was normal any more, least of all her feelings about herself.

Chapter Two

Jane had been at Chalfont for one whole month and had no reason to regret her decision. The servants were not quite sure about her position. The other young ladies who had cared for Octavia in the past had been employed as governesses. Although Miss Mortimer's position filled that role, Lady Lansbury treated her as more of a friend. Miss Mortimer was frequently invited to dine with the family, but she always declined, opting to eat in the rooms she shared with Octavia.

Jane realised she had a talent for entertaining Octavia that surprised her. In spite of her lack of experience with children, she managed to win Octavia's trust and arouse her eager curiosity with the activities they did together. They would walk in the beautiful grounds and at other times Octavia loved to draw and paint, but she was reluctant to learn her letters, so on Lady Lansbury's advice she did not press her.

But it wasn't always easy. There were times when Octavia would be silent for long periods and she was unable to concentrate any length of time on any one thing. She was often wilful and sullen and there were tears if she could not get her own way. But on the whole she brought much pleasure to Jane and Lady Lansbury was beginning to lose that tense, anxious look that Jane had noticed on first meeting her.

Hearing the gravel crunch beneath a horse's hooves on the drive below, she was drawn from her thoughts as she watched Octavia painting pictures in her room. Drawing a deep breath in anticipation of the return of Lord Lansbury from his ride, she moved swiftly to the window and looked down at the man who occupied her thoughts both day and night. He had spent most of the past four weeks in town so she hadn't seen much of him. The moment she fixed her eyes on his tall, powerfully elegant figure, as he dismounted and handed the reins to a waiting groom, she felt that familiar twist of her heart, that addictive mix of pleasure and discomfort.

* * *

Unaware that he was being observed, Christopher entered the house. At best, he was a fiercely private man, guarded and solitary and accountable to no one. At worst, he was a man with a streak of ruthlessness and an iron control that was almost chilling. He possessed a haughty reserve that was not inviting and set him apart from others in society.

There had been other women. He took them to bed, but he did not let them into his life. He could also be cold, calculating and unemotional, which was his attitude to the decision he was about to make regarding marriage to an American heiress, Lydia Spelling. The American dollars she would bring would go a long way to shoring up Chalfont's finances. He was still feeling the effects of his father's ruin, but the returns from his investments were at last beginning to show improvements.

Marriage to Miss Spelling would be advantageous in other ways as well as financial. The Chalfonts had become thin on the ground. To continue the line he had to give some thought to producing an heir. He knew how anxious his mother was for him to marry. If he didn't produce a legitimate heir, the title was in danger of passing entirely out of the Chalfont family. It troubled him more than anyone realised and he knew he couldn't go on ignoring the issue.

When his mother had decided to take Octavia on an extensive tour to visit New York and then Paris, reluctant to let them go alone, Christopher had accompanied them. When he'd embarked on the transatlantic voyage, the phenomenon of seeking to marry an American heiress as the solution to his financial situation and to continue the Chalfont line had not entered his head. He hadn't reckoned on Oswald Spelling.

Spelling, a widower with one daughter, hadn't passed up the chance to socialise with an earl—British aristocrats had become husbands of choice for American millionaires' daughters. Invited to dine at the Spellings's showy mansion on Madison Square, Mr Spelling had seated Lydia on Christopher's right. It wasn't subtle, but then it didn't have to be.

Lydia Spelling was animated and she knew how to assert herself. Encouraged from an early age to express herself and fully confident that she was a worthwhile thing to express, she left Christopher in no doubt that she found him an attractive prospect. As an American heiress she enjoyed a freedom of movement and association that was reserved in Europe solely for married women.

When Christopher finally left New York, he had made no commitment and yet an understanding of sorts had been reached. Lydia was attractive and popular at any event. He did not love her, but making her his wife did not seem such a high price to pay for a lifetime free from financial worry. No sacrifice would be too great if he could restore some of Chalfont's glories and ensure a more stable future.

Christopher was ensconced in Chalfont's library reading the financial sections in the morning papers, one booted foot resting atop his knee,

It was a lovely room. With its beautiful Adams ceiling and Grinling Gibbons chimneypiece, highly polished floor and vividly coloured oriental carpets, it was like an Aladdin's cave—a treasure trove of precious leather-bound tomes. It smelt strongly of polish and Morocco leather. It was a room which encapsulated every culture and civilisation of the universe, where bookshelves stretched from floor to ceiling, broken only by the fireplace and long windows looking out on to the gardens.

Christopher glanced up when the door opened and his mother swept in.

'So this is where you are, Christopher. I thought I'd best tell you that I shall be taking charge of Octavia today. I thought it was time Miss Mortimer took some time off to get on with her work. I really wish she had accepted some kind of reward for what she did for Octavia on the ship. I did think of giving her a bank draft—a reward for saving her life—but she will be undoubtedly offended by the money.'

Christopher smiled disdainfully. 'Perhaps she is not as eager for coin as some of the lower classes would be, who would try to wheedle some sort of monetary reward regardless of the reason.'

'You've become a cynic,' his mother teased blandly. 'But Jane is not like that. She is without guile or greed. She is a lovely young woman, don't you agree?'

Christopher gave her a narrow look over the top of the newspaper. 'She's certainly out of the ordinary—having spent her life, by all accounts, like a wandering gypsy. I've never seen you so taken with any of the other young ladies we have employed to take care of Octavia in the past.'

'You're quite right, and so far I'm thoroughly satisfied. Jane is an absolute treasure.'

'Unconventional and hopelessly peculiar is how I would describe her,' Christopher replied drolly, flicking back the next page of his paper. 'I would have thought that a girl with her background would be devoid of social skills and find it hard to adjust to the kind of world we inhabit.'

'You are too harsh. Jane is a thoroughly charming and engaging and well-adjusted young woman, with a remarkable intelligence. In the short time I've known her I vow she's lifted my spirits considerably. I know you had reservations about her suitability from the start, but she has proved you wrong. The difference in Octavia is quite startling. You must have seen that for yourself.'

That Christopher had misgivings about Jane was etched into the troubled scowl on his face. His mother would hear no wrong said about the girl who had slipped so neatly and effortlessly into their lives, and for the sake of Octavia and his mother's happiness he must accept the situation.

On the other side of the library door, which Lady Lansbury had left ajar, hearing voices and about to enter, Jane paused. Not wishing to intrude, she considered returning to her room, but on hearing Lady Lansbury mention her name, she halted.

Listening to what Lord Lansbury had to say, Jane felt tears of humiliation burn the backs of her eyes. She stepped away from the door, trying to recover her control. If what he said was to be believed, he didn't want her at Chalfont, which meant his initial cordiality to her had all been a pretence. He was rightly protective of his sister, but that did not lessen the sting of his words or the terrible hurt that engulfed her on hearing them.

Fighting desperately to hold on to her rising anger and shattered pride, she raised her head. After all, it wasn't her fault if he found her hopelessly peculiar. Lady Lansbury was happy to have her care for Octavia and was pleased with the rapport that had grown between them.

Taking the bull by the horns, she knocked on the door and pushed it open, forcing a smile to her lips when Lady Lansbury crossed towards her and trying not to look at Lord Lansbury, who had dropped his newspaper on to his knee and was looking directly at her, his face expressionless.

'Come in, Jane. I'm sure you are impatient to begin work. I shall go and see Mrs Collins in the kitchen. I thought we might take Octavia for a carriage ride later if you can spare the time, Christopher.'

'I will try, but I have a lot of work to do today. I have to go over the books with Johnson and I want to inspect one of the farms myself. Johnson claims they don't really need a roof, but it's going to be a rainy autumn and I want to make sure.'

'Johnson is a very efficient and able bailiff, Christopher. I'm sure he can manage without you, but—if you must.'

'I will try. I don't want to disappoint Octavia. I'll have more time this afternoon.'

'This afternoon will be fine,' she said, turning away. 'I won't be gone more than a moment. I'll leave you to set out your work, Jane. Christopher will look after you until I return…'

Her voice faded away into the far reaches of the house and a door was heard to open and close somewhere. Then there was silence.

Without looking at the man lounging in the chair, but conscious of his presence, carrying her things, Jane crossed to a table tucked away in a corner by the window. It would be the perfect place for her to work. Lady Lansbury had introduced her to the library on her arrival at Chalfont, explaining that she would be able to concentrate on her work without interruption.

Christopher watched her pull out a chair and place her files on the surface of the table. With rigid back and head held high, she lowered herself into it. With a mixture of languor and self-assurance, absently drumming his fingers on the leather arm, Christopher let his gaze sweep over her in a contemplative way.

'How do you find Octavia, Miss Mortimer?'

Her face was half-turned away from him. All he could see was the curve of her cheekbone and the long silky flutter of her black lashes. Her hair was drawn unflatteringly into its severe bun. Her face was composed and her eyes clear and untroubled. In fact, she looked as she always looked, unapproachable and detached from those about her. Yet she was paler than usual and he wondered if she was unwell. She was certainly quiet—in fact, she was as prim as a spinster at a church tea party.

She looked up from sorting out her work as though against her better judgement, and Christopher was mystified by her cool reserve. Her face was set in a mould of chill politeness and he could see it was all she could do to answer him. What the devil had he done to earn her animosity, he wondered, and in such a short time? Then he almost laughed. It was all so ridiculous. He was tempted to ask her outright what offence he had committed, then thought better of it. However, he learned the cause of her cold attitude when she next spoke, and he was contrite. His comments had been unflattering and hurtful.

'Lady Octavia is a charming girl,' Jane said crisply. 'Where she is concerned I take my responsibilities seriously. You may not approve of me, Lord Lansbury, but be assured that I am not out to hurt her in any way.'

'Ah. So, you overheard what I was saying to my mother, in which case I can see some form of apology is in order. However, since you mention it I did not say that I do not approve of you. On the contrary. I have nothing but respect for you and the work you do. However,' he said, putting down his newspaper and getting to his feet, 'what my opinions are concerning you has no bearing on the case. My paramount concern is Octavia's happiness and well-being. As you will know, having spent some considerable time in her company, she is not like other twelve-year-old girls.'

'That I do know. Lady Lansbury explained Lady Octavia's situation before I accepted the post.'

'I am sure she did,' he said, moving close to where she sat, 'but naturally I was concerned when I discovered that my mother had decided to employ you without discussing the matter with me first.'

'I understand your concern. Lady Lansbury has shown nothing but courtesy itself, and I give you my word that I shall not abuse her kindness. What you must understand is that I did not seek the position she offered me. Indeed, having just arrived in London—having spent most of my life living the life of a wandering gypsy—to quote your own words, my lord—I was undecided on what I would do next.'

'It would seem my mother came along at the right moment.'

'Perhaps. Time will tell. I dare say the properly reared young ladies of your acquaintance would be horrified and fall into a swoon at the life I have led and liken me to a savage. I may not have been born with blue blood in my veins and all the advantages that come with it, but I have learned much and my life has been enriched by it. Yes, I have been to many places and seen things good and bad, but I would not change a thing. It is not where a person comes from that matters. It's what a person is that counts.'

Christopher stared at the proud, tempestuous young woman in silent, cool composure. Her words reverberated round the room, ricocheting off the walls and hitting him with all the brutal impact of a battering ram, but it failed to pierce the armour of his reserve and not a flicker of emotion registered on his impassive features.

'That, Miss Mortimer, was quite an outburst. Have you finished?'

Pausing to take a restorative breath, wondering if he might order her from the house following her outburst, Jane finally said, 'Yes, I have.'

Cool and remote, feeling a stirring of admiration for this strange young woman who had dared speak her mind with such force, Christopher studied her for a moment, as though trying to discern something. When he had first set eyes on her he had thought her plain. But now, looking at her anew, he found himself revising his opinion. Her eyes were dark and soft and warm and were surrounded by absurdly long lashes. She had fine textured skin the colour of fresh cream. There were tiny lines at the corners of her eyes that told him she was a woman who smiled often.

But she did not smile at him.

Was she really as innocent and prim as she appeared? His instinct detected untapped depths of passion in her that sent silent signals instantly recognisable to a lusty male. The impact of these signals brought a smouldering glow to his eyes. So much innocence excited him, made him imagine those pleasures and sensations Miss Mortimer could never have experienced being aroused by him. If he had a mind, it would not be too difficult a task to demolish her pride and have her melting with desire in his arms.

Briefly, the idea of conquering her appealed to his sardonic sense of humour—if that was what he had a mind to do, which he didn't. The idea of seducing any woman for his own gratification was unthinkable. It would put him on a par with his own father, who had been the most corrupt and debauched man he had known. Christopher was his son, but there the association ended. He was not like his father and he never would be. Where Miss Mortimer was concerned he must remember that for him, because of the position she held, she was untouchable.

The lazy smile he bestowed on her transformed his face. She stared at him, as if momentarily captivated by it, unaware of the lascivious thoughts that had induced it. Hot colour washed her cheeks under his close scrutiny and he had no doubt that she hated herself for that betrayal. He smiled infuriatingly.

With a slight lift to his eyebrows, he said, 'Do I unsettle you, Miss Mortimer?'

'No—no, of course not,' she replied, completely flustered as she lowered her gaze and began sorting out the papers on the table, unable to prevent her hands from shaking.

'Come now, you're blushing,' he taunted gently, being well schooled in the way women's minds worked.

'I am not.' Jane's unease was growing by the second, but she tried not to show it, attempting to maintain a facade of disinterest and indifference.

'Yes, you are.' Chuckling softly, he turned away. 'I see you are busy so I will trouble you no longer.'

The smile disappeared from Christopher's lips and was replaced by a dark frown as he strode from the room. His conversation with Miss Mortimer had unsettled him and he could not escape the fact that already she had caused a rift in his well-ordered routine—a disturbance that had brought a feeling of unease which was beginning to trouble him. Perhaps it was because, despite her ability to stand on her own two feet, there was a vulnerability about her. Or perhaps it was the fact that she had no flirtatious wiles or it was her candour that threw him off balance. Or those eyes of hers that seemed to search his face as if she were looking for his soul.

Suddenly he found himself wondering what it would be like, having a wife to light up his life with warmth and laughter—a woman to banish the dark emptiness within him.

He caught himself up short, dispelling such youthful dreams and unfulfilled yearnings. He had experienced them once before with Lily, foolishly believing that a beautiful woman could make those dreams come true. How stupid, how gullible he had been to let himself believe a woman cared about such things as love and faithfulness.

Striding away from the library, he scowled as he realised Jane Mortimer was suddenly bringing all those old, foolish yearnings back to torment him.

When Lord Lansbury had left her, Jane sat looking at the closed door for a long time, her heart palpitating as a whole array of confusing emotions washed over her—anger, humiliation and a piercing, agonising loneliness she had not felt since her father had died.

Despite the unpleasant things she had overheard him say about her and the forthright manner in which she had retaliated—and the way he had looked at her, commenting on her embarrassment—her heart continued to beat with a chaotic mix of every emotion she had ever felt. And when he had smiled at her it was the most wonderful smile she had ever seen and full of provocative charm.

Even she, as immune to charm as she was to good looks, could feel the potency of both in this man. Feeling her heart somersault, she thought that when he smiled like that and looked at a woman from under those drooping lids, he could make a feral cat lay down and purr. Yet the hawk-like shrewdness of those beautiful silver-grey eyes spoke plainly of a man who would not be easy to manage.

Lord Lansbury's association with the American heiress was all the talk at Chalfont. It would appear that although an understanding had been reached, they were not formally engaged. An announcement was expected soon. Accompanied by her father, Miss Spelling had stopped off in London en route for Paris. They had arrived at Chalfont the day before Lady Lansbury's fifty-fifth birthday celebrations.

Octavia was caught up in the excitement and had talked of nothing else for days. Concerned that her young charge would tire herself out before the party started, taking her hand, Jane led her to the bed.

'You must rest, Lady Octavia, so you are not too tired to enjoy the party later.'

'I love parties, Jane. You will come, too?'

Jane stared into Octavia's face. It was brilliant with hope. Her eyes never moved from Jane's and she scarcely seemed to breathe as she waited for Jane to speak.

Even though Lady Lansbury invited her to attend social events, Jane preferred not to, but since it was Lady Lansbury's birthday and because Lady Lansbury had insisted she attend, she had accepted.

Jane laughed, turning back the down quilt on the bed while Octavia put Poppy in her basket. 'I shall, Lady Octavia. I understand from your mama that lots of people will be coming. Now come along. Into bed with you and go to sleep, otherwise you will be too tired to enjoy the party. When you wake you'll be ready for your bath. I'll lay out your prettiest party dress—the rose brocade with raised pink rosebuds you like so well. You'll be the prettiest young lady at the party.'

'What are you going to wear? Will it be as pretty as my dress?'

'No, Lady Octavia. I have nothing as pretty as that. I don't know what I'm going to wear. I haven't decided.'

Jane tucked the bedclothes around Octavia as she closed her eyes and in no time at all she was asleep. She sat on the bed for a moment, looking down at her young charge. Octavia looked adorable with her curling blonde hair rumpled and falling over her brow, her cheeks flushed and her breath coming softly through her parted lips.

What to wear for Lady Lansbury's birthday party was proving a headache for Jane. It wasn't something that usually concerned her since she was never invited to parties and the like where the guests were made up of fashionable ladies and gentlemen.

Miss Spelling would make her appearance beside Lord Lansbury. Try as she might not to dwell on this, Jane could think of nothing else and would make an extra effort with her appearance. When she tried to picture this unknown American heiress, she was beset with apprehension and a sharp twinge of jealousy—a feeling totally alien to her until now and she rebuked herself for it—all the greater because she had no right to such feelings when Lord Lansbury was going to marry someone else.

A lovely wise old lady she had met in India had told her that whenever a special event occurred, one must cover oneself in silks and perfumes to make one feel secure in one's own being. To do this would send out whatever messages one wished from this simple subtlety.

Jane had taken this advice to heart, but ruefully she thought how simple that advice would be to follow if one looked like some of the fashionable beauties she had seen in London. At twenty-one years old she was capable of self-analysis and knew it would take more than silks and perfumes to stave off the disharmony she felt for herself. She chided herself for not purchasing some new clothes on her arrival in London. Aunt Caroline, eyeing her out-of-date gowns with distaste, had suggested taking her shopping, but Jane had put it off, telling her she would think about it later. She now had cause to regret not doing so.

Looking through her much-travelled battered old

trunk, she drew out a brilliantly hued gown of sapphire silk. It was far more elaborate than her usual day dresses and she was sure it would be suitable for the party. The style was perhaps a little old-fashioned and would not flatter her figure, but it was certainly eye-catching.

The colour glowed and gleamed in the light as though it had a life of its own as she slid the sensuous fabric over her bare shoulders and felt its caress against her skin. The ripples of silk rustled very softly, enticing and provocative. The neckline was modest, the sleeves to the elbow trimmed with the finest lace. The tightly sashed waist and billowing skirt with its layers of supporting underskirts accentuated the feminine shape of her body.

She felt the aura of the old lady very strongly as she twisted this way and that in front of the mirror, assessing herself as never before, as if through someone else's eyes—Christopher Chalfont's eyes.

When Octavia saw her she gasped with delight, reaching out to lightly finger the fine silk.

'Oh, you look so pretty, Miss Jane. So pretty.'

'Do I, Lady Octavia?' Jane asked, looking back at the mirror and frowning slightly as if that image of herself were not quite what she had expected to see.

'It's a lovely dress.'

'This is a very special gown, Lady Octavia. It's travelled with me all the way from India.'

'India was where you lived, wasn't it?'

Jane tilted the child's face up to hers and smiled fondly. 'Yes, I told you all about, it if you remember. It's a country far, far away. Now, I think we had best present ourselves to your mama, don't you? We mustn't be late for her party.'

With Octavia, Jane left their rooms and walked along a wide passage crossing the width of the house. They passed bedrooms and drawing rooms, dining rooms and studies. The Great Gallery was a room of tremendous proportions and a hushed church-like atmosphere. Its floor was of polished oak and its walls supported a huge vaulted ceiling of decorative plaster. Set in rows along the walls were the family paintings, many larger than life and all housed in elaborately gilded frames. They gave the impression to anyone entering the gallery that they were stepping into the presence of nobility.

The afternoon was warm and sunny. Lady Lansbury had opted to have her birthday party on Chalfont's magnificent lawns, where tables beneath parasols had been set out for the guests. Footmen were on hand to assist an enthusiastic stream of guests from their carriages and see that the vehicles and horses were taken around to the stables.

Beneath a red-and-white-striped awning, trestle tables covered with pristine white tablecloths were laden with a magnificent array of food—every delicacy which was considered necessary to tempt the appetite: pâté, lobster, all manner of succulent meats, pies and jellies, bottles of hock and claret, bowls of punch and fortified wine for the ladies. A large complement of servants flitted about to wait on the guests' every fancy.

It was quite a spectacle for Jane when she stepped out of the glass doors which opened on to a broad terrace. Octavia in her pretty pink dress, her pretty bonnet held in place by a wide band of embroidered pink ribbon loosely knotted under her chin, held her hand tightly, an anxious look in her eyes. Jane knew she was always uneasy when in the company of so many people and she had promised not to leave her side for a moment.

The scene that confronted them was a kaleidoscope of colour. The gardens were ablaze with blossoms and islands of rhododendrons and azaleas, the air heady with the sweet fragrance of magnolia. Hanging flowers and a profusion of roses and laburnum climbed and trailed over a covered walkway. Elegant sculptures were set against dark green yew trees and an Italian fountain discharged water into a giant lily pond.

Rising above all this was Chalfont House, standing like a magnificent work of art, the brilliantly lit stained-glass windows of the seventeenth century glinting as they caught the sun. The effect was stunning.

Set against this background of unashamed opulence, the lawns and terraces were swarming with titled, wealthy and influential guests, their beautiful gowns, jackets, bonnets and parasols competing with the flower-filled beds. Lady Lansbury presented an imposing figure in a high-necked gown of eau-de-Nil shot silk with a matching turban trimmed with plumes of a moderate height.

Into this select assembly the proud figure of Lydia Spelling stepped on to the high terrace to make her grand entrance. This was the first time Jane had seen her close up and her heart sank at the exquisite picture of fashionable sophistication she made.

Miss Spelling was sandwiched between the Earl of Lansbury and her father, a short, portly man with mutton-chop whiskers, his face carved in hard lines. With her dark hair perfectly coiffed beneath a plume of tantalising white feathers, and a fitted, high-necked jacket of quilted deep-rose satin that hugged her body and accentuated the full swell of her breasts, Lydia Spelling's appearance was dramatic and could not be faulted. She was not beautiful, or even pretty, but alarmingly arresting.

A hush descended as conversation petered out and every head turned in her direction. Chalfont's gardens offered the perfect stage on which an ambitious young woman might make her mark, but it was a world in which Lydia Spelling's place was already secure. It was a grand entrance carried out as only Lydia Spelling could, with enormous panache, and Jane was grudgingly forced to admire it. She saw before her an experienced woman of the world, at ease with men and determined in her goals.

Watching her, Jane was both resentful and fascinated. Whatever she had expected of Miss Spelling, nothing had prepared her for the remarkable presence of the American woman. Jane remembered everything she had heard about her from the servants and now she could believe it all. Miss

Spelling had the magnetism and the power that Jane could never possess.

Jane felt strangely inadequate, knowing she could never compete with the worldly experience and fascination of Miss Spelling. She felt vulnerable and gauche.

Lord Lansbury fixed his steady gaze on the figure of his mother seated in a high-backed chair beneath a large parasol, presiding over her birthday party. Accompanied by Miss Spelling and her father, he made his way towards her. Without exception the guests stepped aside so that their progress was unimpaired and before the three of them had reached the Countess of Lansbury conversation had resumed.

Octavia immediately grasped Jane's hand and pulled her in the direction of her brother. They were both breathing heavily by the time they reached the group.

On reaching his mother, Christopher bent his head and kissed her cheek before drawing Lydia forward.

Lady Lansbury smiled as her eyes settled on the woman who might well become the Countess of Lansbury, her daughter-in-law. 'Lydia, my dear. How charming you look. I am so pleased you and your father are here to enjoy my birthday party. I am sorry your visit to Chalfont will be brief, although I am certain you will enjoy your trip to Paris.'

'I'm sure we will, Lady Lansbury. We leave tomorrow, but we were keen to attend your party.'

'I hope you have a pleasant few weeks. You will miss her, Christopher.'

'I'm sure I shall,' he replied, smiling at Lydia.

'Perhaps you will appreciate me all the more when I return,' Lydia remarked, trying to catch his eyes, but his attention was caught by Octavia practically jumping up and down to get his attention, bringing a frown of disapproval to Miss Spelling's brow.

Jane thought Lord Lansbury seemed taller and more elegant than ever. Trying to still her racing heart, not wishing to intrude on the group, she hung back, reluctant to put herself forward. Lord Lansbury received her with polite courtesy and Miss Spelling, with kid-gloved hand placed in a possessive manner on his arm, with a practised smile and noticeable coolness.

Laughing gaily, Octavia wrapped her arms about her brother's waist, much to Miss Spelling's annoyance. She took a step back as if she'd been stung when the child reached out to touch one of the flounces on her skirt.

'Please don't touch my dress, Lady Octavia,' she snapped.

Octavia snatched her hand away and stared up at her before sending Jane a look of piteous bewilderment, not liking the tone of Miss Spelling's voice and not knowing what she'd done wrong.

Seeing the hurt and distress on Octavia's face, Jane took her hand and drew her to her side. 'Lady Octavia was only admiring your dress. She has done no harm so please don't shout at her.' Looking down at Octavia, she smiled. 'Don't be upset, Lady Octavia. You have done no wrong.'

Taken aback by the sharp firmness in Jane's voice, Miss Spelling stared at her with severe reproach. 'And why should she not be reprimanded? Spare the rod and spoil the child is what they say, is it not?'

'They can say what they like,' Lord Lansbury said with a deadly calm. 'We like spoiling Octavia.' Turning from her and looking fondly at his sister, he stroked her cheek. 'Are you all right, poppet?' She nodded up at him and he smiled tenderly, hoping that what could have turned out to be an awkward situation had been averted. 'Allow me to introduce you to Miss Mortimer, Lydia,' he said. 'I don't believe the two of you have met.'

Miss Spelling looked at her with a mocking air, making no attempt to hide her scrutiny. Her eyes were hard as she looked Jane up and down that was only a shade away from insolence. She assessed Jane in a manner suggesting she thought she must have fallen on hard times.

'Do come closer, Miss Mortimer. There is no need to be so ill at ease, I assure you. I bark, but never have I been known to bite. Lady Lansbury has told me about you. You are Lady Octavia's governess?'

In that intense moment, surrounded by the opulence of Lady Lansbury's guests, Jane felt some emotion from Miss Spelling, pressing in on her, squeezing her with icy, inflexible fingers. The woman was striking, secure in her own strength and sure of her own incomparable worth.

'I suppose Miss Mortimer does hold the position as Octavia's governess, but she is more of a companion to her,' Lord Lansbury provided. 'We met on the ship when we were returning from France. Her quick actions saved Octavia's life. We have much to be grateful to her for.'

Miss Spelling gave Jane a look which suggested

that her presence devalued the occasion, shaking her head as if pondering what the world was coming to when the upper classes entertained their servants.

'You have been abroad, Miss Mortimer?'

'I have lived abroad almost all my life,' Jane answered. 'My father was an historian—a writer and collector of antiquities. We travelled extensively.'

'Really?' Miss Spelling replied, seemingly unimpressed. The full red smile never wavered, but her eyes were cold. Everything about her was precise and impeccable. 'How very odd.'

Jane managed to retain a cool and unruffled expression as she watched Miss Spelling's diamond earrings flash against her cheeks. She looked in vain for some trace of softness in her, but she was as hard as the trunk of the stout oak tree behind her. 'Not at all. His work was interesting.' Jane felt Miss Spelling's eyes on her once more and an aura of sensuous rose perfume wafted around her.

'And did you assist him in his work?'

'Yes, I did.'

'And do you miss the work?'

'I do, although it didn't end when he died. I still have much to do to complete the work he left unfinished. I enjoyed working with him and we travelled to many interesting places. We even travelled on a camel train from China to Northern India. After that we went to Europe, to Greece and on to Egypt, which was where he died nearly four months ago.'

'It sounds—unusual, to say the least. But what manner of man takes his daughter round the world with no protection other than himself—and then…?'

Jane heard reproach in the deep, husky voice and her spine stiffened. For some mysterious reason Miss Spelling had clearly taken an instant dislike to her. She suddenly resented the rounded curves, the dark hair piled up on the haughty, fascinating head. Her own eyes narrowed.

'What? Died? My father was a good man, Miss Spelling, loving and caring,' she said in his defence, trying to keep her anger at the woman's rudeness in check, 'and you insult me by implying otherwise. Until his death he was a healthy, vigorous man. He didn't know he was going to die. And he taught me well—mainly how to cope when things became difficult. Which I did.'

For one vivid instant the air between them shivered with tense friction. But if Miss Spelling was disconcerted by Jane's abrupt and forthright manner, she hid it quickly under a mask of indifference.

'I see.' She looked towards where a lady seated next to Lady Lansbury was beckoning to her with a hand glittering with sapphires. 'Excuse me, Miss Mortimer. I am being summoned.'

Jane nodded, feeling irritated that she should be so summarily dismissed. 'Of course. Don't let me keep you.'

Lord Lansbury watched Lydia go before turning to Jane. Her violet eyes with their long shadowing lashes were following Lydia. In one quick glance he saw the change her dress had made to her, the long creamy neck exposed. He saw the tiny dimple in her chin and the voluptuous curve of her red lips. He saw the tiny black mole high on her cheek where the rose faded into the gleaming white of her forehead. She was sensuous, provocative, glowing with colour like a country girl, and it seemed to him she was quite out of place among the elegant and sophisticated guests.

His granite features softened as if he understood how angry and humiliated she must be feeling by Lydia's thoughtless remark. 'I apologise for Lydia,' he said. 'She shouldn't have said that about your father. I can see she has offended you with her frankness.'

At any other time she would have been absurdly flattered by his courtesy and concern, but now she was perplexed and shook her head. 'Frank to the point of rudeness.'

'I am sorry you see it that way. Lydia is American and tends to be outspoken.' His voice was polite as he tried to smooth over the awkwardness of Miss Mortimer's strained meeting with his future fiancée.

'That does not excuse her. I am not used to Americans, but I am not prejudiced against the race. Miss Spelling should not have said what she did. I allow no one to speak ill of my father. He was a fine man. A clever man and a loving father. I could not have had better.'

Christopher's entire face instantly became hard, shuttered and aloof. 'You are fortunate in that, Miss Mortimer. More than you realise.' With a slight inclination of his head, he said, 'Excuse me.'

She stepped back. 'Of course,' she said stiffly, somewhat bewildered by the small knot of tension in the centre of her chest.

Jane knew a keen and surprising sense of disappointment when Lord Lansbury left her so abruptly. She watched him join the animated circle of guests that had collected round his mother. The hum of voices and laughter rose. Jane caught Lady Lansbury's eye. The conversation between the three of them had been observed by Lady Lansbury, who was not too lost in her own that she was unable to monitor the situation a few yards away.

Jane let her eyes dwell on Lord Lansbury's face. She had dressed with care, imagining the moment when she found herself in his company. She wanted to do something to make him look at her, and if not exactly see her, then at least realise she had the ability, the mind, perhaps, to capture his masculine attention. She so wanted to see that look in his eyes that he reserved for other females, the look that told them they were the most important person in the world to him at that moment.

Never had any man looked so attractive or so distant, and never had her heart called out so strongly to anyone. She knew she must fight her attraction for him. It would be madness to consider herself anything but out of his class, a social inferior. And his standards were not hers. She tried to pull her wits together, all too aware that the other women were studying her with furtive curiosity. She saw Lord Lansbury smile down into Miss Spelling's upturned face. For one terrible moment she was seized with passionate hatred for the other woman, so terrible and so unexpected that she was shocked by it.

Normally Jane would feel no qualms about joining a group in conversation, but something about the way Lord Lansbury commanded the attention of those around him and the presence of Miss Spelling made her hold back.

She could not hear what he was saying, but she could tell that this was not just polite attention on the part of the listeners. Lord Lansbury held his audience in thrall. A moment later he laughed at a remark thrown his way, looked up and caught sight of Jane. He raised an eyebrow and then resumed his conversation.

'Come, Christopher,' Miss Spelling said, hooking her hand possessively through his arm. 'I care little for standing still in the hot sun. Shall we circulate?'

The two moved off to exchange social niceties and introductions with the other guests, Miss Spelling sailing forth, very much aware of the stir she had created and obviously enjoying it as she and her handsome escort went from one group to the next.

As Jane watched them from across the stretch

of lawn that lay like a rich green carpet between them, Lord Lansbury led Miss Spelling in the direction of a summer house, where several guests were seated, the servants dancing attendance on them. She suddenly realised that although he was perfectly attentive, there was no singular affection between them. There was a distance there and Miss Spelling seemed more interested in nodding and greeting those they encountered than engaging Lord Lansbury in conversation.

As if Lady Lansbury had read her thoughts, moving to stand beside her, she said, 'So you have been introduced to Miss Spelling, Jane.' She sighed deeply, shaking her head as her eyes followed her son and the woman who might be his intended as they conversed with the guests. 'She is an American—which I suppose explains a great deal. And she is attractive, do you not agree, Jane?'

'How could I not? She is very beautiful.'

'Yes,' Lady Lansbury said, somewhat absently on a wry note. 'She has youth, beauty, excellent connections and wealth and a certain fashionable notoriety. What more could a man desire in a woman?'

Continuing to watch the pair, in answer to Lady Lansbury's wistful comment Jane thought perhaps money was a useful commodity, and property. But then, as the only daughter of an American millionaire, Lydia Spelling had all that. But would she be as desirable if she wasn't dressed by France's finest couturiers and wallowing in luxury and wealth? Of course she was as attractive and amusing as any of her contemporaries, but, Jane wondered, was it her money that preceded her whenever she walked into a room? Was it her money that triggered all those sideways covert glances, the conversations that faltered when she approached?

'Her father is very rich,' Lady Lansbury went on, 'made his money in industry—in railroads and armaments and commodities. But he is not a part of the social circle. Some would say Miss Spelling is a good catch, but rich American girls are not accepted by the New York Knickerbocker set.'

'Then it could also be said that Miss Spelling has landed on her feet.'

'Exactly. It appears that American girl's outspokenness and independent spirits are characteristics that Englishmen find charming. On the whole that is the case. Lydia is Mr Spelling's only child. He is ambitious. He wants only the very best for his daughter—a title, which is why he has brought her to Europe to display her like a costly gem to be admired. This gem is destined for a coronet, at least.

Christopher can provide him with that. I can only hope my son knows what he's doing.'

'I'm sure he does, Lady Lansbury,' Jane answered, careful to hide her envy of Lydia Spelling while wishing with every fibre of her being that she was the woman being flaunted on Lord Lansbury's arm.

'I'm not at all sure, Jane. I have great affection for my son, but he does have his faults. I'm concerned about him doing the right thing. But of course I take care not to let such comments reach his ears. It is his affair, after all, who he marries. But if I were a betting woman I'd wager he isn't in love with her.'

'Not everyone who marries is in love,' Jane said quietly. 'In some of the countries I have visited, men and women have their marriages arranged by their parents. Sometimes the couple don't meet until their wedding day. I've heard the opinion that love and marriage are two separate things.'

Lady Lansbury studied her closely. 'And what is your opinion, Jane?'

'That those who expressed that opinion must be sadly cynical people. What other reason is there to marry?'

'Children is a good place to start.'

Jane gave Lady Lansbury a look of feigned astonishment. 'Oh! I did not realise one needed a wedding ceremony to beget children.'

Lady Lansbury laughed. 'What a wicked observation, Jane. Some would say you are quite shocking.'

'Wicked, maybe, but also sensible.'

Lady Lansbury's smile died. 'You are a wonderful revelation, Jane, and I shall enjoy continuing our conversation on marriage at another time.' She glanced once more in the direction of her son, but then, recollecting herself, she looked directly at Jane. 'Forgive me, my dear, for being so forthright, but—what I said about Christopher, I am sure I can rely on your discretion.'

As if reading her mind, Jane said, 'Of course, Lady Lansbury. I never betray a confidence.'

A look of understanding passed between the two women. 'Thank you, Jane,' Lady Lansbury answered.

Considering Lord Lansbury's affairs nothing to do with her, Jane thought it prudent to keep any further opinions on marriage to herself. For the time she had known Lady Lansbury, she had discovered she had a forthright friendliness she liked. They often talked together. Lady Lansbury was very frank. She told Jane how much she admired her Aunt Caroline, who had made quite a niche for herself since her husband's death ten years ago.

Observing Octavia who was watching her brother, Jane noticed her cheeks were flushed and her eyes were larger and brighter than she had seen them. 'Are you all right, Lady Octavia?'

She nodded. 'Can we go and get something to eat? I'm hungry.'

'Of course we can. If you will excuse us, Lady Lansbury.'

'Of course, my dear. Run along,' she said, looking with concern at her daughter as she fidgeted from one foot to the other. 'Octavia is looking a little flushed. Perhaps it's the sun.'

'I'll get her a glass of iced lemonade—and I'm sure an ice cream would not go amiss,' she suggested, knowing of Octavia's love of that particular desert.

'I don't like Christopher's friend,' Octavia said, in a childishly conspiratorial whisper when they were far enough away from her mother to be overheard.

'But why? Why don't you like her, Lady Octavia?'

'She's always cross. I just don't like her. She isn't my friend.'

And just as suddenly her agitation was gone and she looked up and searched Jane's face with her soft blue gaze. There was a gentle elusiveness about her that declared her to be as fragile and vulnerable as a summer flower and she possessed a strange, tragic quality that always touched Jane deeply.

'We shall always be friends, won't we, Jane?'

'Yes, Lady Octavia, I will always be your friend,' Jane said with genuine warmth.

Octavia continued to search Jane's face. 'Truly? Cross your heart?'

Jane smiled, then with her forefinger she made a sign over her own heart. 'Cross my heart,' she promised.

Chapter Three

Taking Octavia's hand in her own, Jane led her towards the terrace, where she asked one of the servants to bring ice cream for Octavia and some fruit for herself. Three governesses sat near a graceful white gazebo, watching several children who had come with their parents playing happily with a ball, throwing it from one to the other. Octavia watched them, showing no sign of wanting to join in their fun as their happy voices rang out, mingling with the deeper, more reserved voices of the grown-ups.

For the next half hour Octavia remained close to Jane. She was quiet, with that odd, faraway look in her eyes Jane had become familiar with. Finishing her ice cream, Octavia became restless, which did not go unnoticed by Lady Lansbury.

'Why don't you take Octavia for a walk, Jane?

Perhaps she would like to go down to the lake to see the swans.'

Jane was more than happy to leave the party. In the field with her father and his contemporaries the difference in rank had seemed irrelevant. What counted was knowledge and expertise and in that environment she had felt equal to anyone. But here among the glittering nobility and gentry where she had not even her looks to recommend her she felt awkward and was glad Lady Lansbury had given her the opportunity to slip away.

Jane took Octavia's hand and they walked along the garden paths to the back of the house. Jane stared ahead at the surrounding countryside with her eyes narrowed in concentration. The view never failed to impress her. Acres upon breathtaking acres stretched out before her and all owned by one man.

Swans drifted gracefully on the still water of the lake and beyond the lake a hill was topped by an ornate building that reminded Jane of some kind of temple. Its entrance was supported by two columns of the Roman Doric order, and above was an open colonnade of Corinthian columns. The entire structure was surmounted by a cupola. It looked extremely interesting and Jane had already decided to take a closer look when she was alone.

They paused to sit together on the grass, looking through a long stretch of fence that enclosed the stables and the large paddock where horses nibbled at the grass. Drawing her knees up to her chest, with a sigh Jane listened to the distant voices and the hum of busy insects in the grass and wild flowers. She smiled with a feeling of contentment. Chalfont was like nothing she had experienced before and she felt herself ensnared by this lovely place that seemed to be closing itself around her and claiming her for its own.

Having a deep and abiding fear of horses, Octavia was always reluctant to go close to them. Big-eyed, she watched them warily.

'That's a mare, Lady Octavia, the brown one with the lovely mane. Is she not beautiful? See how her coat shines with the sun on it. Of course she is groomed every day, so that helps.'

At the sound of her voice the animal raised its head and began to walk towards them. Standing up, Jane went to the fence and, holding out her hand, patted her neck. Out of the corner of her eye she noted how Octavia held back.

'See, Lady Octavia, she's as docile as a lamb. I'm sure she would like it if you were to pat her like I'm doing.'

With her eyes fastened on the horse, Octavia got to her feet and gingerly moved close, her hand resting companionably on Jane's waist as she moved closer to the fence. To Jane's delight she didn't draw back when the horse nudged her head against them.

'Stroke her nose, Lady Octavia, don't be afraid. Watch me, just there.' Taking Octavia's hand, she rested it on the glossy, quivering nose of the animal and the child left it there, unafraid in the confident grasp of her new friend, patting tentatively the patient mare, her bright, long-lashed eyes like cornflowers in the smiling face.

Christopher watched them as he strolled along the garden path in their direction and he began to smile for their laughter was infectious.

On seeing Miss Mortimer leave the gathering with Octavia and with Lydia engaged in conversation with a group of ladies, in view of his earlier rudeness and feeling that some form of polite apology was now required of him, he'd decided to follow.

His face was soft and his eyes warm and adoring when they dwelt on his young sister. Octavia was twelve years old, but she had the mind of a child half her age. While ever he was able he would see that she was cherished and that nothing would harm her. At these times his father's legacy and the responsibility of his inheritance weighed heavily upon him.

He had to give Miss Mortimer her due, for in the short time she had been at Chalfont House she had transformed Octavia. And now here she was, helping his sister combat her fear of horses. No one had been able to get her within yards of one before.

He walked closer, drawn compulsively to Miss Mortimer and to the enchanted child she was bringing, by her own efforts, to everyone's notice. His footsteps made no sound on the grass and she was speaking, unaware of his approach. He stopped to listen to her, bewitched by this new picture of Miss Mortimer in her sapphire-blue dress. What a proud, spirited young woman she was, he thought. He hadn't expected her to blossom into this lovely young woman, simply by shedding those unflattering clothes she wore. Perhaps he had disliked the dismal gowns so much—and her violet eyes reminded him of Lily—that it had tainted his view of her.

'And when you feel confident enough,' Jane went on, completely oblivious to being observed, 'I am sure your brother will teach you to ride and then you will gallop through the fields and the wind will blow away your bonnet and you shall be as free as the lark which soars in the skies.' Her eyes turned in the direction of the open fields surrounded by thick woodland, dotted with hedges and fences that were used to train Chalfont's horses for the hunt. Her voice was soft and dreaming.

'I used to ride once, Lady Octavia. Where I lived for a time, my father and I would ride out together. Sometimes I would ride on and go like the wind. My father would call after me—dear Father, urging me not to go so fast. But I didn't care. I was free. It was wild where I rode and beautiful and there was no one to tell me what I must do or say or think when I rode alone. You will feel like that when you can ride. Would you like that, sweetheart?'

Sweetheart? She had called his sister sweetheart! Christopher Chalfont was known as a hard man, a stubborn, iron-willed man, but he stood now, immensely shaken, terribly moved, feeling more than he liked to feel. He moved closer, mesmerised by the lovely picture the woman and the child created.

He watched her unconscious grace and poise as she moved to stand behind Octavia. Apart from her face and slender hands and lower arms not an inch of flesh was exposed and not a single hair escaped that severe bun. In the soft light her profile was all hollows and shadows. There was a purity about her, something so endearingly young and innocent that reminded him of a sparrow. He tried to envisage what she would look like if the little sparrow changed her plumage and became a swan, and the image that took shape in his mind was pleasing and also troubling. Feeling compelled and at liberty to look his fill, he felt his heart contract, not having grasped the full reality of her appeal until that moment.

Octavia looked from the horse to the face of the woman, understanding little but responding to the joy in Miss Mortimer's voice.

Suddenly Jane became completely still—a young animal which is aware instinctively of danger—then she turned slowly, Octavia turning to look with her, into the face of Christopher Chalfont. Octavia laughed, the horse forgotten, and ran towards him.

'Why, good heavens, Lord Lansbury, you gave me quite a start,' Jane gasped. Except for her treacherous heartbeat, which insisted on accelerating the closer he came, she retained her control. 'You came upon us so quietly I did not know you were there.'

He smiled, placing his arm about his sister's shoulders. Octavia was clinging to his leg and looking up at him adoringly. 'Is that not how one learns the secrets of others, Miss Mortimer, and sees things which otherwise one might miss? If one steps carefully and quietly so that no one can hear or see one's approach the most enlightening facts are frequently uncovered. It can be quite rewarding—as now. I am amazed to see Octavia so close to the horse. She's shown nothing but fear of them all her life and now here she is, stroking the nose of one quite unafraid.'

'And is that not a good thing?'

'It most certainly is. I don't know how you did it, Miss Mortimer—but I thank you. My sister is lucky to have you.'

Jane smiled. 'I think we both might be lucky, Lord Lansbury.'

He dropped his arm when Octavia moved away to stand at the fence, where the horse still stood waiting for another pat. Finding herself alone, she merely stood and gazed at the mare. She made no attempt to pat it again, but nor did she move away.

'Are you enjoying the party?' Christopher asked.

'Yes, very much.'

'Yet I noticed how you seemed to prefer to stand on the fringe.'

'The truth is,' Jane said a little shakily, 'that as a woman of limited importance, I was scared to death of being among so many important people.'

'You were?' he said, sobering. That she would feel like that had never entered his head. 'They won't harm you and I am the last person in the world you'll ever have to fear.'

His words and his tone made her limbs quake and her heart hammer. His dark hair was tousled and she was filled with the impulse to run her fingers through its waves. Gazing openly at him, she decided she liked the crinkles at the corners of his eyes caused by smiling. He had lovely eyes and she wondered if he knew it. Then, pulling herself together, she wickedly chose that moment to lift her head and turn the full impact of her brilliant smile upon him. Lord Lansbury stepped back in amazement.

'I am the proverbial wallflower, Lord Lansbury. I am happy doing that. I confess to feeling a little overwhelmed by it all. I'm unused to such a grand gathering. When I came out of the house it reminded me of a tableau set up to tell a story. I find it rather awe-inspiring, fascinating and compelling to stand on the edge of a gathering such as this and simply watch everyone—how they react with each other.'

'You really are the most unconventional woman,' he said, his lips twitching.

'I suppose I am to someone like you, Lord Lansbury. A conventional person would not have crossed swords with a perfect stranger in front of so many people as I just did.'

'The defence of your father was not just a conventional notion of justice. In order to protect a loved one's reputation what you did was quite understandable.'

'Nevertheless I frequently find the rules of social etiquette and convention tiresome to the extreme, but they are rules which must be obeyed.'

Tilting his head to one side, he said, 'Did you really travel by camel train?'

'Yes, I did—the Silk Road—the southern road from China to northern India.'

'I am impressed, Miss Mortimer,' he remarked with a lazy, devastating smile. 'You are full of surprises. What a truly remarkable achievement for a young woman.'

'I was just twelve at the time.'

'And you rode camels.'

'Yes, indeed.'

'And elephants?' he asked, distracted by a strand of hair brushing against her cheek and resisting the temptation to brush it away.

'I did,' she replied, unaware of the path along which his mind wandered, 'although they are not such temperamental beasts as the camels, which are not at all easy to ride. They also spit.'

He feigned surprise. 'I cannot imagine anyone, man or beast, getting the better of you, Miss Mortimer. Were you not afraid?'

'Not at all, although with deserts and mountains to traverse, the route from China to India is not the most hospitable region in the world. Yes, I have ridden on camels, lived in desert tents and taken part in the excavation of ancient ruins. It was all one big adventure for me.'

'Your whole life appears to have been one big fascinating adventure. I envy you.'

Uncomprehending, Jane stared at him. 'You envy me? But—how? Why? You are the Earl of Lansbury. You live in this beautiful house. You have everything here you could ever want.'

He gave a brief, humourless smile. 'It must seem that way to you. You are right, to a point. I have a certain amount of power, but I do not have the freedom to do as I wish.'

'I do not understand.'

He met her gaze. Henry Chalfont, Christopher's father, had died leaving him with a mountain of debts. His grandfather had been the third Earl of Lansbury with a successful head for business. His running of the estate was crowned with success. On his death Henry had inherited the title and the estate. Henry had committed the grievous sin of believing that the wealth he had inherited would last for ever, with no need on his part to improve or even keep in good repair the estate. He had a talent for one thing and that was how to spend the most money on himself in the shortest possible time.

'My father died before Octavia was born. I was nineteen when I took over Chalfont, old enough to appreciate all that it means. The estate was almost bankrupt—which, to a certain extent, I managed to overcome. Thankfully things are beginning to improve, but they could be better. Had I the means, as the Earl of Lansbury I could have done all sorts of things—the Grand Tour—all the adventurous and exciting things you have done. But Chalfont was at the core of everything.'

Jane was moved by what he said. His voice was soft and warm to her ears. 'You must love it very much.'

He nodded, his gaze slowly sweeping the beautiful green acres. 'Chalfont never changes,' he murmured. 'It smiles, it beckons, it invites and welcomes. I have loved it since I was a child. There is nowhere quite like it.'

'I know what you mean,' Jane answered. 'I am a stranger here, yet I feel it, too. Who could resist it?'

'Who indeed! The estate has to be run,' Christopher went on. 'I get to London from time to time and I have bailiffs and managers to oversee the different aspects of managing things, but I have to be here. I consider running the estate a full-time job and the concerns of my tenant farmers are my own concerns.'

'And is that what all earls do?' Jane asked, her ignorance showing through.

He shook his head. 'Most of my fellow landed aristocrats consider my work habits unseemly and highly eccentric—no way for an earl to act, they say, and that I set a very bad example.'

'And what do you say?'

'I don't care a fig what the rest of the gentry think, but the welfare of my tenants is most important to me. And then there is Octavia. With Octavia being the way she is—both my mother and Octavia depend on me being here.'

'Were you like your father?'

His face hardened and he shook his head. 'No. When you were growing up, were you ever lonely?' he asked, quickly diverting the conversation away from her question.

She shook her head. 'No. We were always with a team of archaeologists and such like. There were times when I was the only English girl for hundreds of miles, with only monkeys and stone statues for company. But I was never lonely.'

'Why did your father take you with him? Why not leave you with Mrs Standish?'

'To be raised like a proper young lady, you mean?'

'Something like that.'

Jane tried to speak as lightly as she could, not wanting the circumstances of her life to shadow the conversation. 'My mother was very young when she married my father. They had been married for ten years before I came along and wherever they went showed an open delight in one another that was as diverting to those who found themselves in their company as it was unusual. My father loved my mother and was loved by her and neither of them saw any reason to hide it, not even when I was born. Everyone was used to their utter devotion. My mother was beautiful, graceful, sweet natured and inclined to laughter. Father was devastated when she died—as I was.'

'How old were you?'

'Eight years old. We were in India at the time. My father couldn't bear to part with me and I refused to leave him. It was suggested he send me to England to live with Aunt Caroline—she was the only family I had left, but to lose both my mother and me was unbearable to him. He grieved for my mother, but he never abandoned his work or me. His work was important to him so he did the best he could. I was educated wherever we happened to be.'

'You must have experienced many cultural changes on your travels.'

'I learned more about countries and people than any schoolroom could have taught me. I was educated by the opinions and manners of the societies in which I lived and to a great degree was taught independence.'

'Is it not the opinion that a woman should not feel herself independent?'

'What? And be governed by the fears and restrictions that blight so many women's lives? I do not share that opinion. I have a mind and will of my own and make my own decisions. I learned a great deal from the many cultures in which I lived, through sheer observation of real life. I was allowed more freedom than if I had been raised in England and many times I had to fend for myself—although Father was always on hand to give me guidance. '

'You've seen a great deal of the world, I imagine.'

'I like to roam.'

'Doesn't it become boring after a while?'

'Not in the least. I loved the life.'

'Nevertheless, it still sounds a lonely life.'

'To someone who has never experienced it, I suppose it does.'

'And marriage, Miss Mortimer? Surely you will want to marry one day.'

'In truth, I've been so busy that marriage has never entered my head. For the time being I am content to carry on as I am, doing what my father did, and to support myself. But when—if—I do marry, then I shall have a marriage like that of my parents—loving and true.'

'Love is not the only side to a relationship.'

'I know. But it is the most important one. I realise that for some money and gain in some way is the only consideration, but there is more to marriage than that. Two people should marry because they love each other, because they are important to each other, because there is a longing to be close to each other.'

'You are a romantic, Miss Mortimer.'

'I suppose I am. When I marry I will settle for nothing less.' When he gave her a sceptical glance she raised her brows in question. 'Do you find something wrong with that?'

Shaking his head slowly, he smiled thinly. 'In my opinion love is a common passion, in which chance and sensation take the place of choice and reason and draw the mind out of its accustomed state.'

'Well—as you said, that is your opinion, but I will not under any circumstances reduce myself to living in wifely obedience in a loveless marriage.'

Christopher gazed at her for a long moment, digesting what she had said and moved more than she could possibly know by her words. 'How extraordinary,' he said after a moment, feigning mockery. 'And all the time I've been harbouring the delusion that all girls yearn to snare wealthy husbands.'

'I am not like other girls.'

'I'm beginning to realise that,' he said quietly. He was deeply moved by her opinions on marriage.

She spoke passionately about things he could not begin to imagine and he was beginning to realise that many more conversations like this with Jane Mortimer could be in danger of derailing his plans to marry Lydia. 'Did you enjoy London for the short time you were there? Were you not tempted to seek the social whirl? Visiting friends of your aunt would keep you busy. I imagine you would be fully occupied from morning till night on the frivolous pastimes with which you ladies fill your days.'

'I should hate that above all things,' Jane said frankly. 'As a matter of fact, I prefer to fill my time with more worthwhile pursuits. I do what I do and I enjoy it.'

'How can you be sure of that?' he persisted. 'You have never known anything other than assisting your father in his work in the wilds of some foreign part of the world. London can be very alluring to an unattached young woman.'

'To some I am sure it is. But not for me. I have very simple tastes. I thank you for your consideration for me and I would not have you believe me ungrateful, but I am like the flowers that you will find growing in the wild. Transplant them, or even bring them into the house, and they die.'

She fell silent, her eyes sparkling. Breathing deeply, she gazed at the lake in the distance. Her senses drank in the intoxication of it all. She suddenly felt like a gilded bird freed from its cage for a few, precious moments. And all the while she was conscious of the man beside her. His closeness lent to her nostrils a scent of his cologne, not overpowering like so many strong perfumes meant to cover the stench of unwashed bodies, but fleeting and inoffensive, a clean, masculine smell. Vividly conscious of her proximity to him, she sharply turned away before he could realise just how much he had affected her.

Octavia chose that moment to walk back to her and take her hand. 'You said we could go to the lake to see the swans. Will you come, Christopher?'

He shook his head. 'I must return to the party. I have neglected our guests long enough. Go with Jane. I know how much you like to watch the swans.'

'Shall we go now?' Octavia looked up at Jane.

'Of course, Lady Octavia.' She turned to Lord Lansbury. 'Excuse us.'

He nodded in silence and watched them walk away.'

'I'll race you?' Octavia suddenly cried, beginning

to run on ahead, her bonnet becoming dislodged and bouncing against her back.

Jane laughed, giving Octavia a head start before she skipped after her, releasing all her suppressed energy.

Christopher watched her go, her bright skirts dancing about her feet as she went, allowing him a tantalising glimpse of slim calves and ankles. Suddenly and completely out of the blue he felt a surge of admiration for the young woman who had just given him an insight into her life. Her purity and the sweet wild essence of her shone like a rare jewel. She was innocence and youth, gentleness and laughter, a wood nymph surrounded by nature, and without warning he felt hot desire pulsating to life within him—unexpected and certainly unwelcome. Ever since she had come to Chalfont he had tried not to think of her presence in the house, tried to resist the way his thoughts turned to her as he tried to focus on his relationship with Lydia, knowing how dangerous those feelings were to him.

Uttering a sound of angry exasperation, he turned away. What was he doing gazing at the girl like a moonstruck idiot? Why had the pleasant mood left him by memories stirred by Jane Mortimer?

On this instinctive thought his anger turned cooler, having recognised part of the cause. It was not her fault that her violet eyes were like those of someone whose memory was laced with bitter pain. Nor, doubtless, was it her fault that she was possessed of a troubling unusual kind of beauty that stirred his troubled soul.

When Jane and Octavia had left the party it had been five o'clock and the guests had begun to disperse—some to private bedrooms, others to drawing rooms and morning rooms. Still others preferred to sit or lie on the lawns, idling away the time between then and the evening's banquet, which would begin at seven. Afterwards the guests would leave for their respective homes and those who lived too far to travel were to stay the night.

It was now almost nine o'clock, with a crescent-shaped moon hanging high in the darkening sky, when Octavia finally went to sleep.

Jane went through to her own adjoining room and drew back the gold brocade curtains of the heavily carved four-poster bed. Undressing and slipping her nightdress over her head before removing the pins from her hair and brushing out the tangles, she seated herself close to one of the windows and looked out at the night sky, letting her mind drift back in time. There was a chill in the air that penetrated her thin cotton shift, so she tied her dressing gown around her before opening the window wide to breathe in the fresh night air. Not yet ready to go to bed, she opened a book and read for an hour.

She was about to put the book aside when a soft tap on the door startled her. She jumped up, not expecting anyone at this time. Crossing through the sitting room adjoining her own and Octavia's room, she opened the door. She stood very still, staring with open amazement at the tall powerful figure of Lord Lansbury. Having removed his jacket, he wore a claret waistcoat over his white linen shirt.

He cocked a brow. 'I know it's late, and you can send me away if you wish, but can I come in?'

At the sound of his voice she experienced a rush of feeling, a bittersweet joy. Her cheeks flushed for she was aware that she was in no proper state to receive visitors. And now, confronted by him, she was only too conscious of her own inadequacy—of her old faded, blue-gingham dressing gown that no elegant lady would ever wear, of her tangled hair and bare feet. She took a deep breath, trying to stifle her rising embarrassment. Lord Lansbury always caught her at her most vulnerable. She could refuse to admit him, but the truth was that she didn't want to turn him away and she could see no harm in letting him in.

'Yes—of course.' Opening the door wide, she stood aside for him to pass.

'Thank you. I won't stay long,'

Christopher was thinking that she looked almost demure in her night attire, high at the neck and gathered under her breasts. But he suspected there was nothing demure about Jane Mortimer. She swept back her abundant hair—the colour, he could only imagine, of a flaming Indian sunset—framing her high, clear forehead with its striking widow's peak. He found himself wondering how it would feel to run his fingers through it. He was drawn to her eyes, with their long black lashes, which were the most definite thing about her face.

At that moment there was a defencelessness about her and the small smile on her lips brought a softening to his heart. It was softness that he felt, a sudden likeness without a feeling of desire for her and he felt a strange urge to protect her. Her face mirrored her confusion on being caught unawares. She looked vulnerable and much younger and she had the innocent appeal of a bewildered child. In fact, she seemed to him at that moment as childlike and pure as his sister. Her long lashes quivered and her eyes no longer reminded him of Lily's for there was in them no appeal—clear and untroubled they looked up at him.

'You have come to see Lady Octavia,' Jane said, 'but she is fast asleep. She was quite worn out after all the excitement.'

'Octavia is not the only one I came to see, Miss Mortimer,' he murmured, his gaze lingering on her face.

'Oh—r-really!' she stammered, his words taking her completely off guard. 'Well—I—I'm honoured.' His manner set her on edge. 'But as you see I am not in any proper state to receive you.'

'You could be wearing sackcloth and ashes for all I care. I imagine your gingham dressing gown is most...relaxing for this time of the evening.'

His voice, low and resonant, beckoned to things inside her that she hadn't even known existed. Tongues of heat curled in her belly. 'Yes—although I would think not every woman would forgive you for entering her room when she is in her night attire.'

The moment the words were out she would have given anything to recall them. Night attire like undergarments were considered an unmentionable subject and she had spoken of them to a man—and to a strange man, at that, who had the incredible effrontery to enter her room when he could see she was in a state of undress. Many ladies would swoon away in horror. Lord Lansbury, however, seemed unmoved. The enormity of her observation appeared to have escaped him and he replied in all seriousness.

'You are quite right and I beg your pardon if my intrusion into your private time has embarrassed you.' His attitude was entirely genuine. 'I must confess that to a large extent I ignore the corroding prudery that muffles and enshrouds almost every aspect of our domestic life in layers of taboo.' He smiled, for the sight of Miss Mortimer's scarlet cheeks brought home to him for the first time the fact that his coming to her room might be considered shockingly unorthodox. A muscle twitched at the corner of his mouth. 'However, it's good to see you at ease—and you do look rather fetching in your dressing gown, Miss Mortimer.'

The embarrassed colour faded from her cheeks. She was unaware that the dark red hair, tumbling unfashionably and wildly about her shoulders, was a hundred different shades and dazzling lights, as her eyes flared to life. He gazed down into her face, a smile beginning to curve his lips. His expression was unreadable, smiling, watchful, a knowing look in his eyes.

What kind of man are you, Christopher Chalfont? Jane wondered and realised she had no idea at all. She suspected he never talked about himself and that he gave of himself sparingly. Despite his self-assurance, she sensed a deep sadness in him, something frozen and withdrawn. What had happened to him to put it there? she wondered.

A light blazed briefly in his eyes and was then extinguished. She gave him a speculative look, deeply conscious that his easy, almost mocking exterior hid the inner man. There was a withheld power to command in him that was as impressive as it was irritating.

'When you returned from the lake, did you enjoy what was left of the party?'

Jane smiled, feeling a treacherous warmth seep through her. 'Thank you, yes—although Lady Octavia was tired, so we didn't stay long. How kind of you to think of me—but you shouldn't be neglecting your guests.'

'My mother is entertaining them in the drawing room. I think they can manage without me for half an hour.'

The door to Octavia's room was ajar and he walked towards it, going inside where he stood by her bed and gazed down at her sleeping face. A book lay open on the bedside table, showing a colourful procession of giraffes, zebras, elephants and other animals making their way on to the shelter of the Ark. Picking it up, he flicked the pages, each one as colourful and interesting as the one before.

He cocked an eyebrow at Jane. 'This book looks interesting.'

'It is—at least Lady Octavia thinks so. She loves stories about animals and is rather fond of this one.'

'I don't recognise it.'

'My—father gave it to me when I was little. It's a bit dog-eared from all the handling and travelling about, but I hoped Lady Octavia would find it as pleasurable as I did. I hope you don't mind.'

'Not at all,' he said, placing the book back on the table. 'It was thoughtful of you.'

Jane knew his eyes were on her as he approached, but after a quick glance at him she dropped her eyes to the floor, angry with herself and with him because, inevitably, whenever he spoke, it seemed to her that his words, however ordinary and commonplace, threw her into confusion.

Shoving his hands into his trouser pockets, he looked at her. 'And how are you getting on with your work?'

'Very well—although I still have rather a lot to deal with,' she answered, leading the way into the small sitting room so as not to disturb the sleeping child.

'You must work very hard.'

'I don't mind at all. I enjoy it, especially when we made extraordinary historical finds. I sent a manuscript and photographs of the assignment my father was working on before he died to his publisher and an illustrator. I am sure they will be satisfied.'

His sudden sweeping smile was disarming and confounded her. 'I would expect nothing less. You strike me as a most competent person, Miss Mortimer.'

She laughed, opening her wide mouth and showing her teeth, white and perfectly aligned. The way she laughed suggested a potential for reckless abandon that drew Christopher's interest.

'Competent? Are young ladies not usually described as accomplished?'

'I would have applied the word had I thought it applied to you. Although I am sure you have many accomplishments to your credit.'

'I don't have many. My dancing leaves a lot to be desired—I have two left feet, I'm afraid. I can't sing and I don't play the piano—and I certainly can't sew a fine seam. But I do have other traits to recommend me.'

'Such as?'

'Excavating sights of historical interest. As well as digging for ancient relics, I hunt. I play croquet—although I suppose that particular game is regarded as civilised—but in fact I do all manner of things which are considered unladylike. I'm afraid I would be frowned upon most severely by society—of which I must confess my ignorance.'

'Where young ladies are concerned, it is defined as those who are eligible for presentation at court.'

'I'm afraid I would be considered a lost cause.'

'Then consider yourself fortunate.' He looked at her for a moment in thoughtful silence, then said, 'What is your opinion of Miss Spelling?'

Jane was completely taken aback by the question and her eyes snapped to his. 'I—I cannot answer that—and it's not fair of you to ask me. Miss Spelling and I are—not acquainted—but—she seems—very nice,' she answered hesitantly.

'Be honest,' Christopher said, amused at the way she tried to equivocate. 'I got the distinct impression when I introduced the two of you that you didn't like her.'

Jane's cheeks flamed. 'Am I as transparent as that?'

'As glass.' He chuckled.

'I think the feeling is mutual. If you know my opinion, why did you ask me?' she retorted crossly. Not for a moment did it enter her head to deny it. 'Forgive me if I appear impertinent, but I could not help noticing that the two of you—don't…'

'Don't what? Look like love's young dream?' he said on a wry note. Seeing the answer in her eyes, he nodded. 'We don't know each other well enough for that. We met in America—in New York. Her father is a self-made millionaire. He is ambitious and interested in all things European—including a title for his only daughter. An attractive girl with a rich father is automatically a treasured being.'

'So—you decided to ask her to be your wife.'

'Not immediately. Nothing was said—it has still not been discussed. Mr Spelling intended stopping off in London en route to Paris, so I deemed it only polite to invite them to Chalfont.'

'But—wouldn't a more select gathering have been more prudent—instead of inviting them to the countess's birthday party with half of Oxfordshire present?' The answer dawned in her eyes when a slow smile curved his firm lips. 'Oh—now I understand. It was to assess Miss Spelling as a possible wife without appearing too obvious. Am I right?'

'You read me too well.' He chuckled. 'But it isn't difficult. Lydia is the kind of woman any man would be honoured to have as his wife.'

'That depends on the kind of wife you want. Although I don't suppose it's every day you meet an American heiress. A tempting prospect indeed.'

Christopher cocked a questioning brow. 'You must think my reason for considering marriage to Miss Spelling is rather mercenary.'

'Of course not. I am aware that it is an accepted fact that in England, society is full of marriages of convenience and political and financial alliances.'

'It is common.'

'I am only surprised that you can be so matter-of-fact about an issue that is supposed to be the most important event in anyone's life. My world is so very different from yours, I'm afraid. But then

I may have got it all wrong. You are probably attracted to Miss Spelling because you think she's a sweet person who worships the ground you walk on—although perhaps she might not be quite so sweet if she were not so rich.'

Jane's forthright manner and the fact that she was not afraid to speak her mind brought a smile to Christopher's lips. 'Miss Spelling may be many things, but sweet is not one of them. However, I will not betray my meticulous standards by bringing to Chalfont an unworthy countess.'

How cold and dispassionate his attitude was towards marrying Miss Spelling, Jane thought, having no wish to discuss it further. The mere idea of them together brought a pain to her heart. 'Then I wish you joy in her.'

For a moment Christopher considered her in thoughtful silence. 'Thank you for your opinion. Nevertheless, Miss Spelling does have some good points.'

'I know. After our conversation earlier, I feel like a pincushion already,' she told him drily.

Unable to contain his mirth, Christopher was laughing now with amusement, his teeth flashing white from between his parted lips. It was a rusty sound, as if he did not laugh very often.

'May I give you some advice, Miss Mortimer?' he enquired.

'If you must,' she replied lightly. 'But I warn you that it will be unlikely that I shall take it, for advice invariably exhorts one to do something that one does not wish to do or to give up something which one enjoys.'

Christopher threw back his head and laughed once more. She realised that when he did that he seemed younger, much younger, than when his face was in repose.

'You are incorrigible,' he said, 'and a complete contradiction in terms and appearance—in fact, in everything.'

'A contradiction?' she queried, looking puzzled.

'Yes,' he answered. 'You look reserved and pliable, yet I believe you are strong and determined and, if the truth be told, more than a little obstinate.'

'That sounds quite dreadful,' Jane said with mock gravity.

'That is a word that can never apply to you,' he replied, turning from her and strolling casually to the door.

Chapter Four

'You said you wanted to give me some advice.'

Christopher turned and looked back at her. 'My advice is for you not to change. To stay exactly as you are. One day you will be a wife and mother any man will be happy to make his own. Oh, and I feel I must compliment you on the dress you chose to wear today—definitely foreign. It was bright—exotic, in fact.'

There was a caressing note in his voice which should have caused Jane to take flight. Instead, perhaps because of the quietness all around them, she merely looked at him a little enquiringly and smiled. 'Like a peacock's plumage, you mean,' she murmured. 'I believe you are teasing me, Lord Lansbury.'

'Not at all. I was being perfectly serious.' He looked down at the table littered with books on

Greek and Roman antiquities and documents and monochrome photographic prints. 'May I?' he asked, indicating one of three men against a backdrop of an ancient temple.

'Please do.'

He gazed at it with interest. 'Would I be right in thinking that one of these gentlemen was your father?'

'The one on the left—with a moustache and wearing a battered old hat.'

'And the location?'

'Al Khazneh, which is one of the most elaborate temples of ancient Petra in Jordan.'

'It looks interesting.'

'It is. Petra is also called the Rose City due to the colour of the stone out of which it's carved. It's of immense historical importance. The artefacts that are being uncovered all the time and my father's writings are of tremendous benefit to scholars and historians the world over.'

'He must have been a clever man.'

'He was. He was particularly interested in ancient scripts and loved delving into myths and legends to find out the truth. He loved the fact that so much remains unanswered. He worked with a team—funded by different societies. Wherever we went, he made sure excavations sites were protected. Everything that was found had to be recorded and catalogued.'

'Which was where you came in.'

'Exactly. With immense buildings hacked into the rocks, Petra is one of the most beautiful places I've been to—like nowhere else on earth.'

The passion she felt for her work shone in her eyes, bringing a smile to his lips. 'I envy you your life, Miss Mortimer—and the special relationship you had with your father.' She had no idea how fortunate she was, he thought. His own father inspired him with nothing but disgust and loathing. 'It's clear to me that you loved your work. And were you in Jordan long?'

'My father was so keen to go there that we spent several months. That was the last picture that was taken of him. It is rather precious to me. It was taken in Thebes—where he died.'

'It must be a consolation to you to have a photograph of someone you care for.'

'Yes—but it is also a reminder of all I have lost,' she said softly. 'Perhaps it would be best to let the memories dim, but while ever I have the photographs I am reminded of how alive he was, how he lived for his work, how vivid he was.'

Jane met his gaze as he seemed to stare at her in a new way, the silver eyes behind the thick lashes crinkling at the corners. She was unaware that she was beginning to stir up his emotions, that he felt echoes of long-forgotten passions—anger, resentment and loss. She would be surprised to learn that before today he might have said that he no longer cared how his own past had affected his future, that somehow, talking to her was reawakening dormant grief.

'Time has a habit of passing,' he said, 'even though sometimes we would hold it back.'

He sighed deeply and looked at her and Jane was amazed by the expression in his eyes. It had a yearning quality, nostalgic almost, as if he was crushed by some scarcely supportable distress. She smiled, taking the photograph from him, unaware that the lights in her wonderful hair changed colour rapidly, from deepest wine to earth-brown to gold, as she abruptly moved her head.

'You are right and I am being sentimental.'

Christopher looked down at her fingers curled round the photograph. 'Perhaps. I was brought up by a father who believed sentimentality was a weakness and anything that was a weakness was abhorrent, forbidden. So was anything that made a man vulnerable, including love. I envy you your closeness to your father. I feel that some atonement for my abrupt behaviour this afternoon is in order. When I introduced you to Miss Spelling, it was rude of me to walk away as I did.'

Jane stared at him, quite intrigued by this confounding man. She was fascinated by this extraordinary conversation and by the very strangeness of having it. To her, his potential attraction was obvious and as she gazed into those cynical grey eyes she felt drawn to him as if by some overwhelming magnetic force. She remembered how, when she had mentioned her father, she had been struck by an undercurrent of intense emotion barely controlled, which, along with subdued whisperings of the servants on occasion, gave her reason to suspect the old earl had been a difficult man.

'Pease don't feel you have to apologise.'

At the sincerity of her reply, humour softened his features and his firm, sensual lips quirked in a derisive smile. 'Why? Because of who I am?'

'It has nothing to do with who you are. It's just that I don't think you have anything to apologise for.'

He laughed softly. 'You are too kind. In fact, you are unlike any woman I know.'

'Am I? In what way am I unlike the women of your acquaintance? Is it because I work?'

He nodded. 'The women I know have nothing to work for—not that they would be allowed to. Little wonder they are all so bored and frivolous. A man has honour for as long as he wishes. All women have is their virtue and once given it is gone. How unjust, don't you think so, Miss Mortimer?'

She hesitated, struck by the cynicism of his words, not certain whether he was ridiculing her. She should have been shocked, but she wasn't. She shrugged. 'I agree with you. You are absolutely right.'

He looked at her curiously. 'Then why do they never attempt to change all that? Has it never occurred to them?'

'I am sure it has,' she answered bluntly. 'Are you saying that women may be as free as men in your world, Lord Lansbury?'

'In an ideal world they would be, Miss Mortimer.'

'That is not what I asked.'

'I know. I shall have to give it some thought.'

'For myself—well—never having reason to question it, I've never thought about it. I just get on with what I have to do.'

'I applaud your honesty. It is a rare virtue in your

sex. Now I will bid you goodnight. I have kept you from your bed long enough.'

Jane watched him go, wishing that he would stay. She thought she must be going mad to have such reckless thoughts about him. She was uncertain what it was she hoped for, since Lord Lansbury was not for her. But something unusual had happened between them today. As yet she had had no time to mull it over, to examine it in depth, to visualise what she would do with it when she knew what it might be. Later she would think about what they had talked about, what he had said, the way he had said it and the expressions on his face.

If he married Miss Spelling, it would be to shore up the flagging finances on Chalfont. She understood why he would do it and she admired his courage and his tenacity. But feeling as she did for him and that marriage should be between two people who loved each other unconditionally, she could not admire him for the sacrifice he was about to make to marry without love for the sake of a house.

The easy interaction between them and the fact that he did not love Miss Spelling had planted a seed of hope in her heart. But she was not so naive as to believe anything could come of it. Things could never be any different between them, feeling as he did about love and marriage, and she was surprised how deeply this pained her. It would be madness to consider herself anything but out of his class, a social inferior. But she knew there would never be any peace of mind for her as long as he remained on earth. Time and distance were of no consequence, for he was already in the heart and soul of her, and there he would remain.

Lady Lansbury was entertaining the handful of guests, who had settled in the large drawing room for talk and music and, for some, a game of whist. Blue-jacketed servants passed among them with champagne, brandy and fortified wines. Mr Spelling and Lydia were among them. They were to leave for London first thing, where they would take the boat train to Dover.

Lydia had taken up her place at the piano and was in the middle of a Chopin nocturne. Christopher walked over to the sofa where his mother was sitting and stood behind her. Mr Spelling sat across the room, his eyes filled with pride as they dwelt on his daughter. They would frequently settle on Christopher, impatient for him to declare himself.

'You have been to see Octavia?' Lady Lansbury

enquired softly without taking her eyes off Miss Spelling.

Bending down, he said quietly in her ear, 'Miss Mortimer said she was quite worn out and went to sleep immediately.'

'Poor dear. It's been a long and exciting day for her. You stayed and talked to Jane?'

'We exchanged a few pleasantries.'

'You were absent a long time. You must have found something of interest to talk about. Did you not think to ask her to join us?'

'She was on the point of retiring.'

'I see. What are you going to do about Lydia? I feel I must ask because her father is growing impatient and everybody is talking about an imminent proposal.'

Something in the soft romanticism of her words irritated and irked Christopher. He did not like being the subject of gossip and speculation. 'I will settle the matter one way or another before they leave in the morning.'

'Whatever you decide I will support you, you know that. But should you decide against it, then take care not to offend Mr Spelling. He won't take kindly to seeing his daughter rejected.'

The Chalfont brow quirked in sardonic amusement. 'At twenty-four going on twenty-five, Lydia can hardly be classed as a young lady, Mother.'

'Then at fifty-five I must seem positively ancient to you. You know nothing would please me more than to see you settle down with someone who will make you happy.'

'I will, but I no longer think that Lydia is the right person for me.' He spoke dispassionately, giving away nothing of his feelings. 'She is beautiful, intelligent and well connected, but I find it hard to swallow that for her, the idea of being the Countess of Chalfont outshines everything else. It's what's on the inside that determines a person, not what's on the outside. Believe me, Mother, I'm beginning to think I'll be doing myself a favour by not marrying her.'

Lady Lansbury turned her head and looked up at her son's stoic features, wondering if the time he had spent talking to Jane might have some bearing on what he said. 'I am surprised to hear you say that, Christopher, and I can see you have made up your mind. You are in a position to choose.'

She gave him a beguiling smile that, ever since he was a boy, had been able to get him to do almost anything she wanted, but on the subject of marriage he remained unmoved. 'When I choose a woman who is most suited to be my wife in every way, there will be affection and respect. When I finally settle down I expect to be made happy by it.'

'And marriage to Lydia would not bring you happiness?'

Christopher looked at Lydia's immaculate profile as her fingers swept with precision over the piano keys. 'I think not.'

'And love, Christopher? Does that come into it? It is necessary if you are to have a good marriage, you know.'

He smiled down at her upturned face, knowing she wanted him to have what had not been present in her marriage to his father. 'I know how much that concerns you. You always were sentimental. I promise you that when I decide to settle down you will be the first to know.'

Lady Lansbury's quiet conversation with her son was noticed by Miss Spelling, who was not so lost in her music that she was unable to monitor the situation on the sofa and that Christopher had returned to the company. It was time to join him.

She stopped playing and called out, 'I have been playing long enough. I am sure someone else would like to have a turn.'

One of the ladies, keen to exhibit her skill at the

keyboard, rose and crossed to the piano, where she began to play a lively tune.

'That was one of my favourite pieces,' Lady Lansbury said when Lydia stood beside Christopher. 'I don't think I've heard it played so well before. Thank you for playing it so beautifully.'

'Thank you, Lady Lansbury. It was my pleasure.' She glanced at Christopher. 'It's a splendid evening, Christopher. I would like to take a walk on the terrace before bed.'

'Of course.' He glanced at his mother. 'Excuse us.'

He escorted Lydia through the French windows on to the terrace. With her hand on his arm they strolled in the moonlight, Lydia doing most of the talking. Christopher heard her, but he did not listen to what she had to say. His attention wandered as the vision of unruly hair tumbling unfashionably about the shoulders of Jane Mortimer, a hundred different shades of red and brown, drifted through his mind. Thinking back to their conversation, he thought it strange that he should have a private and personal conversation with a woman who was an employee. But he sensed in Jane Mortimer someone who was dependable, someone he could trust, who would listen, someone who inspired confidences.

He had no liking for the feelings that were churning inside him—Miss Mortimer had the ability to reach into his soul and open doors he thought were closed for ever. She ignited a desire in him that was beyond anything he could have imagined.

He chided himself for being weak, but earlier, at the party, he could not keep his eyes from following her. He was angry and resentful at her for stealing his peace of mind and placing doubts in his head about asking Lydia to be his wife. He found himself comparing the two women. The more he indulged in this pastime, the more restless he became. With Lydia walking by his side, he felt a fraud. He had thought her beautiful, but now she seemed cold, brittle and lifeless.

She failed to inflame him.

On this thought, realising it was time for truth and honesty, he told Lydia he would not marry her.

When the ladies had retired for the night, one of the gentlemen turned to Christopher.

'What do you say to a game of billiards?'

Christopher shook his head. 'Not tonight. I want

to check on one of the horses before I turn in.' He left them before they could protest.

The temperature had dropped slightly and he shivered as he stepped outside. But he was grateful for the chill, as he needed to clear his head.

Reaching the stables, he paused to gaze at Chalfont's splendid acres awash with moonlight, loving every inch of his inheritance which he had struggled to hold on to with a deep and abiding passion.

In the early days he had sold land to raise the capital for his investments and to pay off debts. His main assets had nothing to do with the estate. Investing in several coal mines and with interests in various industrial concerns and the booming development of the railways which were spreading like veins to every part of the land, at last he was beginning to see rewards. However, he was by no means out of the woods yet and marriage to Lydia would be an excellent way of making sure that Chalfont was safe and that his mother and Octavia remained in a secure and loving environment.

But he had no wish to relinquish having the upper hand. If he married Lydia, it would mean trading his aristocratic lineage for the sake of Chalfont and his family's future security—a commonly accepted practice, but to do so would make him feel less of a man.

Propping his shoulder against the stable wall, he lit a cheroot and let his thoughts wander back over the years as the smoke drifted overhead, back to the tortured years of his life as an adolescent boy and the interminable battles with his father.

Not long after his father had married Christopher's mother, the eldest daughter of a baronet, finances had become an issue. Her own father, Christopher's grandfather, hadn't come from a fashionable set—sobriety, simplicity and respect for those less fortunate than himself had been the hallmarks of his style. Too late his grandparents discovered the man their daughter had married was not the paragon of domesticity they had believed him to be.

Christopher's father, the fourth Earl of Lansbury, had pursued his own interests—horse racing, gambling at various clubs in London, casinos when he was abroad, music halls and extramarital affairs. With his wife tucked away in the country, he spent his life going from bed to bed, uncaring how his indiscriminate infidelities shamed her.

She knew he was committing adultery, but she would not divorce him. She did, however, deny him her bed, until one night, after a bout of heavy drinking and losing heavily at cards, he had forced himself on her, the result being that she fell pregnant with Octavia. She was well into her pregnancy when he again forced himself on her in a vicious and merciless manner. Because of that one, terrible night, she suspected something had happened to the child. Her fears were proved right when Octavia was born and did not progress as quickly as other infants.

And then there was Lily—beautiful, good-natured, fun-loving Lily, with violet eyes, tumbling brown hair and a body that would rival that of Venus. His father was in Paris when Christopher had discovered passion. Lily, who was one of the parlour maids at Chalfont, was twenty years old and he was eighteen. It was easy for him to fall in love with the beautiful maid.

He saw her first when she was in the rose garden picking blooms for the house with her hair unbound. As he watched her, she epitomised for him all the Helens and Guineveres of whom he had read. He soon became infatuated with her and Lily initiated him into the forthright pleasures of sex. Their affair lasted a year, until his father returned to Chalfont after a tour of the Continent.

On finding his son in bed with one of the parlour maids, his father had been highly amused, remarking jovially that at least his son was a truly virile Chalfont—a chip off the old block. When his father had taken stock of Lily and felt the stirrings of arousal warming his blood, the earl could scarce believe his good fortune that Chalfont housed such a beauty. It mattered not one iota that his son was making sport with her. The girl was a member of the Lansbury household and he had the authority to take her.

With anger and bitterness eating away at him, that was when Christopher had truly begun to hate his father.

As for the beautiful, violet-eyed Lily—what would he not have done for her at eighteen? He'd have drunk poison to prove his love for her if she had asked him to, but so awed was she by the attentions of the earl that she lost no time in abandoning the son for the master. Christopher had lost her. How could he ever forgive her, when she had willingly betrayed him in favour of the very man who had destroyed him—and his mother? They had both been broken apart by the cold-blooded cruelty of his father.

Hate and anger had risen in him then, the slow,

deep, moving tremors of an anger so terrible he had wanted to smash something, anything, to release the explosion of hatred, of venomous, perilous, terrifying rage. He had wanted to howl dementedly at the hurt that had been done him, to maim, to kill the man who had done this to him, the man who had taken the woman whom he loved and lived to die for.

The following morning Maisie, the young maid who willingly turned her hand to anything and often took care of Octavia, entered the room carrying a loaded breakfast tray. She set it down on a small table and began arranging cups and plates with a good deal of self-conscious clatter. The aroma of ham, warm bread and pastry filled the room.

Jane was standing by the window, brushing Octavia's hair with idle strokes as she stared into the distance beyond the glass, her thoughts on the conversation she had had with Lord Lansbury the night before.

'Here is your breakfast,' Maisie said cheerfully. 'I'm sorry it's a bit late this morning, but cook's had extra work with the guests wanting to dine early in order to catch the London train.'

Octavia looked at Maisie, her little face expressionless. 'I'm not hungry,' she said quietly, her attention taken by her beloved dog just getting up out of her basket. Falling to her knees, she put her arms about the dog, planting a kiss on its head as it stretched and yawned.

'You must eat your breakfast, Lady Octavia,' Maisie said in a no-nonsense manner. 'Food is strength, as well you know, and I'll thank you to come to the table.'

Jane turned from the window and smiled. 'I'll get her to eat something, Maisie. She was tired after the party and was in no hurry to get out of bed this morning.' Sitting down at the table, she poured herself some tea while Maisie tidied the room. She smiled as she watched Octavia run after her pet into the bedroom. 'Have you worked at Chalfont very long, Maisie?' she asked, helping herself to ham.

'Ever since I was old enough to be employed. My mum worked here all her life, before she became poorly and had to give up.' She stopped what she was doing and glanced at Jane. 'Why do you ask?'

'Oh, no reason really. What was Lord Lansbury's father like?' Before Maisie could give an answer, Jane said, 'I'm simply curious. I find it strange that no one ever mentions him. I get the impression that he might have been—difficult.'

Maisie perched on the arm of a chair and nodded, glancing into Octavia's bedroom to make sure she wasn't listening. 'I don't remember him—not really. Whenever I came to the house he was never at home—abroad somewhere or in London. My mum never said much—she always liked Lady Lansbury, you see, and didn't want to be disloyal. But he wasn't a nice man and when he was here he made Lady Lansbury's life a misery—and his lordship's, whose life was brought low by the behaviour of his father.'

'I'm sorry to hear that.' Jane was genuinely moved by what Maisie told her.

'I'm not saying anything that isn't generally known, you understand. The old earl was an inveterate gambler—besides which...well, there were other things, but his gambling made him notorious. Mum said he was a member of some very unsavoury clubs in town and that Lady Lansbury was forced to put up with his many affairs, which he flaunted shamelessly. Oh, yes, he liked to drink and gamble and spend time with accommodating women of the town—guided by the devil, my mum said. When he died he was in London. Lord Lansbury was with him. Some say he died in dubious circumstances, but nothing is known for certain. It was all very hush-hush at the time.'

Shaking her head, Maisie got up when Octavia came from the bedroom and sat at the table, her dog in her lap. 'I'd better go. There are beds to strip and rooms to clean.'

'And they won't get done while you are talking to me. Thank you, Maisie. When we have finished breakfast I'll take the pots to the kitchen myself.'

When Maisie had left and Octavia was eating her breakfast and feeding Poppy at the same time, Jane reflected on what Maisie had told her. She felt a lump of constricting sorrow in her chest, deeply moved by what she had learnt, which went a long way to helping her understand why Lord Lansbury was reluctant to speak of his father.

Hearing the stable clock strike ten, Jane went down to the great hall to collect some post that had just been delivered. She was expecting correspondence from both her father's publisher and his lawyer.

Seeing that several guests were on the point of leaving, she hung back. Carriages were drawn up outside the house to take them to the railway station. Mr Spelling and his daughter were walking down the steps to one of the carriages, where a footman was holding the door open for them. As they climbed into the back, poker-faced, Miss Spelling looked to where Lord Lansbury was standing with his mother. Having said their goodbyes, they were waiting for the carriage to drive off.

Jane picked up her post and opened a letter she suspected was from Mr Shadwell, the solicitor. It was, and he was writing to inform her that he had at last finalised the details concerning her father's inheritance and he would appreciate it if she would call to see him at her earliest convenience. Folding the letter and replacing it in the envelope, she realised it would mean going to London. She was about to go back up the stairs when Lady Lansbury spotted her.

'How are you this morning, Jane? Not too tired, I hope, after yesterday.'

'No, not at all. It was a lovely party. I expect you will welcome the quiet now your guests have gone.'

'It's always nice to see everyone, but I confess I am ready for a little peace and quiet. Christopher is to leave for London tomorrow afternoon.' A worried frown creased her brow. 'He is to arrange for the sale of our London house. It may have to go,

I'm afraid. We don't spend a great deal of time there so it will be no great loss, but it's a lovely house. Octavia finds the din of traffic along the cobbled streets and the press of people on the pavements nightmarish. She's more accustomed to the quiet isolation of the countryside.'

'When I arrived in London I found it exactly like that, so I cannot blame her.'

'It's the end of July so at least London will be quiet. The aristocracy move out of town at this time of year, on their way to their yachts at Cowes or shooting boxes in Scotland,' Lady Lansbury explained. She glanced at the letters in Jane's hands. 'You have some correspondence, I see.'

'Yes. One of the letters is from my father's solicitor. I'm afraid it means that I shall have to go to London.'

'Then you must go. In fact, I see no reason why you cannot travel with Christopher tomorrow.'

'Oh—but I couldn't possibly—I mean… I couldn't impose myself on him.'

'Nonsense. I don't like to think of you travelling alone. His valet and one of the maids are to travel with him, so there will be no impropriety. And don't worry about Octavia. With Maisie's help I will make sure she is occupied until you return.

But don't stay away too long. The house won't be the same without you.'

Directing her attention to her son who had seen the last carriage on its way and was now walking back to the house, she sighed. 'I must confess that at times I am concerned about Christopher. He works so hard to restore Chalfont to what it was in his grandfather's day. Things are not as bad as they were and he is convinced that his financial embarrassment will be resolved shortly.'

'Perhaps marriage to Miss Spelling will help.'

'Oh, but there is to be no marriage. There will be no proposal.'

Jane's heart lurched with surprised delight. 'But—I thought…'

Lady Lansbury arched her brows. 'What? That he would propose to her? So did I, and he did consider the matter—agonised over it, in fact. But my son is a fiercely proud man, Jane, and he has begun to realise that he cannot allow a woman to take on his debts. I believe Mr Spelling was a little put out when Christopher didn't declare himself but, well, there we are.'

Jane looked past her as Lord Lansbury strode towards them. She had not been mistaken in his character. He was a man of honour and pride, and she admired that.

'Having received some correspondence from her father's solicitor, Jane has an important matter to discuss, Christopher.'

With his eyes as intense as hunting falcon's locked on hers, he was relieved that he had just relegated Lydia Spelling to the past. His decision to do so had more than a little to do with Miss Mortimer and their conversation of the night before.

'Really? Tell me. I'm listening.'

Jane could feel him watching her with that intense stare, but her heart still pounded with the news that he was not going to marry Miss Spelling after all. Surely this was the miracle she had been praying for, even though it would not change anything for her.

'No—I mean, really it should not concern you.'

'But of course it does, Jane,' Lady Lansbury prompted. 'Jane has to go to London to see her father's solicitor. I told her that since you are to go yourself tomorrow, she might accompany you. I'm sure you will agree, Christopher. I would feel so much better if she didn't have to travel alone. Now, excuse me. I'll go and see Octavia while you make your arrangements.'

'Of course you must accompany me,' Christopher said. 'What do you say, Miss Mortimer?'

Impaled on his gaze, Jane stared at him. Perilously close to losing her composure, but unable to shake his, she sighed, lowering her gaze as she considered the matter. She had already decided there was more to Christopher Chalfont than she had realised. Beneath the hard veneer there was an aloof strength and a powerful charisma that had nothing to do with his good looks or that mocking smile of his that was locked away behind an unbreachable wall. That was his appeal—the challenge. He made her—and probably every woman of his acquaintance—want to penetrate that wall, to find the person behind it.

'I—I had not thought of going immediately,' she lied. He had no reason to oblige her, she knew, and she did not wish to seem pushy or rude, imposing herself on him. The thought of being with him for the journey on the train to London should have had her leaping with joy, but instead it filled her with trepidation. But Lady Lansbury had told her Lord Lansbury's valet and a maid would also be going, so she wouldn't be entirely alone with him.

A slow, teasing smile appeared on his lips and

his strongly marked brows were slightly raised, his eyes glowing with humour. 'Why do you hesitate?'

Hot faced and perplexed, a certain innocence in her large, liquid eyes, Jane was suddenly shy of him. There was something in his eyes today that made her feel it was impossible to look at him. There was also something in his voice that brought so many new and conflicting themes in her heart and mind that she did not know how to speak to him.

'I do not wish to impose,' she replied.

'You won't be. I would welcome your company.'

Meeting his gaze, Jane couldn't resist smiling. 'Very well. Thank you.'

He arched a sleek black brow, amused. 'Good. Then that's settled. We'll leave here after lunch to catch the two o'clock train.'

Jane felt a sudden quiver run through her as she slipped away from him, a sudden quickening within as if something came to life. She went up the stairs in awed bewilderment, feeling his eyes burning holes into her back as she went. It was a while before she could breathe properly.

In deep reflection, Christopher watched her walk away. Angrily he attacked his sentimental thoughts until they cowered in meek submission, but they refused to lie down. His fascination with Jane Mortimer was more disquieting than his decision not to propose to Lydia—in fact, it was damned annoying. If he wanted an affair or diversion of any kind, he had a string of some of the most beautiful women in the country to choose from—so why should he feel drawn to a twenty-one-year-old woman who had infiltrated her way into his thoughts and his home? He liked her. He liked her company. He liked talking to her.

He tried to put her from his mind, but failed miserably in his effort. If he wasn't careful, he would make a fool of himself, he knew it, doing his best to get some order into his mind to discover why. Why she would keep creeping into his thoughts when he least expected it. Why he found himself looking out for her whenever he was in the house or the park or the garden. The sweet fragrance of her soft perfume lingered, drifting through his senses. He cursed with silent frustration, seized by a strong desire to go after her and cauterise his need by holding her close and savouring those full, soft lips of hers.

Instead he strode into his study and attempted immersing himself in his work. Sitting at his desk, he set himself the task of going over the estate accounts, multiplying and subtracting and adding long columns of figures. With a keen, mathematical mind, under normal circumstances this was a simple procedure, but slowly, a face with wide velvety violet eyes thickly fringed with curling black lashes, a wide expressive mouth and full lips and cheeks as flushed as a ripe peach crept unbidden into his mind—teasing him, taunting him.

At this thought Christopher leaned back in his chair and set down his pen. After a moment of further confusing, uneasy thoughts concerning the young woman who took such good care of his sister, he thrust himself out of his chair, strode across the study and within minutes was galloping away from the house to ride off his frustrations.

While Octavia was with Lady Lansbury, Jane opened the bulky envelope that had been delivered from Aunt Caroline. She had enclosed some correspondence from Phineas Waverley—or Finn, as Jane and everyone else affectionately called him. Her aunt's letter was lengthy, giving her a detailed account of her day-to-day activities. Finn's letter informed her that he was shortly to begin work on the exhibition he had told her about for the Antiquities Society in London, and would she like to help him prepare for it?

Jane was excited by the idea of being involved in the work once more and she would write back telling him she would give serious thought to accepting his offer. After all, in the beginning she had told Lady Lansbury that her care of Octavia would be only temporary. But could she bear to leave Chalfont?

The warm afternoon drew Lady Lansbury outside. It was quiet and still but for the hum of busy bees among the flowers. Seated on the terrace in the shade, she had been reading for several minutes, but now she lowered her book so that it rested, forgotten, in her lap. Her eyes fixed themselves on Jane. She sat on a bench on the lawn, watching Octavia walk back from the lake with Christopher.

There was an intense expression on Jane's face. Jane, Lady Lansbury could see, was looking at the man rather than the girl. There were times when, believing herself unobserved, Jane would gaze at him with all the quiet longing of a woman who loves deeply but with small hope of ever possessing the object of her desire.

Already Christopher has enchanted her, Lady

Lansbury thought with a sigh, feeling a swift stab of helpless sympathy for the naked sorrow and longing she saw on Jane's face. She had a tremendous amount of admiration for the young woman. Everything about her was in complete contrast to Lydia Spelling, who had set out to ensnare Christopher as soon as he entered her sphere. Barely a smile or a word had passed Lydia's lips without contrivance. Each turn of her head, every flash of her eyes was carefully calculated to delight, to amuse, to captivate the English earl. She was a true American daughter of a self-made millionaire, and with that special tenacity peculiar to her breed, she had set her heart upon the prize and become single-minded in winning it.

On the other hand, Jane rose to every challenge and opportunity life had to offer in spite of the grief that had lowered her spirits when her father had died. Lady Lansbury noted that today she seemed to have taken more time over her appearance than usual. She was wearing a feminine dress of delicate pale blue muslin. Her bonnet was held in place by a wide band of ribbon loosely knotted under her chin, its ends left hanging so that they moved in the breeze.

Although her haughty manner and often bold

stare marked her as strong of character there was also a softness about her, an elusive gentleness that declared her to be fragile and vulnerable. Jane was a woman of shifting moods and subtle contradictions, and while she could not be described as a classical beauty, it was this spectrum, this baffling, indefinable quality that drew attention to her and held the beholder captive. She had somehow managed to infiltrate the very fabric of the household with her enormous reserves of friendliness and charm.

Her gaze went to her son. These past weeks Christopher had battled over whether or not to propose marriage to Lydia Spelling. Lady Lansbury was relieved he had decided against it. She loved Chalfont dearly and she could not see Lydia Spelling within its walls as its chatelaine.

Whereas—*Jane?* She became thoughtful. She was a young woman who seemed to know her own mind, and she would stand up for what mattered to her. Her background might be frowned upon by those in the upper echelons of society—for centuries the bloodlines of this family had been unsullied—but what did that matter if she could make her son, who had endured and borne so much misery and pain in the past, happy.

Her thoughts began to run off at a tangent.

Maybe…

Chapter Five

After lunch the following day the carriage took Lord Lansbury and Jane to the station, just half an hour away. It wasn't until Jane had climbed into the carriage and enquired after the maid and valet who she thought were to travel with them that Lord Lansbury casually told her they had left on an earlier train with the baggage to open up the London house.

The impropriety of travelling alone with Lord Lansbury gave Jane reason for concern, but with the carriage halfway to the station, it was too late to do anything about it.

When they arrived at the station, the yard, littered with boxes and trunks, was noisy with the influx of passengers who were waiting for the train. Christopher had a small carriage bag made from the softest leather. Impatient for the train to arrive and not liking to be kept waiting, frowning, he took out his pocket watch, a gold hunter which had been a gift from his mother, and flicked open the case to look at the time. The watch caught and reflected the sun, which also lit the diamond in the ring which he wore on his little finger.

He was dressed immaculately in dove-grey trousers and a fine worsted dark-green-coloured coat, his pristine white shirt contrasting sharply with his dark hair and dark countenance.

As the train to take them to London pulled into the station, in a cloud of smoke and soot, Jane watched as it came to a halt in a hiss of steam. They stood back as passengers began to get off and drift away.

Moving towards the first-class compartments, Christopher took Jane's hand to assist her. The gesture was unexpected and Jane quivered in response. His smoky stare homed in on her as though he, too, had felt the shock of electricity that bolted through her when they touched, and Jane's heart skipped a beat. Her cheeks coloured as she turned her head away and entered the empty compartment.

Keeping her eyes lowered and making herself comfortable, Jane took a book from her reticule that she had brought to read on the journey. Lord

Lansbury sat across from her and, keenly aware of his presence, she knew it would be difficult concentrating on the book's content. She knew he was watching her. She could still feel the pressure of his hand on hers. This was insane, but her body was throbbing.

The silence between them stretched as the station master blew his whistle to send the train on its way to London.

'Miss Mortimer?'

'Yes?' she asked at once, swallowing hard.

'Are you comfortable?' he enquired softly.

'Yes, thank you,' she replied, favouring him with a brief smile before lowering her head over her book.

'What are you reading?'

'A biography of Marie Antoinette.'

'Indeed?' He glanced at the slim blue volume. 'Do you find it interesting?'

'Yes. Not only is there real historical value to it, but it's also about the kind of woman she was, which is what I like.'

'And what kind of woman was she—apart from being the queen of France and having her head removed?'

'By all accounts, not only was she beautiful, there

was something undefinable about her—a magical, captivating quality. She did have a certain allure.' Meeting his eyes, she noted the little smile twitching the corners of his lips. 'Why do you smile?' she asked, slightly indignant. 'Do not mock me, Lord Lansbury.'

'I'm not. Quite the opposite, in fact. I imagined that all young ladies read romantic poetry and insipid novelettes—which I am certain have a deleterious effect on their impressionable minds—whereas I find a woman who prefers reading about historical heroines. I have no doubt you've read anything I care to name and are conversant in French, Greek and Latin.'

'Yes,' she replied, as though it were the most natural thing in the world for a young woman to be so accomplished. 'My father taught me.'

'I am impressed.'

'You seem surprised.'

'I confess that I am. There are few ladies of my acquaintance who are familiar with the classics—and I am hard-pressed to think of any one of them who is conversant in any language other than their own native English and perhaps a smattering of French.'

Now it was Jane's turn to be surprised. 'Then

I can only assume that your experience with the female sex is somewhat limited, Lord Lansbury.'

A gleam of supressed laughter lit Christopher's eyes and Jane could only guess, correctly, that her remark about his inexperience with women had not been taken in the way she had intended.

'No doubt you consider my reading material quite boring, Lord Lansbury. Usually I read for enlightenment, for knowledge, but I often read something light. In fact, I often read those insipid novelettes you mentioned and enjoy them enormously.'

The journey went quickly as Christopher asked her about the countries she had visited, fascinated by the ease of their conversation. Her tastes were many and varied and she was knowledgeable about most things, answering his questions and listening to his comments with interest, speaking to him as an equal and enjoying the debate when his opinion differed from her own, laughing when the discussion was in danger of becoming heated.

She talked with relish and held him rapt with sparkling tales of her travels so that he could almost smell the scented breezes of India and the Mediterranean. He listened in fascination to stories of her adventures and experiences in exotic Asian countries and Europe, marvelling when she told him of the splendour and treasures of Florence and Rome, and trying to imagine the beauty of the Swiss mountains, of the individuality of the many people she had met.

Absently she tucked a stray lock of hair beneath her bonnet that had dared escape its strict confines. Christopher was distracted. The unconscious gesture caused him to study her closely. He remembered how her hair had looked when he had seen it unbound—the colour of rich mahogany with highlights of red and gold, making him think of harvest corn, chestnuts and autumn fires. He had the absurd desire to reach out and remove her bonnet and set her hair free and let it spill about her shoulders, convinced it would glow with the glorious vibrancy of autumn leaves.

She fell silent and gazed at the passing scenery. In the subdued light of the compartment her eyes were captivating. Their violet depths, aglow with the warmth of glorious purple velvet-soft pansies, looked so dark to be almost black. His gaze dipped to her mouth, an enigmatic mouth, ripe and full of promise.

Christopher decided then that Miss Mortimer did not do herself justice. He strongly suspected that the ill-fitting russet-coloured travelling dress she wore hid a female form that was faultless, slim and strong, with long legs and curves in all the right places. Her face was alluring, interesting, and overall there was an innocence and vulnerability about her that would put a practised seducer beyond the realm of her experience.

Jane became uncomfortable beneath Lord Lansbury's watchful gaze. He sat across from her with his long legs stretched out, studying her imperturbably. His body, a perfect harmony of form and strength, was like a work of Grecian art and most unsettling to Jane's virgin heart. Unable to endure his scrutiny a moment longer, she looked across at him, her eyes locking on his.

'Why do you look at me so closely, Lord Lansbury?'

Quite unexpectedly he smiled a white buccaneer smile, and his eyes danced with devilish humour. 'You don't have to look so uneasy to find yourself the object of my attention. As a matter of fact I was admiring you.'

Unaccustomed as she was to any kind of compliment from the opposite sex, the unfamiliar warmth in his tone brought heat creeping into her cheeks.

To divert the conversation away from herself, she

said, 'Do you often go to London?' She wondered how he could bear to leave such a lovely place as Chalfont for the hurly-burly of the city.

'Frequently. I have business meetings to attend, as well as taking my seat in the House of Lords occasionally.' A faint smile touched his lips when he observed Miss Mortimer's expression of bewilderment. 'I realise that spending all your life travelling foreign parts, you will know very little about English politics.'

'You are a politician?'

'No—at least not in the professional sense. It is simply that I, and all peers of the realm, have been trained to regard it as our right and duty to participate in governing the country. We enter Parliament as we do university and gentlemen's clubs.'

Jane was impressed. 'It all sounds very grand to me.'

'I imagine it does, and I take my duties very seriously, but I prefer Chalfont to London. Octavia is a constant worry so I try not to be absent for any length of time. Although I am happy to say that my mother has not looked so at ease for a long time. She has come to rely on you, as bright and quick-witted as you are, Miss Mortimer, and Octavia is happier away from her. I am grateful to you.'

'It's a pleasure, Lord Lansbury.'

'Although Octavia is probably already missing you. I can see that you will have some explaining to do when you get back.'

'With Lady Lansbury and Maisie fussing over her, I do not think that Lady Octavia will have noticed my absence.'

'My mother informed me you look on your position as only temporary. Do you intend to leave us soon?'

'Eventually I think I must. A colleague of my father's is putting together an exhibition of antiquities. He's asked me to help him.'

'And will you?'

'I don't know yet. I shall have to give it some thought.'

'But you are tempted?'

'Yes. Yes, I am. It's what I know, you see. What I'm good at.'

Christopher was unprepared for the disappointment that washed over him. 'You're relentless.'

'I'm not sure you meant that as a compliment.' Resting her head back on the upholstery, she closed her eyes.

'You can sleep if you wish. I promise not to disturb you. I'll wake you when we reach London.'

'I don't feel in the least like sleeping. Besides, we'll soon be at Paddington. Anyway, I could not sleep with you across from me,' she told him quietly.

'Why not?'

'It's not often I'm alone with a gentleman.'

'We were alone together in your rooms the other night.'

'That was—different.'

'But why?' he persisted.

Jane also asked herself the question and to her consternation found the answer. It was because he encroached so closely upon her, because he seemed too near, because she was afraid of him coming closer still. Her body reached out to his, wanting to feel his lips on hers, but if that were to happen it would be her undoing. However difficult it would be, she must learn to resist these feelings.

Quietly, in answer to his question, she said, 'Because you had come to see Lady Octavia.'

They were fast approaching Paddington Station.

They fell silent. As the train was reaching its journey's end, Jane lifted her face and smiled at Christopher. For him it was as though a shutter had been flung open and the sunlight rushed in. He sat quite still, looking across at her and no longer seeing her as the woman who looked after Octavia. He had never truly seen her beauty before, nor had he ever seen a smile like that, compounded of a luminous tenderness in her violet eyes, and yet in the lift of her lips, her even, perfect teeth and the dimple near her voluptuous mouth there was a hint of seduction.

The scent of her gentle perfume filled the compartment with a subtle fragrance that was as potent as the sound of music and there was a strange magic in the warm air. Quite suddenly, and with a queer stunned amazement, Christopher was conscious of a fantastic, overwhelming impulse, an impulse to reach out and take Miss Mortimer's face between his hands and draw it to his own. For a long moment it was almost as though he could feel her thick hair under his fingers, the shape of her head and the touch of her warm mouth.

Then a shrill sound of the train's whistle shattered the spell, bringing him back to reality as though from a drugged sleep. A tide of incredulous horror engulfed his mind. His nostrils flared on a sharp breath and his thoughts darted in confusion. Why had he sent his valet and the maid on ahead to prepare the house for his arrival? In doing so he had known that he would have to travel with Miss Mortimer alone, but he had not thought he would find himself fighting his attraction for her. And now he was afraid where it might lead. Why must she sit there in her ill-fitting russet dress through which he could just make out the outline of her breasts and the curve of her long supple waist?

Suddenly the train lurched, propelling Jane out of her seat and across the distance that separated her from Lord Lansbury, sending her crashing into his steely warm chest.

Christopher's eyes captured Jane's with some considerable surprise and Jane looked into his face and for a long moment could not look away again, held by something she was unable to name but which her female body instantly recognised. His eyes had narrowed in sudden concentration and he looked faintly surprised at something *his* body was telling *him*.

Unprepared for the sheer force of the feelings that swept through her, she knew, with a sort of panic, that she was in grave danger, not from him but from herself, and was aware that she must, absolutely must, pull back. But she was too inexperienced and affected by him to do that. Her eyes became fixed on his finely sculptured mouth as he came closer still and she knew he was going to kiss her.

She was trapped and she knew it. She was mesmerised by him, like a moth to a flame, and she felt her heart suddenly start pounding in a quite unpredictable manner. He was looking into her eyes, holding her spellbound, weaving some magic web around her from which there was no escape.

The darkening of his eyes, the naked passion she saw in their depths, seemed to work a strange spell on her and conquered her, and, without knowing what she was doing, moving within his arms, her entire body began to tremble with desire and fear. There was nothing she could do to still the quiver of anticipation as he lowered his head and covered her mouth with his own.

The shock of his lips on hers was one of wild, indescribable sweetness and sensuality as he claimed a kiss of violent tenderness, evoking feelings she had never felt before as she was half sitting, half lying across his lap. Any notion that she should fight never entered her head. Her eyes fluttered closed and, for a few seconds, time ceased. What he was doing to her was like being imprisoned in a cocoon of dangerous, terrifying sensuality where she had no control over anything. Particularly herself.

His kiss deepened, widening her lips for the slow, exploratory stroke of his tongue in her mouth, and the sensations inside were like tight buds that burst into blossom, filling her with splendour.

In the haze inside her head, the train came closer to its destination, but Jane had wandered away from what had happened to propel her into his arms as her bonnet became dislodged and fell on to the seat. His fingers slipped through the tight strands of her hair, pulling it loose from its confinement and tangling sensuously in among its glorious mass. He gripped her nape as his mouth slanted over hers in hungry demand.

Imprisoned within his embrace and seduced by his mouth and strong, caressing hands, burning wherever they touched, Jane clung to him, her body responding eagerly, melting with the primitive sensations that went soaring through her, her lips beginning to move against his with increasing abandon as she fed his hunger, unwittingly increasing it.

Her hands held on weakly to his broad shoulders and she clung to him as ivy might cling to an oak. The strength in that hard, lean body gave her strength and gave promise of pleasure she had never imagined, promising far more than this first hungry contact between them. His tightening embrace crushed her breasts against his chest.

Often Jane had dreamed of such a kiss, but this, her first, made those insubstantial dreams seem like shadows in this delirium of delight. She gave herself up to the magic of this first romantic kiss, savouring the difference with a sensual awakening as Lord Lansbury's arms held her captive, her body moulded to his. Warm and moist, his lips tenderly caressed her own, pressing gently, probing, firm, growing more and more insistent, demanding the response she instinctively gave.

But although he held her firmly, Jane experienced a sensation of falling weightlessly to earth like a drifting leaf. Then she seemed to soar into a void of violent pleasure, and the delirium mounted moment by moment until nothing existed but this man, this magic, this miraculous new world of sensation exploding within her.

He went on kissing her for several delicious seconds more before he withdrew his lips and she caught her breath, gasping. Then he buried his lips in the soft curve of her throat and her fingers clutched the cloth of his jacket. She threw her head back, her hair spilling behind her in heavy waves.

After what seemed like an eternity he raised his head. When he released her, dizzy and disorientated, she would have fallen from his lap on to the floor of the compartment if he had not immediately steadied her. She was too innocent and naive not to let her emotions show on her face and for a long moment Christopher's gaze held hers with penetrating intensity. The clear grey eyes were as enigmatic as they were silently challenging. She had no immediate thoughts. She had only the memory of something immense, of incredible joy, beyond which nothing was comparable.

'So,' Christopher said softly, a lazy grin sweeping over his handsome face, 'I was not wrong about you, Jane Mortimer. You see what you do to me?' Meeting her gaze, he saw that her eyes were naked and defenceless.

His voice was no more than a breathless caress, but at the sound of it the passionate spell broke and dissolved before the cold inrush of reality. They exchanged a shocked glance as he gripped her arms and sat her on the seat beside him. His eyes had darkened to a stormy dark grey. The smile widened on his lips.

'Why do you look so worried?' he asked, reaching for her once more.

Jane's face flooded with colour and she lowered her head, mortified. For a moment she was thrown into such a panic she could not think coherently. She knew he, too, had felt the sudden excitement of physical contact. Jane had never been kissed in her life and she could not have imagined how pleasurable it could be. His kiss and his embrace had been like being wrapped in a cocoon of dangerous, pleasurable sensuality where she had no control over anything. Not even herself.

'Please—let me go,' she implored helplessly. 'My—my head is in a turmoil... I—I can't think straight.'

The train had come to a halt. Doors opened noisily and the engine gave a shriek, but Christopher Chalfont, who had just kissed his companion, did not notice as he stared at Jane, reeling with the unexpected bounty of her kiss and too intoxicated by her sweet lips to care. Her unsullied inward beauty fed his soul and those plump, soft lips were every bit as luscious as he'd briefly fantasised.

He raised a finely arched brow and chuckled softly at her distress. 'It was but a kiss,' he murmured.

'To you, maybe, but not to me.'

Jane was shocked by the explosion of passion between them, shocked by what she had done. What had happened surpassed anything she had ever known. She tried desperately to control her raging emotions and match his casual mood. All her adult life she had wondered what it would be like when she was kissed for the first time, but never had she believe it would be like that. Lord Lansbury should never have done so, nor should he be so insufferably composed about it.

'It—it should not have happened. It should not,' she stressed.

Taking her hands to still them as they fluttered about arranging her clothes, Christopher looked closely at her face. 'But it did. It did happen and nothing you can do or say will change that. Accept it.'

'I will have to,' she whispered, drawing her hands from his. 'But it was a mistake all the same.'

He was passing the kiss off as some light occurrence, but Jane began to feel that something momentous had happened and her life from this point on had changed beyond recall. Her face was suddenly pinched and all colour seemed to have faded from her cheeks. Then, without speaking, she hurriedly fastened her hair and snatched her bonnet from the floor, placing it on her head and securing it with the ribbon beneath her chin.

'The train has stopped,' she murmured. 'We should get off.'

Standing up, she picked up her bag and shoved her book inside. Her thoughts wandered as she did her utmost to avoid Lord Lansbury's questioning gaze, unable to believe what had just happened. Ever since she had set eyes on him he had haunted her, as did the passions she held for him. She watched him whenever he was close with what she felt to be a most improper and uncomfortable ardour, studying furtively the handsome face, the full curve of his strong mouth, the fierce dip of his dark eyebrows.

And now he had kissed her she felt completely at odds with herself. She could see the irony of it and would have laughed had she not felt so wretchedly ashamed.

She tried not to look at him when he assisted her off the train on to the platform. Walking side by side, they left the station where a row of horse-drawn cabs waited, some wearing nose bags, and there was a smell of straw and the stable.

'Thank you,' she said primly, about to climb inside the nearest cab. 'I can manage perfectly well now. It isn't far to Aunt Caroline's house in Kensington.'

'I know that,' he uttered brusquely, tossing his bag on to the seat and taking hold of her elbow. 'But what kind of gentleman would I be if I abandoned you now? We will share the cab. I will see you to your aunt's house.'

Having no wish to argue the point and eager to reach Kensington, Jane let him hand her inside. As the cab moved on she was still trembling in the aftermath of his kiss, unable to believe what had happened and that she desperately wanted him to repeat the kiss that had stunned her senses with its wild sweetness. Seated across from her, he held her gaze and she looked with longing at his lips.

'Don't look at me like that unless you want me to kiss you again, Miss Mortimer,' he murmured huskily, his eyes darkening with renewed passion.

With her heart beating hard against her ribs, she averted her eyes. 'I don't—I mean— Oh, what have I done?' She forced herself to draw a deep, uneven breath. 'It was as if something—' or someone, she thought '—had cast a spell on me and made me behave totally out of character, for I would never have behaved in such a bold manner before…'

Christopher saw that her lovely eyes were apprehensive and deceptively innocent. 'It was not entirely your doing. If you have to blame someone, then blame me. You are too hard on yourself. Calm down,' he said gently. 'We will soon be at your aunt's house. Don't let her see you like this.'

Her eyes were drawn back to his. 'Like what?'

'With your eyes aglow with passion and your lips trembling.' Unable to resist teasing her, he smiled, leaning forward and touching her cheek.

'She—she will think I am pleased to see her—which I will be, of course.'

'If seeing your aunt makes you look like this, then you should come to see her more often.' His expression became serious. 'You are not angry with me, are you?'

She shook her head. 'I am not angry,' she replied quietly, meeting his penetrating gaze. 'Only afraid of what might happen as a consequence of this indiscretion.'

Christopher put out a hand, as if to draw her to his side of the cab.

'No,' she cried with a hint of anger. 'Do you enjoy inducing feelings in me that can come to nothing?' She thrust his hand away as the cab came to a halt outside her aunt's front door. 'We have arrived at my aunt's house. I must go.'

Flinging the door open and stepping down, she walked towards the house without a backward glance, feeling extremely conspicuous after what she had done. No decent, upstanding woman would have done what she had just done, she thought, chastising herself most severely. No, indeed. Any moral, respectable, God-fearing twenty-one-year-old would not have allowed her employer to kiss her like that and, worse, enjoyed the experience. She was horrified and afraid of the feelings unfolding inside her.

Aunt Caroline was delighted to see Jane so soon after writing to her.

'You take me by surprise, but it's so nice to have you back. I've missed having you to talk to,' she enthused as she poured them tea in the drawing room. 'I imagine Lady Lansbury will miss you—as well as Lady Octavia.'

'I don't intend staying away too long,' Jane said, sitting back in her chair and gratefully sipping the tea her aunt handed to her.

'Was that Lord Lansbury I saw leaving in the cab?'

'Yes. We travelled to London together. He's thinking of selling the London house.'

'So,' Aunt Caroline said, shaking her head, 'it's finally come to that. His father certainly has a lot to answer for. Ever since he took over the reins Lord Lansbury's been struggling to keep afloat.'

Despite still feeling quite wretched over what had occurred between them, Jane felt a stirring of admiration for Lord Lansbury. 'It must have been extremely difficult for him at that time.'

'It was, but he was determined to succeed, to recoup his father's losses, pay off the creditors and make Chalfont what it once was.'

'It's a beautiful house, there's no denying that.'

'And the earl is a terribly attractive man. It's easy to see what women see in him. There isn't a woman alive who isn't impervious to him. Christopher Chalfont is one of the most attractive men on the social scene—when he deigns to favour society with his presence, that is. Wherever he goes women strive to please him, for despite his cynical attitude, there is an aura of virility about him that does dangerous things to their hearts.'

'And how does Lord Lansbury react to these adoring females?'

'That's the trouble. He doesn't.' She gave Jane a sideways, questioning look. 'What is your opinion of him, Jane? After all you must have formed one, living in his house and taking care of his sister.'

'I—do not know him well, Aunt Caroline, but in my opinion he is much nicer than he appears.'

Aunt Caroline looked at her curiously, noting the delicate flush that had sprung to her cheeks. 'Why, Jane, what is this? You aren't by any chance enamoured of Lord Lansbury, surely?'

'No,' Jane replied in a rush, averting her eyes. 'At times he can be quite insufferable, but I have seen some of the qualities you speak of.'

'I dare say he is no more immune to a pretty face than the next man, but since the family fell upon hard times he has conducted his affairs with absolute discretion. It is rumoured that he is to marry a rich American woman to shore up his finances. Do you know anything about that?'

'Only that he has decided against it.'

'Then perhaps things are looking up for him and he doesn't need a rich American after all.'

Jane got little sleep that night. Her body was restless. Her thoughts of what had happened on the train became a sharp disturbance and she could not put it out of her mind. She ceased chastising herself for her weakness, for the potency of how it had felt to be held in Lord Lansbury's arms and almost kissed into oblivion took precedence over any regrets she might have had at the time.

She saw the image of Lord Lansbury. The darkness was full of him. She knew every detail of his powerful presence, the unforgettable moulding of his face, his body, the eyes so full of light, the beautiful mouth curling at the corners caressing hers. He was in the room, haunting her like a wonderful memory she did not want to let go of.

Turning over, she pressed her hot face into the pillow. Closing her eyes with the remembrance of his kiss burning in her mind, she was seized by a nameless, crushing longing for him to kiss her again. Until Lord Lansbury had kissed her she'd had no real inkling of the intensity, the sheer force of passionate love, and now it had touched her she would not deny herself the pleasure of it again if the occasion and the opportunity arose.

The following morning she dressed with special care in a light brown skirt and dark green jacket. Accompanied by her aunt, she was very calm as she took a cab to Westminster and arrived at the offices of her father's solicitor, Mr Shadwell, shortly before noon.

They were shown into Mr Shadwell's office. Large and solid, he stepped forward to greet them, smiling broadly. 'Good day to you, Miss Mortimer. I'm pleased you could see your way to coming so soon. Please be seated. There are important matters we have to discuss.'

She allowed him to seat her at the table while her aunt took a seat at the back of the room and looked on. Mr Shadwell sat in a leather-covered chair across the desk.

Jane was so awed by the occasion and what he had to say that she took little notice of her surroundings. When she had received Mr Shadwell's letter asking her to attend his offices in London now that her father's affairs had been finalised, she hadn't known what to expect—though, of course, she didn't know enough about lawyers and wills to make comparisons.

What she did know was that her father had been a wealthy man when he died. In India the opulence of the Moghul Court and the princely states was legendary, and their dazzling jewels attracted a great deal of attention. Through his work her father had made many influential friends, which had led to substantial gifts. They had meant nothing to him. What could he do with rubies and diamonds and precious sapphires from Kashmir? He wasn't interested in accumulating wealth for himself. But he was a shrewd and careful man, and to take care of Jane's future some of the gifts bestowed on him he turned into readily transportable capital. This was his legacy to her, for when the day came when he would not be there to guide her.

A shiver of apprehension ran through her as Mr Shadwell glanced down at the folder in front of him. As briefly as possible he explained the terms of the will.

'As you know, Miss Mortimer, you are your father's sole heir, and he has left you a very wealthy woman indeed.'

He went on to talk further about her father's legacy and that she would need advice on investing her money wisely. She asked brief questions now and then, and when she finally left her head was spinning with the enormity of her wealth.

Jane and her aunt made scant conversation on the journey back to Kensington. They were both preoccupied in the privacy of their own thoughts. Their visit to Mr Shadwell had been brief but eventful. For Caroline Standish it had been a day of sudden concern for her niece. For Jane it had been an experience that would, she knew, alter the whole pattern of her life.

'You always knew your father had accumulated wealth.'

'I did, but I am quite staggered by the amount.'

'Have you any idea what you will do now?'

'Nothing for the present. I shall have to give the matter some thought and take advice from those who know about such things.' She smiled. 'I shall begin by making a generous donation to your charities, Aunt Caroline. I'm sure you will be able to put it to good use.'

'I would be most grateful, Jane. There is a home for unmarried mothers…'

After saying goodnight to her aunt, Jane rested in the gathering darkness, listening to the night sounds beyond the open window. Too restless to sleep, she lay on her bed beneath the covers, willing her body to relax. She was now faced with an enormous dilemma and decisions about her future had to be made. She would shortly be able to access her inheritance—a great deal of money, it would seem. Too much. She was forced to consider seriously what she must do next. It was a time for calm and reflection.

One thing she was sure of was that she would have to abandon her care of Octavia. How could she remain working as a hired help when she was an heiress in her own right?

Suddenly she had the stirrings of an idea. It was perhaps ridiculous, and if she had any sense at all she would discard it without a second's thought, but all her feelings were heightened. The more she thought about it, the more plausible it seemed. Lord Lansbury and his family needed help. She would like to see Lord Lansbury given a helping hand in his resolute determination to restore his family wealth.

But would Lord Lansbury accept her offer? He was a proud man and would probably show her the door. She had seen how reluctant he had been to marry Miss Spelling for her money, why would he accept hers? All she knew was that she would like to try. Besides, unlike Miss Spelling, her offer would be unconditional. What use was all that money to her when it could do so much for Chalfont?

Aunt Caroline was apprehensive and wasn't sure she was doing the right thing when she told her what she had decided. 'Are you sure you know what you are doing, Jane? Let good sense and not sentiment rule your emotions.'

'I have done nothing else but think about it all night. Trust me,' Jane said, smiling confidently. 'Lord Lansbury's situation can only be improved by my offer.'

Chapter Six

Jane took great care with her appearance for her visit to Lansbury House. Even though she knew she would not attract stares of admiration and envy, she sensed in herself a new thing, an extra quality that set her above the realms of mere physical attractiveness. Today she felt different, somehow more alive than she had ever been before. A peculiar inner excitement touched her cheeks with a flush of delicate pink, which added a special sparkle to her eyes and caused the promise of a smile to hover at the corners of her mouth.

Her eyes were shining with expectation when she arrived at Lansbury House in the heart of Mayfair. She was admitted by a footman and told to wait a moment while he informed Lord Lansbury that she wished to see him. She looked around, her brilliant smile encompassing the magnificent chequerboard-tiled hall floor with its curving marble staircase and crystal chandelier suspended from the ornately plastered ceiling. She almost laughed out loud. She felt like a good fairy in a children's fairy tale, thrilled to the core to be about to bestow a gift on an unsuspecting being who was waiting for a miracle.

She was admitted to find Lord Lansbury seated behind a leather-topped desk. Giving it a quick glance, she noted every pen and every sheet of paper was in symmetrical order—and what she thought to be his desk diary, scrupulously maintained in his neat handwriting, a daily record of meetings and commitments. Shoving back his chair, he got up and walked round the desk.

Overwhelmed and ridiculously nervous, Jane stared at him. He was looking every inch the handsome, elegant earl today, with his blue coat and darker blue trousers, gold-striped waistcoat and his immaculate white linen. Dark hair brushed back, his handsome features were thoughtful as he contemplated her. He stood for a moment beside the table, and she looked at him with admiration before recollecting herself.

'I—I— Forgive me,' she said haltingly. 'I wanted to see you, but I can see you are busy.'

'Not at all. You took me by surprise, that is all.'

The words, spoken softly, were as potent as a caress. Jane stared into his brooding dark face. Confusion pressed around her heart. This was the first time she had seen him since he had kissed her and she didn't really know what to do or how to feel or even how to behave at this precise moment, which was unlike her since she had always said and done the first thing that came into her head. She had tossed and turned in her bed until the early hours on her first night back in London because of this man and his kiss, and then her dreams had been filled with such longings and yearnings as she had never thought to experience.

'I—I hope I am not disturbing you,' she said.

Since their parting Christopher had wondered how she was and if she had recovered from their shared kiss. She had been filled with such innocent, unselfish passion when he had drawn her into his arms. On reflection he remembered how shocked she had seemed afterwards. He smiled. Perhaps she had never been kissed before. That would explain it.

But it didn't explain his own reaction, he thought, as his gaze lingered on her lips, remembering what it had felt like to kiss them. Kissing Jane Mortimer was something he knew he was going to remember for a long time. The first touch of her lips, so seemingly chaste, and yet it had sent arousal pulsing through him in an instant.

He'd known he was kissing a virgin and that his kiss had awakened carnality inside her for the very first time. Try as he might he could not banish her from his mind so easily. She had a way of getting under his skin and insinuating herself into his mind with an intelligent sharpness of mind and a clever wit that he admired, making her pleasant company and interesting to be with.

'Not at all,' he answered. 'I am genuinely happy to see you.'

Noting her lovely eyes, richly lashed under excellently marked eyebrows, and the way in which she looked at him, she suddenly looked so young and defenceless to Christopher. He stared at her, at her lips, wanting to taste them once more, to feel their softness, but it was an impulse he would not succumb to.

'What is the reason for your visit?'

'I have something to say to you.'

'Given this shameless conduct on your part—seeking me out at my home—I hope it is something of an important nature. Or,' he said quietly, his dark brows rising a notch, a teasing glint igniting in his eyes, 'naughty.'

Jane tensed, forcing down a rush of panic, hoping she was not utterly wrong in her judgement of Lord Lansbury. 'I—I said I wanted to talk,' she reminded him.

'And that's all? How disappointing.'

'That depends on what I have to say.'

He chuckled. 'Fair enough,' he acknowledged. 'Talk it is, then. Although I was right about you.'

'In what way?'

'You are not like any woman I've met before, which is why I am all the more intrigued by you.'

She frowned. 'Don't be. I am not in the least intriguing.'

'I beg to differ. You are the most fascinating young woman I've ever met. There is quite a fire under that cool, detached, practical exterior of yours.'

Suddenly Jane felt uneasy. In order to gain time and marshal her thoughts, she said, 'You—you appear to be busy. Perhaps I should come back some other time.'

'I'm in London to decide whether or not to sell the house. It's in a prime location. If I do decide to sell it, I have no doubt that once it goes on to the market I'll soon have it off my hands.'

His smile became ironic. After attending a meeting with his lawyer and auditors and turning them loose on Chalfont's well-kept books and ledgers, for the first time in years it would seem that after all his hard work he was at last beginning to see some reward for his efforts. He might not have to sell the London house after all. But that was not Miss Mortimer's concern.

'So, tell me why you wish to see me. Is it important?'

'Yes, at least I think so.'

'Have you concluded your business with your father's solicitor?'

She nodded.

He motioned her to a seat. 'Then you'd better sit down.'

'No,' she said quickly. 'I would rather stand, if you don't mind.'

'As you wish.' Thrusting his hands into his trouser pockets, he rested his hip against the desk and tilted his head to one side, looking at her intently. He was intrigued. 'Don't you think you should get to the point?'

Jane swallowed nervously, meeting his gaze beneath his close scrutiny. She knew her next words could be the turning point in her life—that it could be for the better or she was about to make a complete fool of herself.

'First of all I would like to tell you that throughout his life my father accumulated a great deal of money. He—he dealt with it in a rather haphazard way. He was never interested in money, you see—not really—but he did consider my future very carefully. Now his lawyer has finalised his affairs, it—it would appear he did rather well for himself—he even bought into some profitable diamond mines in Africa, among other things. All are paying healthy dividends. He has left me very well provided for.' Realising she was letting her tongue run away with her, she fell silent.

'I see. I am happy for you, but what is it you are trying to say, Miss Mortimer?'

Jane took her time, wanting to create the impression of unhurried calm, but her pulse was racing. 'I have to decide what to do next—with my money, that is.'

'You don't have to do anything with it. I am sure your lawyer and bank manager will advise you regarding investments—and I imagine your aunt would welcome a donation for her charities.'

'I have already taken care of that.'

'So what is it you want from me?'

'Nothing. It's—it's just that I know how difficult things are for you at present—financially, that is. I—I have money, and I thought...'

As he realised exactly what she did think, Christopher's attitude changed immediately. Humiliated and shamed beyond bearing, he was silent, looking at her hard, incredulously, as though she had suddenly changed before his eyes. His eyes glittered with a fire that burned her raw and his voice was deadly calm when he spoke.

'Is this your idea of a joke?'

Bemused, she shook her head. 'A joke? No, of course it isn't.'

'Good. It would have been in excruciatingly bad taste. You are not wanting in audacity, I'll grant you that.'

Jane felt a prickling of fear that escalated to panic the moment she looked into his eyes. In contrast to the deadly quiet of his voice, his face was a mask of savage fury. She watched him struggle to contain it.

'I—I don't understand...'

'Then listen carefully. I don't want your money, Miss Mortimer,' he said in a terrible voice, standing up straight. 'I will not be obligated to you. I think what you are about to suggest comes under the heading of charity. Is that what I am to you—a charity case, an object of pity? If you think that, then you have a low opinion of me. The day I need pity from a woman is the day I walk myself off a cliff.'

'I do not pity you.' Jane's eyes were huge with genuine horror that he should think that. Half-turning from his burning gaze, she put her hand to her head. 'As a matter of fact, I have a very high opinion of you—and Lady Lansbury. She has been very kind to me. I wanted to help you and your family.'

'What can you possibly do for my family that hasn't already been done?'

Jane rounded on him with fire in her eyes and a challenge to the world in the arrogance of her stance. 'I can save you from ruin. I am offering you a way out of debt. Don't let your masculine pride stand in your way.'

His eyes slashed her like razors. 'The state of my finances is not your business, Miss Mortimer. My father might have exhibited a proclivity towards all manner of expensive vices—gambling was his addiction—he lost astronomical sums and once offered Chalfont in payment of one particular enormous debt. At the time I was a wealthy man in my own right. I stepped in and paid it. Unfortunately it almost ruined me. Everything was mortgaged up to the hilt. The banks and creditors became like scavengers, calling in loans and taking everything that was not entailed. When they scent a failure, they are quick to close in to ensure that they get their share of what is left. I dug myself out of a hole and I am still digging, but I am climbing to the top of that hole without help from you or anyone else.'

Panic jolted through Jane's entire nervous system—her heart began to race wildly. He spat the words at her. At this cruel attack she fell back and put her hands over her face as if he had hit her. For one dreadful moment she had seen the rage in his eyes, in his stance, in his hands clenched by his sides. In fact, the very air between them sizzled with it and she became quiet inside her where the memory of their kiss was hidden, the remembrance of it soothing the anger, understanding at last why he was reacting like this to her offer.

She had humiliated him and because of it he could quite simply not stand the sight of her in this room where he was forced to look at her, knowing she was the cause of that humiliation, hurt pride and shame.

Her courage and her anger seemed to have abandoned her all of a sudden. The whole situation had turned into a grotesque and humiliating farce.

'I see, but—'

'But nothing. I think you forget yourself and your station. You may find yourself elevated to a position to be envied, but your sole concern in my house is for the care of my sister. However, since you have come here to make me an offer of your money, what exactly would our arrangement be? You want to give me some of your money. Why would you do that? For what reason? Explain yourself, Miss Mortimer.'

'Oh, I— Indeed, I have given no thought to—'

'Come now,' he persisted, beginning to pace up and down the room impatiently. 'You are not usually lost for words. Nor are you so stupid as not to have given the matter careful thought before making me the offer. A loan comes with interest.'

Suddenly it dawned on him what it was she might want. Had this foolish young woman read more into their amorous embrace on the train than he realised at the time? Was it possible that she had aspirations to be his wife and she was making the offer of her money to tempt him? He was used to being pursued by rich heiresses in pursuit of a title. It looked as if Jane Mortimer was no different after all.

He stopped pacing and stared at her. For a moment his expression was blank, then the uncompromising line of his jaw hardened. His eyes, which had been cold and harsh, became colder still, and his stern mouth tightened. 'Just what interest would you require in return for your money? Would it be of the monetary kind or something else?'

'Something else?' she repeated. 'I don't know what you mean.'

'Don't play the innocent. It won't work.' He moved closer, halting in front of her, his eyes glacial and pinning hers. 'One minute you're an independent young woman taking care of my sister, and today you're oozing good will and awash with excitement over the prospect of sharing your newfound wealth with me. I think you read more into our embrace than I realised.'

A dozen rejoinders sprang to Jane's mind, only to lodge in her throat behind a lump of confusion that swelled unbearably as she regarded him. 'I did? I just don't know where to begin.'

His face hardened into an expressionless mask,

but his eyes were probing hers like twin daggers that impaled her, looking for answers. 'Let's stick to the salient points. What are you really doing here? What do you want from me?'

She glanced at him, her eyes dark with pain and disillusionment. 'I haven't thought… That's a little awkward to explain,' Jane said. She was so off balance from his anger that her mind went blank and she uttered disjointedly, 'I merely thought that since you are having to sell your London house—and you can no longer rely on Miss Spelling—'

'What?' he ground out. 'That you would put yourself forward in her stead?'

Jane's head whirled with the most dreadful confusion. She had done nothing to invite this. 'Put myself forward? No—I…'

'Please tell me you didn't expect me to offer to marry you because of what happened between us. Tell me that you aren't that naive or that stupid. Had I wanted to marry for money I would have married Lydia. But when it boiled down to it—although I was a little late in realising it—as lovely and fortuitous as it was, her money alone was not enough. May I ask why the hell you would think I have any desire to marry you? Why should I take yours?'

Flinching from the sting of his tone, Jane wished she could sink into the floor and disappear. In that warm, elegantly furnished room all reality seemed to have been suspended, leaving her to hang in the numbing vacuum of her own uncertainty.

'Oh, dear,' she said, choosing her words with great care in the hope of preserving what little was left of her pride, 'you have got it wrong. You have misunderstood me completely, and if you'd waited a little longer instead of running off in a temper, you'd have heard me say how…'

One eyebrow lifted in sardonic, arrogant enquiry. 'What would I have heard? What an excellent mistress of Chalfont you would make?' Seeing fire flame hot and sure in her eyes, he smiled mockingly. 'Ah, I appear to have touched a nerve. I see you have a temper.'

Jane could feel the anger begin somewhere in her breast, a hard knot just where her heart lay. Having come to his house with nothing but good intentions, she found his hostile manner and egotistical attitude outrageous. She also felt a dreadful resentment that he should feel he had the right to speak to her as though she were nothing at all. But she kept her temper subdued, which she found, as the moments passed, to be reasserting itself. Her father had said she had one, and Finn, after the not-so-good times wherever they happened to be. She had not believed it, not even remembered it, and though so far she had found no reason to show it, she knew it was there, simmering beneath her outward calm.

Stiffening her spine, she raised her head defiantly. 'I do lose my temper and I am hurt just as easily as anyone else. Not until afterwards do I remember and try to understand why the person who made me lose my temper might have belittled me in such a way. When I came here my intentions were honourable and completely honest. I did not expect to have them flung back in my face.'

'It's unfortunate you've wasted your time, but it's hardly a tragedy.' Christopher would allow himself a moment's weakness, but not now, not in front of Jane Mortimer. His pride was his strength. 'Did you really think I was so desperate for money that I would accept yours? You can turn around and go right back to your aunt.'

His words sliced through her, laid her open and left pain in their wake. His taunting smile seared her and brought a rush of colour to her face. He was cruelly laughing at her and her stung pride would not allow that. It brought her chin up defiantly. She glared at him.

'It will be my pleasure, Lord Lansbury. I'm sorry I came here. I can see I have wasted both your time and mine. I am beginning to feel that Miss Spelling has had a lucky escape.'

'I couldn't agree more. I have a reputation to protect, a certain standing in society to maintain. Imagine the hilarity should it be discovered I had taken money from an employee to help settle my debts.'

'Well then, you will have to make more suitable arrangements when next you look for a wife.'

His eyes were almost silver, the grey draining away in his anger. 'Be careful what you say,' he said harshly. 'And don't be misled by the fact that I once showed myself indulgent in my dealings with you—'

'One might say more than indulgent!' Jane bit back. 'It infuriates me that I allowed such liberties to be taken by a man who thinks of me as no more than a moment's pleasure when you get me alone.'

'I don't recall you complaining at the time.'

Something welled up in Jane, a powerful surge of emotion to which she had no alternative but to give full rein. It was as if she had suddenly become someone else, someone bigger and much stronger than her own self. Her eyes flashed as cold fury drained her face of colour and added a steely edge to her voice.

'Which is to my regret. As a matter of fact it did mean something to me. To you, what happened may have seemed commonplace,' she upbraided him, her words reverberating through the room. 'Just another one of the many flirtations, romances and infidelities that give society something to gossip about. But I am not in the habit of kissing gentlemen who are relative strangers to me, or any other kind for that matter.'

'I was not accusing you of such.'

'What you did accuse me of was quite absurd. You, Lord Lansbury, are way above me in every aspect and not for one minute would I aspire to marry you. But after saying that, your lofty rank does not intimidate me. You may be an earl, but you are not the sun around which the world revolves. I know who I am and what I am and I do not need you to remind me. Anyone with the least instinct for class differences could tell I am not a born lady. My background testifies to that.'

'Which was down to your father.'

'Do not bring my father into this,' she replied

fiercely. 'He did not belong to any particular class of society. Clever and dedicated, he represented working-class men, yet when he was in the presence of foreign nobility, he had the same confident manner as they. It was not easy to tell whether he was an upper-class gentleman who chose martyrdom among the workers or a working-class gentleman who had risen in life.'

'Be that as it may, Miss Mortimer, I think that when you met my mother and she offered you the position to look after Octavia, you simply seized on a brilliant ploy to lead a better life for a while, and the deal was sweetened when you came into your inheritance and you realised how—desperate as I am for money—you saw your circumstances changing for the better and decided to test the boundaries. But I am not about to fall like a rock for it!'

In an attempt to shut out the torment of his words, Jane found herself watching his mouth, the lips that had kissed hers so gently, so passionately. It seared her.

'How dare you say that to me?'

'I do dare, Miss Mortimer. You are nothing but a shallow, scheming, calculating little opportunist. With your talent, you should be on the stage, along with—'

He would have continued but his angry diatribe was cut short. Jane was on her way to the door. She could be roused to a primitive and savage rage by an act of wanton cruelty and injustice. Unable to let the injustice pass, borne on the tide of her own anger, she turned and strode quickly back to him. Beside herself with rage, her colour gloriously high, her eyes stormy with hurt indignation, with all her strength she dealt him a stunning blow across the face. The sight of the sudden redness calmed her down, but did not cause her the slightest twinge of regret or compunction. He had insulted her basely and she had been far too patient with him.

A scheming, calculating opportunist.

The words hung in the air like an acrid smell.

She felt obscurely happy at having been able to inflict pain on him. She could even have wished it were greater. She would have liked to lash out at him with her teeth and nails and tear out those insolent eyes in which, for the moment, surprise had taken the place of contempt.

Mechanically, Christopher raised a hand to his cheek. To all appearances it was the first time such a thing had ever happened to him and he could not get over it. The slap had reduced him to silence and Jane, realising this, contemplated him with satisfaction.

'Perhaps now,' she uttered sweetly, 'you will remember me. You are a heartless, inconsiderate, arrogant monster and I cannot believe I let you touch me. I will never be able to forgive my stupidity for making you an offer of my money—without strings—no games. I regret my own foolish naivety in thinking you would have welcomed my offer with open arms. It is your loss, Lord Lansbury. Not mine.'

Spinning on her heel, she swept from the room with all the majesty of an outraged queen, leaving her aggressor to his own thoughts. Outside she climbed into the waiting cab. Progression was slow as the streets were crowded. There were horses ridden by top-hatted men and side-saddled women, dozens of carriages of every type, open and closed, but she saw nothing. She was too dazed to think, too numb to feel, but she could hear over and over again the carelessly brutal opinion of her uttered by the man she adored. How cold he had been, how hard and implacable his eyes.

Entering the house, like a moth floundering in lamplight, she stumbled her way up the stairs to her room. Once inside she turned the key in the lock and leaned her head against the hard wood of the door frame. Not even her aunt was allowed to witness the collapse of her brave facade as all her courage drained away and she sank to her knees, weeping as if her heart would break. She could hear Lord Lansbury's words ringing in her ears, muted only by the sound of her own weeping as her heart was shredded into pieces.

Christopher stared at the door that Jane had just disappeared through, feeling bewildered and consumed with anger. Feeling the minutes ticking by, he stood perfectly still, unable to shake off the image of the tempestuous young woman with blazing violet eyes and a face alive with fury and disdain. The picture branded itself on his mind. She'd actually looked and sounded as if she'd meant every single thing she'd said to him.

He thought of what he had accused her of and knew he shouldn't have. Instinct told him he had gone too far and was close to making a mortal enemy of a woman who was a loyal friend to his mother and his sister.

Was she ambitious?

Had she hoped that he would offer marriage in

return for her money? And just how much money had she inherited?

Was she innocent of deviousness all along?

He didn't know what to think—but, he thought, feeling the sting in his cheek from her slap, it might be interesting finding out.

The morning following her bitter altercation with Lord Lansbury, Jane awakened feeling oddly refreshed after a night of tearful recriminations. She was surprised to find that she was no longer in the throes of wrenching heartbreak. The previous morning, everything had seemed so simple and predictable. Now everything had changed. Getting out of bed and remembering how she had gone to Lansbury House, ready to lay her generous offer at Lord Lansbury's feet, now she tried to shut out the images, but it was no use. They paraded across her mind, tormenting her with vivid scenes of the mindlessly besotted girl she had been.

How could she have been so foolish, so incredibly naive? The bitter confrontation had almost destroyed her, but as she went about her morning routine of bathing and dressing, more in defiance than sincerity she told herself that she was free of Christopher Chalfont now. Oh, yes, she had feelings for him still, she felt sure she always would, but she knew now that as far as he was concerned she had been just another woman who had fallen into his arms—so very gullible—and now she would pay dearly for it if she let it, which she was determined she would not do. Some vestige of pain still lingered, but she did not feel sad or foolish. In a strange way she felt liberated. A wry smile touched her lips as she sat before the dressing-table mirror and brushed her long hair before securing it at her nape.

In the clear light of day she vowed that everything would be different. She was determined not to look back on her grievous mistake of offering Lord Lansbury some of her money, because it hurt too much to remember. At twenty-one years old and rich beyond anything she could have imagined possible, she was her own mistress. From this day forward, her life was going to change. For better or worse she was going to put Christopher Chalfont from her mind. She was going to enjoy herself.

About to leave her room to join her aunt for breakfast, glancing at herself in the long mirror, she paused, her gaze sweeping over her not-so-fashionably turned out reflection with a critical eye. It was as if she were really seeing herself for the first time. She glanced in the mirror every morning to see that her hair was tidy, her face clean, but she was always too preoccupied with other matters to really see herself.

What a sorry sight she looked, she thought, spreading the folds of her skirts between her hands. It had seen much service. She was dressed neither well nor fashionably. It was drab, the grey colour seeming to drain the colour from her face. It also hung badly on her tall frame. Remembering with envy the flounced dresses the ladies had worn at Lady Lansbury's party, she realised that if she wanted to turn her life around she needed some new clothes very badly. She realised she should have paid a visit to the shops before now, but clothes had never been high on her list of things to do—until today. Her mind was made up. A visit to the shops would not go amiss—not that she had any experience of the buying of fashionable clothes.

'Come, Aunt Caroline, admit it,' she said, when she broached the matter with her aunt and observed the elevation of her eyebrows. 'My wardrobe is hardly up to town standards. I have no real flair and, to be completely honest, I've never been all that interested in fashion, but something needs to be done. I need a complete new wardrobe.'

'Oh, dear—yes, I do see your problem. You dress very—individually, I will grant you, but you are not completely without taste.'

Caroline thought it was a splendid idea that they should begin right away—in fact, she was quite excited at the thought of a shopping trip to the dressmakers and milliners in Bond Street, a thoroughfare of potential wealth and luxury. Jane had given her a brief account of what had transpired between herself and Lord Lansbury at dinner the night before and Caroline had half expected her to appear red-eyed and puffy-faced with weeping. She was pleased to find her looking none the worse from her ordeal and looking forward to moving on with her life.

'I will enjoy accompanying you to the shops. And jewellery,' Caroline suggested. 'You'll need something decorative to set off your new wardrobe.'

'I have several lovely necklaces and earrings and bracelets given to me by my father.'

'I'm so glad you're being positive about all this, Jane.'

'I have to be. Of course, now my situation has changed I shall have to go to Chalfont and explain to Lady Lansbury why I can no long take care of Lady Octavia,' Jane said, as she placed her bonnet over her hair, making a mental note to arrange her hair differently when she had taken care of her clothes. 'She has been extremely kind to me. I have no intention of disappointing her by leaving without an explanation.'

'I am sure Lady Lansbury will be sorry to lose you, but considering your new status as a wealthy young lady, you have no need to work. You will soon be parading through Hyde Park with the best of them.'

Jane laughed, fastening the ribbon of her bonnet beneath her chin. 'I don't know about that, Aunt Caroline. One thing I do know is that I do not intend being idle. I'm used to being busy. Phineas Waverley will be arriving in London shortly to prepare for his exhibition.'

'Do you still intend helping him to prepare for it?'

'Yes—absolutely. He needs someone who's familiar with the work.' Seeing the apprehensive look in her aunt's eyes, she smiled to reassure her. 'Don't worry, Aunt Caroline. I know what I'm doing. I do love it. In a way it will be like carrying on my father's work. It will also give purpose to my life. I think it's just what I need to occupy my mind at this time.'

* * *

Jane drifted through the perfumed air of Mrs Ainsworth's elegant salon, an establishment that had been recommended by one of the ladies who worked with Aunt Caroline's on the board of charities. Mrs Ainsworth, who employed a number of experienced seamstresses, dressed the well-to-do in her own exquisite and clever designs.

Ordering a whole new wardrobe, Jane was twisted and turned for the best part of two hours in the sumptuous salon as she was measured for the simplest dresses for morning, dresses for leisure, coats and tea gowns, some with long fitted bodices, all in a variety of colours and exquisite materials—gowns that emphasised her figure to advantage and flattered her vivid colouring. On the whole they were plain, but sculpted to Jane's fine-drawn slenderness by the clever fingers of Mrs Ainsworth. Jane was glad the bustle was falling out of favour, which she considered quite hideous and unflattering.

Like a child in a sweet shop she ordered draped overskirts and ruffled underskirts, delicate lingerie, wraps and coats, shoes and boots, and she was unable to resist purchasing beautiful beads and fans and mother-of-pearl combs and any accessory that caught her eye. She even ordered two ballgowns to be made and a riding habit in a colour of velvet that matched her eyes—not that she believed for one moment she would ever wear the ballgowns or the riding habit. She had never been to a ball in her life and she didn't have a horse and didn't believe she would get the chance to ride one again—and if she did, she would have to sit on one of those ridiculous side saddles like all the other ladies.

Mrs Ainsworth kept a quantity of ready-made gowns of different styles and sizes. When Jane purchased a rather lovely green brocade with a contrasting darker green jacket to wear immediately, with high-heeled cream boots and kid gloves to match, she was quite indistinguishable from any of the other well-bred young ladies who frequented Mrs Ainsworth's establishment. Indeed Mrs Ainsworth privately considered Miss Mortimer had a style, a certain unique something to which she could put no name. She had seen it on very few, but it set them apart from the others, who were merely fashionable. As she was being fussed over, Jane asked herself why she was doing this. It had seemed like a dream when the expensive fabrics had brushed her skin and, as she looked at herself in the mirror attired in her gorgeous new green outfit, her glossy hair arranged in an elegant chignon, she no longer saw the plain young woman who faded into the background. It seemed like a dream in which a girl she recognised as herself but who had nothing at all to do with the real Jane Mortimer. In fact, she looked rather pretty.

'You look so lovely,' Aunt Caroline enthused. Her eyes full of admiration suddenly became rueful. 'And so tall—just like your dear father. Unfortunately I took after our mother's side—she was small and verging on the plump side. When I was your age, how I wish I had been as tall and slender as you.'

Jane could not believe that silks and satins adorned with ribbons and frothing lace could bring about such a change. Yes, she thought, with her colouring, her high cheekbones and her violet eyes, she really did look quite wonderful. She no longer looked like the drab Jane Mortimer.

Chapter Seven

Jane had written to Lady Lansbury letting her know when she would be returning to Chalfont. Lady Lansbury sent a carriage to meet her off the train. It was mid-afternoon when she arrived. Chalfont was enjoying the last days of summer, while leaves still clung to the trees in the park. On entering the house she was told by the butler that Lady Lansbury had taken a chill and was confined to her bed.

Instructing to have her bags taken to her room, Jane went directly to Lady Lansbury's suite, knocking gently on the door. Lady Lansbury's maid admitted her.

'How is Lady Lansbury?' Jane asked, unable to conceal her concern.

'She is resting, but I know she will be pleased to see you back. I was about to go and get her some tea, so I'll leave you for a moment.'

'I've just arrived, but I will be happy to sit with her for a while.'

Jane crossed the richly patterned carpet to the bed. The curtains were partly drawn over the windows to keep out the bright light. Lady Lansbury lay propped against a mound of pillows, her face drawn. Jane was startled by her condition. Her eyes were closed and there was a hollowness about her cheeks. Jane had not expected to find her so ill. When she opened her eyes, on seeing Jane she smiled. Her eyes warmed and at once she was as she had always been—kind, sweet-natured, gracious, affectionate, even despite the difference in their rank.

'Jane! I cannot tell you how pleased I am to see you back at Chalfont—and how lovely you look. I hope things went well for you in London.'

'Yes—yes, they did.'

Lady Lansbury coughed a little, then sighed deeply, her hands fluttering like pale flowers on the lace-edged bedspread.

Jane was concerned by her pale face and the bleak expression in her eyes. 'I had no idea you were ill. Had I known I would have returned sooner. How long have you been like this?'

'Please don't concern yourself, Jane. I'm all right.

I took a chill after getting caught in the rain three days ago when I took Octavia down to the lake. It had been threatening rain all morning. I should have known better than to leave the house without a coat.'

'Have you been seen by a doctor?'

Lady Lansbury closed her eyes. 'Yes, yes I have,' she replied wearily. 'Doctor Boynton, our family physician, came to see me yesterday. He left some medicine and told me to remain in bed for a few days. Have you seen Octavia?'

'Not yet. When I was told you were poorly, I came straight up. How is she?'

'The same. Maisie has been looking after her in your absence. Octavia will be overjoyed to see you back. Christopher isn't back from London yet, although he is expected any day now. It would appear that things are beginning to look up at last. He's been meeting with the auditors and others who look after his finances. He wrote telling me he might not have to sell the London house after all.'

'I'm happy to hear that. It must be a tremendous relief.' Having no wish to discuss Lord Lansbury, whom she had struggled day and night to put from her mind, Jane averted her eyes and said quickly, 'Is there anything I can get you?'

'No, thank you, Jane. I am sure you will want to settle in. Come and see me later—and bring Octavia with you. She will be overjoyed to have you back.'

As Jane made her way to her own room, she knew she could not tell Lady Lansbury she was planning to leave Chalfont until she was feeling better. She had no wish to cause her further upset. Her hopes that she would have left before Lord Lansbury returned from London were dashed.

Octavia was delighted to have Jane back at Chalfont and in no time at all their days fell into a familiar pattern. Unable to shake off her chill, Lady Lansbury kept to her room, where Jane would visit with Octavia twice a day.

Almost a week after Jane had returned, Lord Lansbury arrived. The first thing he did was to see his mother, who informed him that Jane was back. He was relieved his mother remained in ignorance of what had transpired between Miss Mortimer and himself in London. At the very least he was grateful to Miss Mortimer for that.

Determined to speak to her immediately, he went to the suite of rooms she shared with Octavia, where he was told by Maisie that they had left earlier to walk to the lake.

One hour later, from the window of his bedroom he saw Miss Mortimer crossing the lawn with Octavia dancing along beside her, Poppy yapping at their heels. After looking fondly at his young sister for a moment, his eyes, as though drawn by a magnet, became fixed on the young woman who was causing such disruption to his life.

What a proud, spirited young woman she was, he thought, and she was wearing a new gown. Ever since he had laid eyes on her she had slowly blossomed before his eyes. Now this tall, stylish goddess of a creature was as rakishly elegant as a fashion picture.

She was wearing an informal day dress in lavender. The front was flat, the back full; the elegant cut accentuating her slimness. Her hair was also different. Swept upward away from her face, it showed to advantage her long slender neck. Curling tendrils drifted about her face and neck as he had never seen them do before.

The loveliness of her smiling face was flushed with her exertions and when she moved her slender, though softly rounded, form floated with a fluidity and grace over the freshly mown lawn. In the simple elegance of her dress, chosen to blend with the soft warmth of her skin and hair, Christopher's breath caught in his throat as he watched the irresistible curve of her generous lips as she laughed with Octavia. He had never thought to see her looking so at ease, so provocatively lovely, glamorous and bewitching. He already yearned to hold her in his arms, to feel her warmth, smell her hair, her flesh.

As he recollected himself his dark eyebrows dipped alarmingly and his lips thinned. Every time he thought of her, of kissing her, he felt a sharp needle of exasperation drive through him, directed at her, as though, like a witch, she had cast a spell on him, which was totally absurd. It was not her fault that he couldn't seem to put her out of his mind. No woman had clouded his judgement and stolen his peace of mind so completely. Never in his life had he felt a bond so great and a feeling so all consuming.

Jolted from his reverie when the centre of his attention disappeared inside the house, with a soft curse he turned from the window. After their angry encounter he had believed her to be a scheming little opportunist, driven by nothing but her own ambition. Had he been wrong about her? If it turned out that he had made a mistake, then he would have to bear the load of self-recrimination for the accusations he had heaped on her.

The humiliation that had engulfed him when she had made him the offer of her money had clouded his judgement and it had been wrong of him to condemn her out of hand.

When the summons came for Jane to attend Lord Lansbury in his study she went directly. Unaware of what awaited her, she was apprehensive but determined to stand her ground. Perhaps he had decided to send her away from Chalfont to be thoroughly rid of her. He had good reason for doing so. But in any case she had to leave. To be near Lord Lansbury, to continue to work in his house with no other prospects, knowing the disdain with which he regarded her, was an intolerable thought. Thank goodness she could make choices about her future.

Although, as she made her way to his study, she found that she felt the same longing to see him again. Looking back, she had no idea what had possessed her when she had found herself alone with him on the train, for she had been unable to stop herself. It was as if Jane Mortimer—plain,

God-fearing Jane Mortimer—had undergone an extraordinary transformation beneath that intense silver-grey gaze and become some kind of shameless Delilah. Every time she thought of it, her acute embarrassment came flooding back, along with an odd, breathless excitement that she was certain could not be anything but wicked.

When she entered the study, Lord Lansbury was working at his big desk and did not look up, even when the door was shut. As she stood, she looked at him, recalling the days and nights she had struggled to keep him from her thoughts, to forget him, which had all been for nothing. The memories came and with them the emotions she had felt before she had left him in London. The feelings she had wanted so desperately to deny swept over her and she knew that what she had felt for him before was not dead, was still very much alive inside her. How could she have thought that she could forget him?

'You asked to see me,' she said.

'Yes, I did. Please sit down. I will be with you in a moment.'

Hearing that terse, cold, impersonal voice, Jane felt her heart contract as she moved to sit down on the chair at an angle to the fireplace and some distance away from the desk. The room opened directly on to the terrace, colourful with roses and pots of geraniums. A sweet scent of honeysuckle and mown grass wafted through the open French windows, along with the call of a blackbird above the constant hum of buzzing bees.

Jane sat quite still, practically holding her breath. The silence was so complete that the swift scratching of the pen across the paper seemed to her to make a shattering noise. He went on writing, eyes down.

Looking at his bent head, despite her determination not to think of him ever again in any romantic sense, Jane felt such a pang of longing and need that she wanted to confess her feelings. How her blood stirred at the sight of him. During the time they had been apart she had hoped she had managed to conquer the debilitating effect he always had on her senses, but his potent sexual magnetism was like a palpable force. How had she allowed him to do this to her? She was scandalised by the stirrings inside her that the mere sight of him commanded and she resented this hunger, this need, that held her captive to her emotions.

She could not allow herself to continue in this way. The sooner she left Chalfont and put Christopher Chalfont behind her, the better it would be for her peace of mind.

Suddenly he put down his pen, looked up and their eyes locked. The eyes that met hers were hard, his face expressionless. Shoving back his chair, he stood up and walked around the desk. Not wishing to be at a disadvantage by remaining seated, Jane got to her feet and gazed at him wonderingly, forgetting in an instant all that he had made her suffer—the unjust, insulting accusations he had flung at her.

As he strode towards her, the room seemed to shrink. He was so tall that she thought he must surely have grown since she had seen him last. But otherwise he was unchanged. There was still the same masterful face and silver-grey eyes, the same brushed-back dark hair. As he came closer a knot began to form inside her chest. He was politely frightening and bore down on her with the predatory grace of a stalking beast.

Considering the turmoil within her, her voice was curiously calm when she spoke. 'What is it you wish to speak to me about?' He halted in front of her. She drew a deep breath and inhaled the sharp scent of sandalwood and with it an added scent of him. It disconcerted her. Did he have to stand so close?

'Do you really want me to spell it out? We cannot avoid one another. It is best that we clear the air between us.'

Jane's proud, disdainful violet eyes met and held Lord Lansbury's grey ones without flinching. She was discovering, agreeably, that now she was face to face with him, the vague terrors which had haunted her ever since their last encounter had melted away. The remembrance of her feelings at that time made her forget her momentary wrath. Her face relaxed a little.

'Yes, that is the sensible thing to do.'

'I feel as if I have been in some kind of bizarre limbo since our meeting in London,' he said, moving away from her. 'You really are quite extraordinary. You shouldn't go around giving your money to strangers.'

'You're not—I mean, a stranger—and I've never done this sort of thing in my life. But then, I didn't have any money of my own before.'

He chuckled softly. 'It was like something out of the Arabian Nights tale when, like a genie out of a bottle, you appeared on my doorstep, intending to solve all my problems with your money.'

'Why are you laughing?'

'Because, on reflection, you were beginning to sound like an American girl.'

Jane bristled. 'Like Miss Spelling, I think you mean.' She frowned. 'Are you making fun of me?'

'Perhaps a little.'

'Then please don't.'

Jane could feel his eyes studying her as he circled the desk, to stand on the opposite side.

'It seems you are not quite as I thought you to be, which I find disconcerting,' he continued. 'My preconceived ideas of you are falling away, Miss Mortimer.'

'And what preconceived ideas might they be?'

'I thought you were mild tempered, not easily roused to anger. It appears I was wrong on both counts.'

'Yes, you were,' Jane admitted calmly.

'You have a temper, with no compunction about speaking your mind and attacking those who make you cross.'

'Only those who provoke me. I understand perfectly if you don't want me here. Indeed, when I returned I fully intended telling Lady Lansbury that I was leaving—to be gone before you returned.

Unfortunately she was unwell and I had no wish to upset her.'

'For that, at least, I am grateful. I must confess that after what occurred between us on our last encounter, I was surprised to find you had returned to Chalfont. It did enter my mind that you had returned to provoke me.'

'Provoke you?' Jane replied, doing her utmost to remain calm, determined not to let him draw her to anger and cause her to lose her fragile grip on her emotions as she had done the last time. 'Why on earth should I do that? Do not judge me by your own behaviour. It would never occur to me to stoop to anything so shallow. I told you—knowing how abhorrent my presence in your home would be to you now, it was my intention to leave before you returned from London. I considered it best to avoid any confrontation that might end as our last meeting did.'

Fury flared in his eyes. 'Whenever we happen to meet in the future, Miss Mortimer, it will never end like that one. I do not suppose it occurred to you to inform me before you left Chalfont.'

'No,' she answered with characteristic bluntness. 'It was Lady Lansbury who engaged me to care for Lady Octavia. It would have been extremely rude on my part to leave without explaining my reason for doing so. When Lady Lansbury engaged me to come to Chalfont I was wholly committed to caring for Lady Octavia, but I did explain to her that it would only be a temporary arrangement.'

'And naturally your change of circumstances means you have to leave.'

'Yes—although I do have other reasons,' she told him, thinking of Finn, 'along with the fact that after what transpired between us has made my situation untenable. You must see that.'

'Nevertheless, this is my house, Miss Mortimer. You may feel you have to answer to my mother, but I insist on knowing what goes on.'

'And do you always get what you want?'

Jane watched his dark brows lift in surprise at her impertinence and she could not suppress a hint of satisfaction.

'Usually,' he replied. 'Perhaps because I am a heartless, inconsiderate, arrogant monster. Or so I have been told.'

Having her own words quoted back to her was a bit disconcerting, but if he expected an apology he was going to be disappointed.

'All aristocrats are the same,' he went on. 'I suppose it's down to the way we were raised. It comes with a lifetime of being surrounded by people who wait upon our every whim. Do not expect an earl to behave otherwise.'

'With you as an example, Lord Lansbury, I assure you I will not. And if you are reminding me of your lofty rank to try to intimidate me, then please don't. It will have no effect on me whatsoever. Earls, dukes, call them what you like, are not the sun around which the world revolves. What I did in London—offering you money—was stupid beyond belief. I realise that now.'

'It was. I did not put you down as being reckless.'

'I am not. I am impulsive at times, but never reckless. It was quite out of character for me. But Lady Lansbury has been so kind to me—and I have become extremely fond of Lady Octavia. When I realised how wealthy I am—I thought I might be able to help in some way. I assure you, Lord Lansbury, I had no ulterior motive when I made you that offer and it was quite wrong of you to assume otherwise. It was hardly my fault if you jumped to the wrong conclusion. Unfortunately I hadn't thought it through.'

'Clearly. I hope you understand my reasons for refusing your—generous offer. Try to see it from my point of view. Had I accepted, I should have lost all respect for myself—and for you, too, for putting me in a position of feeling obligated to you and for that I should not forgive you.'

'Yes, I can see that now. Believe me, Lord Lansbury, the last thing I wanted was for you to feel obligated to me in any way.'

'Good,' he said, walking slowly back to stand in front of her, 'and since you are so concerned about Chalfont, you will be pleased to know that things are beginning to improve. After meetings with my lawyer and the bank manager and several other people who are involved with the running of the estate, I find I do not have to sell the town house after all.'

'Then I am happy for you, but please do not feel you have anything to explain to me.'

'I don't. I just thought you would like to know.'

'Lady Lansbury must be relieved.'

'Very much so. However, that said, I want to thank you for your offer—which I should have done when you approached me, instead of losing my temper, for which I apologise.'

There was silence, a silence occupied by Jane in examining what Lord Lansbury had just said. She was astonished. She stared into those clear eyes, searching for mockery, veiled contempt, but found neither. A formidable, exacting man he might be, equal to any risks, brave enough for anything, but one thing he would not do—he would never deal dishonestly with himself or others. There was no arguing with such determination.

'Thank you,' she said at length. 'I, too, lost my temper—which does not happen very often. I accept your apology.'

'And you, Miss Mortimer? You certainly made your feelings clear. As I recall you lost more than your temper that day. You were quite eloquent about passing your opinion of me. Am I to expect an apology, also?'

'If you are referring to the slap I gave you, then no. I make no apology for my actions,' she said emphatically. 'I never apologise when I am provoked about giving an honest opinion. You deserved it. Had I been a man I would have hit you harder. Have you any idea how shamed and insulted I felt when you accused me of being a scheming, calculating opportunist? The accusation was unreasonable and unjust and most unworthy of you.'

Her words brought Christopher up sharp and he stared at her. She looked so young, so vulnerable, facing him with those mutinous, appealing violet eyes locked on to his, that his anger was defused.

His senses were jolted into life by the elusive, perfumed smell of her and he recalled how pleasurable it had felt when she had been in his arms, her lips clinging to his. Half-smiling, half-frowning, he looked into her eyes.

'I stand rebuked. Whatever might have been going through that head of yours, I am sorry you were hurt.'

Jane smiled inwardly to herself with satisfaction. The knowledge that he was sorry warmed her and made up for a good deal of his abominable treatment of her. But threads of anger still coursed through her and she had no intention of letting him off lightly.

Christopher gazed down at her, at the seductive swell of her breasts beneath the confining fabric of her bodice, and he ached to caress the womanly softness of her, to embrace her as he had done once before and ease the ache at the pit of his belly. Strange lights danced in her hair and the womanly essence of her filled his head, stirring and warming his blood.

Jane, almost overawed by his nearness, tried to break the contact he was beginning to stir inside her. She didn't move as he ran a finger slowly down her upper arm. It was a gentle caress that awoke tingling answers in places she tried to ignore. The betrayal of her body aroused vexation in her, even though it seared into her heart, reminding her how deeply her feelings still ran for this insufferable man. It was a hard fact for her pride to accept, especially when she would never see him again when she left Chalfont.

Christopher lifted a brow as he regarded her and she read in the depths of his eyes and the heat of his stare the same thing she had seen when she had fallen into his lap on the train. Calmly she met his gaze.

'Cool your ardour, Lord Lansbury,' she warned, giving no hint of the heart beating a fierce tattoo in her breast brought about by his close proximity and his touch.

'Come now. You were not so ill-disposed to me on the train to London,' he said, his tone silky, easy, his eyes regarding her with fascinated amusement. 'In fact, you were rather amiable, as I remember.'

'You remember too much,' Jane snapped, two sparks of anger showing briefly beneath her lowered lids.

'You were tempted, then.'

'I was stupid.'

'And now?'

'I am no longer foolish enough to get carried away by you.'

'And you are sure of that, are you?' he asked, smiling, his eyes gleaming with expectation as he moved closer to her.

Jane stood perfectly still, unable to look away, knowing that she was very much in danger of becoming overwhelmed by him once more, by his lean, muscular body emanating raw power and his sternly handsome face hovering so very close.

Slowly Christopher's eyes moved down from her face and over the bodice of her gown and the gentle swell of her breasts. A lazy appreciative smile twisted his lips and he found himself dwelling with a good deal of pleasure on the tantalising delights underneath.

'I would be a fool if I thought you had nothing more to offer than your money,' he murmured, meeting her gaze. Seeing shock mingle with fear in her wonderful eyes, he moved away a little, becoming less threatening to her sensibilities. He grinned infuriatingly. 'Don't look so worried. I was just testing the waters, so to speak,' he said softly, but his instinct told him she was no more immune to him and her own vulnerability now than she had been on the train.

'Then don't venture too deep, Lord Lansbury, otherwise you might find yourself out of your depth,' Jane retorted coldly.

His eyebrows arched and his silver-grey eyes danced wickedly. 'There's little danger of that, Miss Mortimer. 'I am an extremely good swimmer. I never take advantage of defenceless young ladies—but you did not give me the impression of being defenceless when you allowed me to kiss you.'

Jane stared at him, her mind trying to adjust to his words. No man had ever spoken to her like this before. She had never had the opportunity to fall in love before. 'It would be interesting to know how much of a gentleman you are, Lord Lansbury—had the train not arrived at Paddington when it did.'

'Were I not a gentleman, Miss Mortimer, it would not have mattered a damn where we were.'

Jane was infuriated. 'How dare you speak to me like this? This is neither the time nor the place and most certainly not part of the agreement I made with Lady Lansbury. You really are the most appallingly rude man I have ever met.' Backing away, she half turned from him. 'I am glad to say she is feeling much better now. I intend telling her tomorrow that I am leaving.'

Trying to regain her composure she struck a stubborn pose, the look in her eyes as she silently met his sardonic gaze one of pure mutiny. 'I think we have said all we have to say. Please excuse me,' she said, as a breeze blew into the room through the open windows. 'It's becoming decidedly chilly all of a sudden.' Stepping away from him, she walked quickly out of the room, unaware of his infuriating smile of admiration as he watched her go.

'Jane? What did you say?' Lady Lansbury looked up at her from her chair. She was still in her night attire, but she was feeling well enough to sit out of bed. 'And do sit down.'

Jane took the offered chair. 'I said I have to leave, Lady Lansbury. I am so sorry but I did say at the beginning that my position could not be permanent.'

'I remember, but I thought you loved it at Chalfont—and Octavia has become extremely fond you.'

'I know, and I am fond of her, but I have to leave.'

Lady Lansbury suddenly stiffened in her chair and gave Jane a sharp look. 'Has something untoward happened, Jane?'

'No, not at all,' she hastened to assure the other

woman, hoping she sounded convincing. She could not bear it if Lady Lansbury learned what had transpired between her and Lord Lansbury. 'I have enjoyed my time at Chalfont, but since I came into my inheritance it has changed things. Besides, I intend to help with the opening of the exhibition I told you about.'

'I see. Then—what can I say but to wish you well.'

There was a hint of dismay in Lady Lansbury's voice and Jane's heart sank. 'Lady Lansbury, I am grateful that you gave me the chance to come to Chalfont—to get to know Lady Octavia—but I think that the time has come for me to move on. I don't know what path my future will take. Perhaps I'll buy a house of my own where I can enjoy good society and make friends—although I can't bear the thought of having nothing to do.'

'You could help your aunt with her charities. I'm sure you would be a valuable asset.'

Jane laughed. 'That isn't what I want to do, but I shall make sure Aunt Caroline and her charities are taken care of. Perhaps I'll go abroad and continue with what my father was doing. I really have no idea. But what I do know is that I need to consider my future very carefully and that I cannot do while I am at Chalfont.'

Lady Lansbury smiled and, reaching out, she squeezed Jane's hand affectionately. 'I understand, Jane. It's been lovely to have you here. I am only sorry you can't remain with us. Octavia is not the only one who is going to miss you, you know. I, too, have become extremely fond of you. I shall miss you greatly.'

Jane heard the emotion in Lady Lansbury's voice she was trying hard to conceal and she was deeply moved. 'Maybe you could both visit me in London. When the exhibition is up and running I would love to show Lady Octavia some of the artefacts.'

'Of course. She'd love that. And you must visit us—now we don't have to sell the London house, and you can always come to Chalfont. We would like that.'

Jane didn't point out how difficult it would be for her to come and go from a place she had grown to love, when she was no longer a part of it. It would be too painful.

'Perhaps when Christopher—I had hoped—' Breaking off, Lady Lansbury frowned, not voicing whatever she had been about to say. Instead she looked down, fingering the ribbon of her dressing gown, lost in thought. Jane waited, silent. Raising her head after a moment, she gave Jane a considered look. 'I must tell Christopher you are going—unless you have mentioned it to him already.'

'I—I felt I must speak with you first.'

She nodded. 'I am sure he won't want you to leave. He might even try to persuade you to stay longer.'

Jane averted her eyes, biting back the bitter reply that Christopher Chalfont would not waste one moment grieving her departure. 'What possible objections could Lord Lansbury possibly have to my leaving?'

'You are to be commended for the care you have taken with Octavia. Like myself, he will not want to lose you.'

'I am sure someone else can be found for the post.'

'But not someone as excellent as you.'

'Would—would you like me to remain until you have found someone else?'

'Jane, I am reluctant to see you go. I don't want to lose you, so of course I would like you to remain until someone else is found—someone suitable. But you cannot wait about indefinitely. No, you go when it suits you.'

'Well, I don't have to return to London immediately. Finn won't be arriving in London for two or three weeks, which means I could remain at Chalfont for the next two weeks. It will give Lady Octavia time to get used to the idea of me leaving.'

Christopher watched Jane enter the conservatory. She had on a new gown with trailing skirts that was simple and elegant, the colour a deep ink that showed off the creaminess of her skin and the fullness of her mouth. Swept upward and away from her face, the height of her hair somehow emphasised her long elegant neck. It also meant that her ears were more exposed along with the drop-pearl earrings brushing her cheeks. The arched wings of her eyebrows and the thick rows of dark lashes emphasised the brilliant violet of her eyes.

Hidden behind the fronds of a splendid potted palm tree, she was unaware of his presence as he watched her. She appeared to be searching for something and, looking down at the book he had picked up from the white-wicker table in a corner of the conservatory, he realised he probably had what she was looking for.

He had been avoiding her. During the two weeks that followed the day she had left his study, he had found any excuse to stay as far away from her as possible. But he had been conscious of her presence in his house. There was an atmosphere of well-being, of calm and order where anything to do with Octavia was concerned, which came from the centre of Jane Mortimer's own nature and which he knew she had brought to his home.

That was the moment when he realised he did not want her to leave Chalfont.

But why? What could possibly be achieved by her remaining?

The truth of it was that the smooth running of the estate and the recent improvement in his business affairs inspired him with a most gratifying sense of solid order, security and accomplishment he had not felt before. And yet he was plagued by a deepening awareness of a large hole in his life, an emptiness, which had sharpened since he had decided not to make Lydia his wife.

He had been unable to shake off the image of a tempestuous young woman with blazing violet eyes and a face alive with fury and disdain when she had left his London home. She was so unlike Lydia Spelling in every way—and not in the least like Lily. There was no comparison between Jane and either of them.

Lydia was sophisticated and sure of herself and her own place in life, clever enough and ambitious enough to find another man with a title to marry. Lily, who had learned to use her attraction cruelly and for pleasure, had been a woman with an eager body and an empty heart, whereas Jane Mortimer was in possession of a bright intelligence, stunningly direct, polite but candid, and she also had a provoking sensuality and was brimming with deeply felt emotions. She was a decent young woman with a decent woman's need for marriage, which he was not able to give her.

He was an earl, a peer of the realm with a position to uphold, each of his ancestors marrying a woman from a good family, usually with money. It would be madness even to consider taking as his wife a woman who until her inheritance had worked for a living.

But he could not cast aside the picture she had made as she had run after Octavia on the day of his mother's birthday party, the swing and sway of her body, strong and vibrant, and the slenderness of her calves exposed by her raised skirts. Nor could he forget how it had felt to place his mouth on hers, the sweetness of her breath, the eagerness of her response, and the softness of her body in his arms.

These things were beginning to come between him and his everyday life, the remembrance of them stirring him in a way he had never known before.

Lady Lansbury had gone to visit friends and had taken Octavia with her. With the great house around her still and silent, Jane had come to the conservatory to search for a book. She often brought Octavia into the conservatory to read to her, until Octavia's mind began to wander and she lost interest. With its glass walls and high dome it was filled with rare, exotic plants—an explosion of flowers, colour and fragrance. It was a lovely place to sit.

After their visit yesterday afternoon, a book had been left behind, one that Octavia was particularly fond of. If only Jane could remember where she had put it, she thought with frustration as she pulled out chairs, looked under cushions and nearby plant pots.

She didn't turn when she heard sharp footsteps on the tiled floor, but her back stiffened.

'Is this what you are looking for?'

Turning slowly, Jane watched him approach. He held out the book she had been searching for and she took it from him.

Not since the day he had summoned her to his study had Jane come face to face with him. She had caught glimpses of him outside the house, heard his voice within the house, the clatter of his horse's hooves on the gravel drive. Every day he spent hours in his study working, often with his bailiff or estate manager present.

Looking at him now with his shoulder propped against the door frame, she noticed that he always wore his impeccably cut clothes with a careless sort of elegance. Looking so dapper in his tan jacket, fawn breeches and waistcoat and shiny brown riding boots, his arms crossed imperturbably over his chest and his eyes glowing, there was something undeniably engaging about him, a powerful charisma that had nothing to do with his powerful physique or mocking smile.

There was something else, too, something behind that lazy smile and unbreachable wall of aloof strength, behind his piercing silver-grey eyes, that told her that Lord Lansbury had done, seen and experienced all there was to do and see, that to know him properly would be exciting and dangerous, and therein lay his appeal. He made her feel alert and alive, and curiously stimulated.

'Yes, thank you,' she said, in reply to his question. 'I was reading to Lady Octavia yesterday and I forgot to take it with us when we left. She has accompanied Lady Lansbury to visit friends.'

'And you? I suppose you are feeling at a loose end.'

'Not at all. I'm leaving for London the day after tomorrow. I have to get my things together. What I can't take with me Lady Lansbury has kindly offered to have sent on.'

'She is sorry that you are leaving.'

'I—cannot stay.'

'No?' The idea that he would miss her company when she was gone was a sudden and startling realisation. 'Then since Octavia is not here, do I get to spend time with you?'

'Why? Are you telling me that you find my company pleasant?' she asked with an underlying hint of sarcasm.

'When you're not being stubborn and temperamental.'

'I am never temperamental.'

'I disagree.'

'Well—only if you drive me to it.'

Laughing softly, he shrugged himself away from the door and sauntered towards her. What a glorious creature she was. Her lips were moist and parted slightly. Her chest was rising and falling softly and the thought of her soft, warm flesh beneath the fabric of her dress was causing his imagination to run wild. Jane Mortimer was an unusual female, intelligent, opinionated and full of surprises. She was also the epitome of stubborn, prideful woman. Yet for all her fire and spirit, there was no underlying viciousness. She was so very different from the sophisticated, worldly women he took to bed—experienced, sensual women, knowledgeable in the ways of love, women who knew how to please him.

'Tell me, Miss Mortimer. Has there been no young man in your life?'

'No, I'm afraid not.'

His eyes gleamed with devilish humour. 'Do you mean to tell me that surrounded by archaeologists and antiquarians all your life, not one of them caught your interest?'

'No—I mean I had my work, which was important to me.'

'And you would allow nothing to interfere with that. Not even love?' he murmured softly, his gaze capturing hers.

'No.'

'Why? Are you afraid of love, Miss Mortimer?'

A pink flush infused her face. 'No—it—just never happened.'

'I don't believe you.'

'Whether it's true or not, I—I would not admit something of such a personal nature to you.'

'Miss Mortimer, as a woman you are truly unique.'

Jane looked at him warily. 'You are not trying to seduce me, are you, Lord Lansbury?'

'Would you allow me to seduce you, Miss Mortimer?'

In spite of the fact that his eyes were touching her like she had never been touched before, Jane gave him a defiant look. 'Now you're mocking me.'

'I wouldn't dream of it. You are far too clever to mock.'

How could Jane be angry with him when he smiled that engaging smile? It was no longer possible. Her lips curved in a smile of her own. 'And you really are a complete rogue, Lord Lansbury, arrogant and overbearing.'

He grinned. 'I admit it. What I need is an attractive, patient and extremely tolerant young woman to take me in hand, to make me see the error of my ways and reform me.'

'Then I wish you luck. Intolerance and impatience have always been two of my failings, but there must be a female somewhere who will fall for a silken tongue and be willing to expend so much energy, time and effort on such an unenviable task.'

'Then I take it you would not be willing to accompany me on my ride if I asked you to?'

Jane stared at him with amazement. 'Ride? You are asking me to ride? A horse?'

'What else?' He grinned. 'We are fresh out of camels.'

'Why—I—you are jesting.'

'No. I am being perfectly serious. I recall you saying how you would ride like the wind. Octavia won't be back for hours. Would you like to join me? Although I cannot promise that it will be as exciting as what you're used to.'

The temptation to be back on a horse was too tempting for Jane to resist. 'Why—I—I'd love to. But—it looks like rain.'

Christopher glanced out of the window. Dark clouds were gathering, but he refused to be put off.

'Do you only ride in fine weather?'

'No, but I will have to change.'

'I'm in no hurry. Come to the stables when you're ready.'

Something in his heart moved and softened as he

watched her scamper off in child-like glee before going outside and heading for the stables. Where she was concerned, nothing made sense, for nothing could explain why he was beginning to enjoy being alone with her.

He thought she was unlike anyone he had ever met. She was different, a phenomenon. He sensed a goodness in her, something special, sensitive—something worth pursuing. There was also something untapped inside her that not even she was aware of—passion buried deep. What would happen if she allowed it all to come out?

Chapter Eight

Christopher looked up from tightening the girth on a tall black stallion and noted that Miss Mortimer entered the stable yard with a spring in her step. She wore a tweed jacket over a silk shirt and a hat clamped to her head, her hair secured at her nape by a green ribbon. Stable lads were going about their work and a groom was leading a rather fine, tall chestnut mare with a black mane out of one of the stalls.

Drawn to the mare, she crossed the yard and ran her gloved hand over its coat, which rippled like satin. The horse whinnied and nuzzled her with affection, blowing warm breath on to her cheek.

'What a splendid animal,' she murmured when Lord Lansbury came to stand beside her. Eyes aglow, she looked at him with unconcealed excitement. 'Please say I can ride her?'

'If you like.'

His gaze swept over her. Her skirt was long trained and full and, as if she was about to spring on the back of the horse, she bundled the skirt up to her knees and, horror of horrors, showing beneath it were a pair of buff-coloured trousers and glossy riding boots. His initial look was one of shock, which slowly turned to open admiration.

'I see you've come prepared.'

'Of course. It's so rare for me to get a chance to ride these days that I don't want to spoil it with any restrictions whatsoever. Tell me about the horse.'

'She's highly strung and not easy to handle—she'll also bite you as soon as look at you. Her name's Duchess, by the way.'

'She won't bite me—will you, Duchess?' Jane whispered, rubbing her nose. 'I'm not afraid of her. I'm sure we'll get on very well.' She turned to the groom. 'Saddle her for me, will you? And I don't ride side saddle,' she was quick to add. Having already had a glimpse of the trousers beneath her skirt, he gave her an appalled look. 'I love to ride, but that saddle will take all the pleasure out of it. I consider it a serious handicap. How on earth can anyone be expected to communicate with the horse on such a contraption—let alone stay on! I shall probably become unseated at the first obstacle and break my neck—which I am sure will fill Lord Lansbury with morbid delight.'

'Not at all,' he said, laughing at her description of the side saddle. 'Although I must point out that if anyone should see you, you will be ostracised from society before you've had the chance to enter it.'

Running her hand over Duchess's glossy flank, Jane tossed her head, indifferent to his words. 'That doesn't concern me in the slightest.'

'No.' He chuckled, admiring the way she defied convention and cast decorum to the four winds. 'I did not imagine for one moment that it would.'

'What would you have me do, Lord Lansbury?' the groom asked, certain his lordship would not give his permission for such an outrageous breach of protocol.

Seeing Miss Mortimer was determined, and that it was plain she was comfortable with the horse, Christopher laughed and nodded. 'Do as the lady says, Robert. I'm sure we don't have to worry about Miss Mortimer falling off.'

With the appropriate saddle and eager to be off, Jane turned to a grinning Lord Lansbury. 'Help me up, if you please.

'My pleasure.'

Bowing his head to the inevitable, he linked his hands to receive the well-polished boot of his companion. She was up in a flash, her feet feeling for the stirrups.

When they entered the park the wind had risen and the odd spot of rain brushed their faces. Christopher knew that Miss Mortimer was aware that she had created a stir in the stables and cared little. He sensed that the need to ride and to taste complete freedom for a little while was so intense inside her that she refused to let anything get in the way of her ride. She had told him that she hadn't been in the saddle for a long time and it was clear that she intended to make the most of it.

The mare was fresh, her spirits high. Christopher set an easy pace. He observed that his companion had her hands full for the first five minutes. When the mare had settled down, she bent and whispered words of encouragement in the horse's ear. Then, after Jane put her heels to the glossy flanks, Duchess, nostrils flared wide, swiftly exploded under her and she was gone in a blur. Sure-footed, the horse moved like a dream as they fairly flew over the ground. Miss Mortimer's skirts ballooned out, her eyes a radiant deep violet in her poppy-cheeked face, her grin wide and triumphant.

Christopher kept pace with her, aware of the black clouds gathering pace and the rain beginning to fall. He kept his eyes on Miss Mortimer as she rode the courageous Duchess hard and as no lady should, bringing a gleam of admiration to his eyes. She was having a wonderful time, tearing over the terrain at such a pace. Her hair came loose from its confinement, her ribbon flying up and away like a bright green kite. She cleared a hedge, which had been a gamble even for Christopher—but she had taken it with ease.

Christopher had not entirely believed her when he had heard her telling Octavia that she could ride like the wind, but he saw for himself that not only could she ride, but she could ride as well as himself. He couldn't think of many men who could have taken that hedge, let alone a woman. When she turned her head and looked at him he could not take his eyes off her. Never had he seen her so animated, so aroused. There was a passion in her so potent that it seemed to alter the very atmosphere of the ride. In that moment he thought she was the most striking-looking woman he had ever seen in his life. Raising his crop to her in congratulation, he was fascinated by this extraordinary young woman.

Cresting a hill, they slowed to a canter. Exhilarated by the ride, Jane came to a halt, Christopher drawing rein beside her. He smiled broadly, his white teeth gleaming from between his parted lips.

'Well, young lady, you are full of surprises. If my eyes do not deceive me, there is not much anyone can teach you about a horse. One can tell a born rider by watching the way he…' he paused and smiled '…or she, performs in the saddle.'

Seeing the way Lord Lansbury controlled his animal effortlessly, without thought, as fluidly and as softly as the horse himself moved, Jane was thinking the same thing about him. She returned his smile and for a moment there seemed to be only the two of them in the whole world.

'Thank you. I'll take that as a compliment—although Duchess is a splendid horse.'

Suddenly the wind rose and whipped about them. Christopher looked up at the sky, already half-drenched by the rain. 'We have ridden further than I intended. We'll soon be drenched to the skin.' Reaching for his cape rolled up at the back of his saddle, he draped it about her shoulders. With his crop he pointed to the temple that crested the hill overlooking the lake. 'Ride for the temple. We'll take shelter there until the rain lessens. Stay close to me,' he shouted above the wind. 'If we hurry, we'll soon have a roof over our heads.'

The rain, which they had hoped would refrain from falling heavier until they reached their destination, offered them no such respite. The heavens opened, water slanting down out of a sky the colour of pewter. Had he been alone Christopher might have carried on the two miles or so to Chalfont, but it was evident to him that Miss Mortimer was saturated beneath the cape and no doubt chilled to the bone.

Reaching their destination, they dismounted and Christopher tethered the horses to a tree, the stout branches heavy with foliage offering them some degree of shelter.

Inside the folly Jane stared around her. It was not a large structure, but it was dry and surprisingly clean.

'At least we're out of the rain,' Christopher said, removing his wet jacket.

Jane pulled off the shrouding cape, shook it out and draped it on one of the stone benches built into the wall before removing her jacket.

Looking at his companion, Christopher lowered

his gaze and his smile faded. Her clothes, soaking wet, clung to her in a most provocative way and he took a moment to appreciate the shapely figure beneath.

'Look at you. You're soaking wet—and cold, I expect.'

'A little.' She tried to remove her gloves, but they were plastered to her hands.

'Here, let me,' Christopher murmured, taking hold of her hands with a gentleness Jane had not expected of him. Freeing them from their confinement as if they were so fragile they would break, he put her gloves aside and enfolded her small hands in his own and tried to rub the circulation back into her frozen veins.

Jane looked at those hands holding hers and wondered how a man's hands could be both strong and gentle at the same time.

With his head bent and intent on his task, Christopher raised her hands to his lips, holding them there in the hope that the warmth from his mouth would help with the thaw, leisurely caressing the cold flesh with his lips.

Wholly dependent on him for the moment, Jane watched in rapt amazement. A pulsating heat began to throb in her hands, spreading outwards, and she felt shooting, tingling sensations travelling to the tips of her fingers. With her hands still enfolded in his, Christopher's gaze swept upwards and regarded her in silence, and for a moment his eyes held hers with penetrating intensity.

The mysterious depths were as enigmatic as they were silently challenging and unexpectedly Jane felt an answering response. She could feel tension rising inside her—a thick, strange sort of tension she'd never felt in her life before. It unfolded within, warm and slow, but it also strengthened and deepened with each second that passed. The darkening in his eyes warned her that he was aware of that brief response and his eyes narrowed, a hint of a smile tugging at his lips. No words were spoken, but in the pale light of the folly their eyes locked, each probing and searching the innermost thoughts of the other.

When she would have pulled her hands free Christopher refused to relinquish his hold. Taking one hand in each of his own, he placed them against his cheek.

'Are they warmer now?'

Her lips trembled into a smile of thanks as she pulled her hands free and took a step away from him. 'Much warmer, thank you.'

'I apologise for the rain,' he said, returning her smile. 'I wasn't expecting it.'

Jane laughed, removing her sodden hat and shaking her hair loose of its ribbon. 'I don't mind. Having lived all my life in countries with a tropical climate, in deserts and in heat and drought where rainfall is minimal and water precious, the English rain is quite wonderful,' she said, closing her eyes and running her tongue over her lips as if to savour the taste of the rain.

Christopher could not move. He could only stare at the upward curve of her mouth and the exposed creamy skin of her neck, his body taut. His smile faded slowly as he looked at her and as it did he wondered if right now her heart was pounding as hard as his, if her body had the same burning ache as his and her mind the same torrid thoughts.

'I've never been to a desert so I wouldn't know,' he murmured. Lust hit him with such unexpected force that he stood rooted to the spot. She opened her eyes. He felt certain his thoughts must be written on his face, but she only smiled at him, seemingly unaware.

'It can be most unpleasant. The sand gets into your eyes and sticks to the skin and gets into everything. There isn't even enough water to wash it away. I must say I don't miss it.' She looked around the folly. Stone built, it was square and had mullioned windows on three sides. 'What a strange place this is. Why was it built?'

'For no particular reason,' he replied, his eyes following her as she went to the glassless window overlooking the lake, seeing how her wet skirts were plastered to her legs.

And her legs. Dear Lord! How long they were.

'The second Earl of Lansbury had an interest in building follies all over the estate,' he went on, trying to focus on what she had asked him and not dwell on the outline of her lithe body beneath her skirt as desire began flooding into his own. He tried to stop it, telling himself that what he saw beneath was in his imagination, but that didn't seem to help. 'No two are the same. Some, sadly, are in dire need of repair before they fall down. This particular folly was the last to be built and he would come and sit in the doorway and survey the house and lake most days when he was at Chalfont.'

Tearing his gaze away from her legs, he reminded himself that this was Miss Mortimer, with the body of a goddess concealed beneath her wet clothes.

'I can understand why. The view is lovely,'

Christopher had to agree, but he was not looking

out of the window. 'On a good day, when not obscured by rain.' He moved to stand beside her and she turned her head and looked up at him. 'You are a strange young woman, Jane Mortimer,' he murmured, focusing his eyes on a wisp of hair against her cheek.

Without thinking he reached out and tucked it behind her ear, feeling the velvety softness of her skin against his fingers. She stood still as he ran the tip of his finger down the column of her throat, along the line of her chin to her collar.

'Suddenly I find myself wanting to know everything there is to know about you—what you are thinking, what you are feeling. You are still very much a mystery to me.'

'In the short time we have known each other I think you've learned a great deal about me.'

'Maybe. I have learned that you are not the prim and proper miss you purported to be at first, that you are learned and much travelled, that you see nothing wrong in offering gentlemen money and that you kiss very well—but I have much to learn.'

'Lord Lansbury, please!' Taking a step back, Jane was aghast. 'Stop it, now,' she retorted, her face heating. 'It wasn't like that and you know it.'

'No? Are you saying you didn't enjoy kissing me?'

'No—yes…'

Christopher laughed. He was by no means finished with her. 'Don't be embarrassed about it. It was just a kiss and harmless enough.'

'Kissing is never harmless,' she shot back. 'It can lead to…'

Christopher folded his arms across his chest and looked at her with one raised eyebrow, waiting for her to finish.

She pressed her lips together and turned to look out of the window once more. 'It can lead to all sorts of things,' she finally said.

'How many times have you been kissed, Miss Mortimer?'

She didn't answer. He studied her rigid back, thinking of their kiss, remembering the moment when he had first touched her lips. He wondered if she had ever been kissed in her life before that. Suddenly, he wanted an answer to his question. He wanted it badly. 'How many?'

'I don't think that's any of your business.'

'And I don't think you had been kissed before I kissed you. Does it bother you?'

'In a way,' she confessed. 'But wherever we were I was always surrounded by foreigners and older men who accompanied us on the expeditions. Sometimes they were accompanied by their wives.'

'Were they not accompanied by their children?'

'Only the very young children who needed looking after. The older boys and girls were sent away to schools in England to further their education.'

'Is that what you wanted? To go to school in England?'

'Sometimes, but it was never an option for me.'

'So you missed out on the parties and balls.'

She laughed lightly. 'I doubt I would have been able to attend such frivolous events had I been here in England. No, my father needed me to assist him with his work. I was content.'

'So,' he said, smiling down at her, 'I am the first man to have kissed you.'

She nodded. 'Which is why I'm not very good at it.'

'Would you like me to show you?'

Thinking he was complaining, lifting her chin, she scowled at him, her back to the wall. 'I'm sure you must have been disappointed. You must forgive me.' As Jane saw the wicked smile on his lips a pained expression crossed her face. 'There's no need to make fun of me. Not all of us have the benefit of your experience and expertise.'

She started to turn away, but he lifted his arms to brace them against the wall, trapping her. He leaned closer, inhaling the scent of her. 'You did not disappoint me, Jane,' he said softly, using her given name for the first time, sending a warm thrill through her. 'Quite the contrary. I liked it so much that I would like a repeat performance.'

Her face took on a look of panic, but she tilted her head back and met his eyes. The closeness of his body was making her feel warm. 'You would?'

He grinned. No woman could stick her nose in the air better than Jane Mortimer. He nodded. 'Don't be afraid that my sinful ways will corrupt you.' He bent his head until his mouth was an inch from hers. 'After all, you might like it better a second time.'

His gaze lowered to her lips. Jane felt a sudden rush of anticipation and denial, pleasure and panic. Her pulse beat frantically in her ears.

The corners of his mouth lifted in the ghost of a smile and he reached out and traced the line of her lips with the tip of his finger.

A quivering began deep inside her. Her lips parted, and she knew she should speak, should protest, should pull away. But she remained motionless and silent, awash in the sensation of his light caress. What was he doing? she wondered. What was this raw ache, this intense pull she was feeling? *He knows the effect his touch is having*, she thought, watching his gaze follow the deliberate motion of his finger back and forth across her lower lip.

His hand moved to cup her chin, then to caress her throat. Then, slowly, he pulled away, leaving her in the aftermath of the sensations he had created, bereft and dazed and still waiting for a kiss that never came.

'I think the rain has lessened,' he said. 'We should be getting back.'

Slowly the sound of his voice penetrated her mind. 'Yes, I suppose we should,' she murmured, staring at him, her cheeks burning, the aftermath of his touch lingering. Her heart was pounding in her chest. She was not used to being touched, she told herself. That was all. But the unbelievable pleasure of it had taken her by surprise. She could not believe the melting sensation he could evoke when his fingertips touched her.

Neither of them made a move to leave. The sound of the rain dripping in the doorway ticked away the seconds as they looked at each other.

Jane knew they should leave, but she stood rooted to the spot.

Taking the initiative, Christopher exhaled sharply. 'Jane.'

She watched his eyes turn smoky. His lashes lowered. Instinctively she swayed towards him, willing him to kiss her.

Raising his hands, he buried his fingers in her hair, wrapping its thick strands in his fists. Drawing her face closer to his, he gazed down at her in wonder. Her magnificent eyes were naked and defenceless.

With her heart pounding turbulently, Jane saw his eyes translucent in the dim light, his lean features starkly etched.

'A kiss, then, Miss Mortimer—to confirm what your lips told me the first time.'

Jane shook her head in feeble protest. The insistent pressure of his body, those feral eyes glittering with power and primeval hunger, washed away any measure of comfort she might have felt. A strange, alien feeling fluttered within her breast and she was halted for a brief passage of time when she found her lips entrapped with his once more. Though they were soft and tender, they burned with a fire that scorched her. Closing her eyes, she yielded to it, melting against him.

'I cannot stop myself doing this, Jane,' he murmured, raising his head a little. 'I am not made of stone and, God help me, I cannot stop wanting you.'

Lightly brushing her lips, he felt them tremble beneath his, but she did not move or push him away. He ran his tongue across her closed lips, tasting, coaxing, until she yielded, until her mouth opened beneath his with a wordless sound of surprise.

Something told him he ought to stop, that he had gone too far, but when she made a tiny sound, a fluttering, purely feminine mixture of innocence and invitation, his last vestige of reason dissolved.

Jane's lips clung to his and she closed her eyes, remembering how it had felt to have his mouth on hers.

After what seemed an eternity, Christopher raised his head and looked at her upturned face. His stare travelled over her, consuming her with unnerving intensity.

Frank, open lust.

His senses were invaded by the smell of her. It was the soft fragrance of her unbound hair—the sweet scent of jasmine mingled with the musky female scent—that made his body burn. Curling his long masculine fingers round her chin, he tilted her face up to his. Her eyes were large, black and soft, her eyelashes still moist and glistening with rain.

It seemed a lifetime passed as they gazed at each other. In that lifetime each lived through a range of deep, tender emotions new to them both, exquisite emotions that neither of them could put into words. As though in slow motion Christopher drew her to him. His gaze was gentle and compelling, then his arms were around her again. As though in slow motion, she was melting against him as his warm, fine mouth moved inexorably over hers. Unable to pull away, Jane lost herself in his wondrous kiss, so deep and drugging and slow.

She clung to him, her arms around his neck, one leg trapped about him as though to hold him even closer. Their bodies fitted together, breast to breast, thigh to thigh, their mouths fused, moving, caressing. She lifted her chin and his lips slid beneath it and along her jaw, taking the lobe of her ear between his lips. Suddenly he loosened his hold and reached out to grasp the discarded cape, quickly spreading it on the floor. Taking her back in his embrace, with a groan they both sank to their knees as though the strength had gone from them. She held his head, wrapping her arms about it as his mouth slid to her breast, then his hands went to the buttons and unfastened them, releasing the fullness of them, the hardness of her rosy nipples in his mouth.

'Dear God, Jane,' he gasped and she was made to realise there was no going back, no escaping what was to happen.

Seizing his waistcoat in her fists, she pulled him closer. In response, he deepened the kiss, tasting her with his tongue. Wrapping one hand around his neck, she tangled her other hand in the thick, short strands of his damp hair.

He broke the kiss pulling back to look at her, his expression strangely resolute. 'You want this,' he said, lowering his hands. 'Say it.'

Jane stared into his eyes with all the ardent emotions she had kept tightly reined for weeks. She thought of all the ancient frescos and pictures she had seen in the ancient places she had visited, in Greece and Egypt and Rome, of men and women, their bodies locked together, and she decided it was time for her to decide what it was she wanted. This was real. This was happening to her now.

At that moment she wanted so badly for her life to be different, to be daring—perhaps even a bit shocking—to taste all that she had missed. That day on the train he had given her a taste of what it could be like. She wanted another taste. That was what he was offering her now. Could she just reach out and take it? And could she live with the pain afterward, loving him and watching him walk away?

She suffered only a second of uncertainty. She was going to feel the pain anyway when she went away. But she didn't want to go without feeling the passion first, the passion he could offer her, the passion she'd never even known she could feel until she had met him. She was to leave Chalfont and she knew she would probably never have another chance like this. She felt an unabashed sense of regret and made up her mind there and then that she was not going to let this chance slip away. There was not the slightest chance she could deny herself the opportunity to finally feel like a woman. Just once, she promised, sliding her hands over his chest, revelling in the exhilarating experience.

'Stop talking.' She recaptured his mouth. 'Don't spoil it. I want the same thing you do.' Her inexperienced fingers began to loosen the buttons on his waistcoat.

Christopher pulled away her hands and did it himself, never taking his eyes from her face. Removing his waistcoat and cravat, he threw them on to one of the stone benches. Impatient to hold her once more, he drew her to his chest and placed his mouth over hers. Sliding her hands through the front of his shirt, Jane slid them over the hard contours of his chest. Removing her lips from his mouth, she lowered her head and kissed his warm flesh. He didn't move, but she could feel his gaze on her face as she looked up and studied him in the silver light.

He laid her down on his jacket. The dusty floor felt like soft silk beneath her, but she was so wrapped up in the moment that she gave it no thought. She watched as he stripped himself of his clothes and revealed his beautiful male body. It was quite magnificent. Long, graceful bones and flat muscles that flowed smoothly from the curve of his chest to the slight concavities of his belly and thighs. For a moment Jane felt her insides lurch, she didn't know why, and her mouth became dry and in the pit of her stomach something flared.

He was large and powerful, hard and eager, and she had but a moment to admire it before she had scrambled to her feet and he had done the same for her, removing her skirt and bodice—laughing when he peeled the confining trousers she wore beneath over her thighs and cast them aside. Her undergarments, all but her stockings, went the same way and he placed lingering kisses on each new portion of flesh he revealed, breathing in the warm, womanly scent of her. She was mesmerised by his seduction and wouldn't let herself think how skilful he was in this department. She didn't want to wonder how often he had done this before. She was the one he was doing it to now.

His warmly glowing, hungering eyes seemed to brand her as he ensnared her gaze before he tore it away and swept it over her body. Jane felt it, uncaring now whether or not he could see the heat in her cheeks and wanting only to be perfect for him.

Had she issued an invitation for him to peruse the sights, Christopher couldn't have been more eager to respond. Tall and glorious, her body was a lustrous shade of burned honey and polished amber in the wavering blur of the light filtering through the windows into the folly. Her long sleek limbs, sheathed in dark silk stockings, did much to rouse his admiration and desire so that he could barely contain it.

'Has anyone ever told you how beautiful you are?' Christopher murmured huskily.

A smile curved her soft lips as relief washed over

her. He didn't think she was disappointing or plain. He thought she was beautiful. 'Only you, my lord.'

'Christopher. My name is Christopher.'

'Christopher,' she murmured, liking the sound of it, even though it evoked all the feelings of her lovesick former self.

They lay on the large cape spread over the floor. It wasn't the most comfortable of beds, but so great was their need that they thought nothing of it. Christopher swept his hand along her thigh as she pressed alongside him. Jane lay in quiescent stillness, indulging in every blissful, delectable delight he stirred within her as he worked his magic upon her womanly softness, and when his mouth claimed her breasts once again, she felt almost consumed by the pleasure he wrought.

The exquisite sweetness of it spread through her body like warm honey, creating a desperate longing that made her ache and unlocking something inside her, releasing all the repressions and restraints she had imposed on herself ever since she had first met him. She uttered a startled gasp at the carnal pleasure as he pressed a kiss to her stomach, feeling the quivering sensations that rippled through her as he continued to trail kisses across her flesh, tasting her skin with his tongue.

His hands moved upwards along her hips, following the curve of her waist, across her ribs to cup her breasts, his thumbs brushing light back and forth across the tips. She tilted her head back with a moan, closing her eyes, and her hands tightened convulsively on his shoulders. Then his hands were moving lower and she forgot to breathe as he touched her in that most intimate of places. She jerked against him, feeling hot little shivers race through her body. Shocked by the intimacy of it, she thought she ought to push his hand away, tell him to stop, but she could not. She could not think past the touch of his fingers and the tension that was building in the pit of her stomach.

'I cannot bear it,' she gasped, feeling that she was hovering on the brink of something glorious and wonderful as everything inside her seemed to explode in a white-hot flash, sending incredible sensations to every part of her body. 'Please, Christopher, whatever you are waiting for, I beg you to wait no longer.'

His eyes shone with unmistakable ardour as she felt his weight and strength above her and he overwhelmed her with the power of his body. His face slowly lowered to hers and soon his lips and tongue took possession of hers, demanding, consuming the delectable sweetness until his delicious assault left her feeling faint. Almost consumed by her womanly warmth, he drew her naked body against his, his arms tight about her, her breasts against his chest, his flaunting manhood searching between her open thighs for she was as eager as he.

There was no gentleness in him, nor in her, and when she wrapped her legs about his, his body pierced hers. She moved her hips beneath him.

'Jane,' he groaned against her ear, 'don't move, for God's sake.'

'I'm all right. Truly. Please—don't stop now.'

She tried to keep still, but it was no use. He was the first man she had known and he knew it, too.

Christopher closed his eyes, glorying in the joy of being at one with her, letting the mindless pleasure overtake him. He was lost, without sight, or hearing, or thought. Wrapping his arms around her, he began to move against her, forcefully now, sinking himself so deep inside her she moaned with the pain of it. His breathing was harsh and ragged as she took away his desperation, his restless and wild longings, serving him, holding him. He took her mouth in a stormy demanding kiss and felt her hands shifting softly over his shoulders, gentling him at the same time her melting body welcomed him, sheathing him, offering them both release.

Jane clung to him, conscious of a heat inside her that she had never known before as he moved slowly, seductively initiating her into the art of love. She was almost delirious with the new sensations and the powerful response of her own body. It seemed to have a will of its own, exquisitely pulsating. Finally she felt Christopher gather her into him when he climaxed, almost sending her over the edge.

Afterwards he held her in his arms, smoothing her trembling body. He kissed her forehead, helpless again to withstand the supple, willing loveliness of her body. He said nothing for a few moments and Jane could hear his ragged breathing against her cheek. It endeared her to him even more, knowing that a woman could still make a man vulnerable.

Christopher pulled back and looked into her face, watching as she slowly opened her eyes. He had never seen her look lovelier than she did at that moment, with her hair spread about her head in lustrous waves, an extraordinary smile of contentment curving her soft lips. One long leg was wrapped across his body. He did not want to lose the feel of her, the warmth of her, the passion of her, not yet.

He touched his lips to hers and whispered against her mouth, 'Are you all right?'

'Perfectly,' she replied. And she was. She felt no regret, no shame. Just an incredible, overpowering joy that made her feel alive, vibrant, beautiful and absurdly happy. They had pleasured one another and she ached for it to happen again. How wonderful, that making love could do that to a woman. Christopher Chalfont had discovered the woman in her, the latent desire of which she had always known, deep down, that one day she was capable of knowing.

Christopher kissed her once more. Still dazed and enchanted that making love was such a sensuous and wondrous experience, she kissed him deeply, placing her hands on either side of his face.

'No more, Jane,' he whispered softly against her lips before rolling away from her. 'Though God knows it wouldn't take long for my loins to recover with your wonderful body beneath me. I will stop while the pleasure of this first time is still warm within you. But we must get up and get dressed.'

'Must we?' She sighed and stretched, lifting her arms above her head, displaying her proud breasts.

Getting to his feet, he held out his hand for her to do the same. Picking up her clothes, she gathered them to her, for without the warmth of his body, the folly was cold, but just thinking about what had happened was enough to keep her warm. For the first time in her life she felt feminine, completely happy and content with the world and everything in it.

It wasn't until they were dressed, assisting each other with buttons and the like and Jane was tying her hair back with her ribbon, that Christopher came to his senses, reminding himself of the inevitable consequences of what he had just done.

Looking at Christopher, who was seated on one of the stone benches pulling on his boots, and unable to resist touching him, Jane threaded her fingers through his hair. Not only did she see his body stiffen, she felt it. Immediately she withdrew her hand.

'Christopher? What is it?'

His boots on, he barely glanced at her as he got to his feet and bent to retrieve the cape, shaking it out. Then he faced her. 'You must forgive me, Jane. I hurt you. When we came here I had no intention of seducing you.'

Bewildered, she stared at him and managed to

smile even as she blushed, unable to feel properly guilty, but at the same time an uneasy disquiet was setting in. 'Hurt me? Do not distress yourself on my account. You didn't hurt me,' she hastened to reassure him. 'Well, maybe only a little, which was to be expected, but I am perfectly all right.' She lowered her gaze, for the remembrance of what they had done made her flustered and a bit shy, but venturesome, too. 'In fact, I feel quite wonderful,' she confessed.

'I am relieved to hear it. However, the consequences of what we have done—what I have done, for I take full responsibility for this—must be faced.'

Still in a state of euphoria, Jane was unable to make sense of what he was talking about. 'But—what is there to face?'

Picking up her hat, he handed it to her. 'Marriage, Jane. We will be married as soon as it can be arranged.'

She stared at him as realisation of what he had said became clear. 'Marriage? You would marry me?'

'Yes, of course I will.'

He became still, observing her reaction to his suggestion, unable to believe what he saw. Dear

Lord! He had asked her to marry him and she was looking at him as if he had grown horns, hooves and a tail.

Jane swallowed; eyes wide and disbelieving. She did not look exactly pleased. More bewildered, confused, uncertain. Her hands went to her hair, twisting it back into some sort of order.

'You must not feel…you must not think… I do not expect you to…'

The words sounded sensible to Christopher, reasonable. And yet the silence that followed was long and heavy.

Jane closed her eyes. When she opened them again, they had turned hard and cold and distant. 'No, I cannot accept. I suppose your offer is kindly meant, but…' She could not quite believe she had heard him right, but there were certain matters—matters that were important to her—that must be discussed before she could even consider marrying him.

'Why have you asked me, Christopher? Are you saying that you have fallen madly in love with me? Is that why you want to marry me?'

He turned away, focusing his eyes on something outside. 'I have come to have a high regard for you.

You must also know by now that I am attracted to you and have a passionate desire for you.'

'I see.' Having no idea of the proper etiquette of refusing a proposal of marriage and wanting to give him her answer to his face, she moved to stand beside him. 'Please, look at me.' He turned his head slowly and looked at her. Although it was one of the hardest things she had ever done, she said, 'First, I thank you for your proposal. I was not expecting it. Second, as wonderful it is to know that you desire me, it is not enough. I will not marry you, Christopher.'

Chapter Nine

Christopher stared at her, unable to believe she had turned him down. Pain and desolation entered his eyes, but it quickly disappeared and his expression was suddenly guarded. He rushed on to reason with her before she could express her indignation. 'I see no other option open to you, Jane, or to me.'

'What are you saying, Christopher? Are you telling me that you love me?' *Please, Lord*, she thought, *let it be so.*

'Love?' All trace of gentleness disappeared from his face. He slowly shook his head. 'How does one define love? I no longer know what the word means. I care for you—a great deal, as it happens—but don't confuse physical desire with love. I have lived through one disastrous relationship, which taught me that it is an unpleasant experience I have no desire to repeat. The woman in question burned almost every emotion out of me when she betrayed me with another.'

'And so you judge every woman to be the same,' Jane said quietly.

'Maybe not all of them, but I realised a long time ago that poets may write about love and balladeers may sing about it. It exists for others—but not for me. Despite the feelings and emotions we aroused in each other just now, the depths of passion we reached, do not fool yourself into believing it had anything to do with love. Just because I made love to you does not mean you touched my heart.'

Jane's heart plummeted. Everything had suddenly begun to go so very wrong. She wondered what the unknown woman had done to cause so much hatred—or what he was guilty of as far as the woman was concerned that had made her turn from him to someone else.

'I see. Well—thank you for being honest with me. But I would have imagined you would have too much common sense to attribute to all women what you have experienced in one.'

'You would say that. You, who showed me so much vulnerability, so much generous passion—a woman who in her loving was so like…' He fell silent, cursing himself for thinking of Lily when he hadn't mentioned her to anyone in years. 'However, this changes things between us. After meeting you it didn't take long for me to realise that we have something in common. Like me, you like to make your own choices. I owe no man a living and I owe no woman a duty. In short, I am my own man, free to do what I choose. I am asking you to be my wife and the mother of my children. I will never fail you, Jane.'

She inhaled sharply. The impact of his words was like a punch in the stomach. 'I know that, but the answer is still no.' She knew she was mad to refuse him. Mad with desperation and panic. But she did not feel particularly flattered or complimented by the manner of his proposal or his definition of love. What he offered was not enough.

'There must have been other women in your life, Christopher. Have you offered to do the honourable thing by any of them?'

'The women you speak of were experienced women of the world. You are the first woman I have made love to who was untouched—the first woman since…in a long time, I have feelings for.'

'I see. Well, it doesn't change anything. I won't marry you,' she said with a proud lift to her chin and in a tone made carefully neutral, feeling the need to give back hurt for hurt. 'Marriage is important and serious and not something to be undertaken lightly—especially for me. I comprehend perfectly how you feel. But what makes you imagine I want to be your wife when you make me an offer of marriage so unwillingly? You have certainly said nothing that can tempt me into accepting your proposal. I reciprocate your feelings. I am strongly attracted to you and desire you, but without love I see no reason for us to marry. Besides, we're from two different worlds. You should marry according to your station. I would be a total failure both as the wife of an earl and in society.'

'You can learn. My mother will be there to guide you and explain everything you would need to know.'

'I do not doubt it,' she said caustically, feeling more hurt than she cared to admit. In his expression there was no affection, only a resolute determination to have his way. 'Isn't marrying me a bit extreme? What we did—I was equally to blame. I knew what I was doing. I confess to being somewhat ignorant of these matters, but is it not the usual custom for men of your position not to marry the women they seduce, but to pay them off? I gave you freedom with my body, but I think you've carried it too far.' She could see that her words had pricked his anger. Holding her gaze, he stood before her, tall and powerful, his face austere, his eyes challenging.

'You insult my honour and your own. Damn it, Jane! I'm not asking you to become my mistress. I am asking you to be my wife.'

'Because you feel obligated. Well, you needn't,' she said coldly. She didn't want him to ask her to be his wife because he felt obligated, as if it were some kind of duty. She wanted him to ask her because he loved her. But he did not. Perhaps he felt a little affection for her, but no more than that. That realisation was what hurt the most. 'Please do not feel you have a duty towards me. Whatever I want, it is not that—to hold you through some obligation that would make a mockery of what we have just shared, however brief it was.'

'You must realise you have no choice in the matter,' he said. 'It's the sensible solution.'

'Solution? Solution to what? A solution means there must be a problem and I don't see one. I'm not some foundling you're obliged to propose to every time you have a touch of guilt. I understand that in such cases marriage is the accepted mode, but there are other alternatives. I shall go to London as planned and take up my work at the exhibition.'

She looked at him, coldness about her now, of fixed, unbending resolution that would not be denied.

'And if there is a child?'

Jane stared at him. She hadn't thought of that, that there might be a child from their union. Unconsciously her hand went to her abdomen and for a moment she could think of nothing more wonderful than to give birth to his child. But she would not have her life or that of her child dictated by circumstances.

'There may not be a child,' she replied. 'If there does happen to be one, then we will discuss the matter again. I have the means to take care of a child myself, but you have my word I would not deprive you of seeing it. You are an honourable man. Illegitimate children of men in your position do not suffer any great setbacks in life.'

Christopher stared at her, his eyes like chips of ice. 'What are you saying? That I set aside my own child? To my knowledge I have never fathered an illegitimate child and I have no intention of doing so.'

Jane's body stiffened and Christopher saw a wall come up between them like a physical barrier.

'Ah, so it is your conscience that is bothering you. Christopher, please listen to what I am saying. You don't have to sacrifice yourself on the altar of matrimony for my sake. I doubt there will be a child. If there is we will deal with it. Accepting your support for any child we might have is one thing. Marrying me is something else and completely unnecessary in my opinion. I want nothing from you. Do not feel under any obligation.'

Christopher's jaw tightened and his eyes burned furiously down into hers. 'I don't. My obligation will be towards the child—should there be one. I could make some money over to it and put some in trust until a later date—but I would despise myself if I did not try to do better than that. I would insist that boy or girl, any baby, must be spared the stain of illegitimacy. I will not disown a child of my blood.'

'Please stop this. You are being premature. There may be no baby.'

Her stubbornness provoked Christopher's eyes to blaze with renewed fury. 'If there is, you cannot bring it up on your own. You will never endure the disgrace and humiliation when it becomes public knowledge. People can be extremely cruel in such situations. The scandal will be intolerable. You will never withstand it. I will have a say in how it is reared. I refuse to have a child of mine brought up a bastard just because its mother—in her abominable pride—refuses my offer of marriage. It is not an offer I make lightly.'

'And with sentiments such as these you expect me to agree to become your wife?' Jane flared incredulously. 'You have my answer. I will not marry you and I will not let you stampede me into it.'

'For heaven's sake, Jane, you were a virgin,' he said more gently, his expression grave as he combed impatient fingers of frustration through his hair. 'If you think I would take your innocence and not do right by you, then you do not know me, of my position in life or my honour as a gentleman.'

'I do and it matters to me that you have some regard for me. For myself, I don't want to marry you. I see no reason to. I want to manage my own life. I want independence and autonomy. I want to be accountable to no one.'

'And as my wife you would be accountable to me.'

'Yes.'

She pressed her lips together. Resistance was in every line of her, in her pose, in the stiff rigidity of her body, in the distance between them. They stood four feet apart, and yet the gap between them seemed wider than the Atlantic Ocean.

'Your ability to wound my vanity, Jane, is boundless, it seems.'

'I am sorry about that, but that's how it is. You owe me nothing and I will take nothing from you. I don't need your money. If I did, it would make no difference to my decision. I don't want to be kept by you or by any man. I am fairly self-sufficient. I prefer it that way.'

Christopher sighed heavily. 'You are a stubborn woman, Jane Mortimer. You're being unreasonable.'

'Unreasonable? Because I won't marry you? We made love, Christopher. That does not mean you have to marry me.'

'What is wrong with that?' he demanded to know, his voice harsh with his disappointment. He had expected her to react with delight to his proposal, not with what looked strangely like offence.

'I—I don't know exactly, but…'

'What? Tell me and I'll put it right.' His face worked with some emotion, but he was not a man who liked to plead. 'Your reputation may be greatly compromised. Have you not thought of that?'

'Why? Because I'm a fallen woman?'

'I didn't say that.'

'No, but it is what you implied.'

'If word of this gets out you will be ruined.'

'We are the only two people who know. I won't tell.'

'I won't either. It's not the kind of thing one bandies about. But if you don't marry me and marry someone else, you will have some explaining to do on your wedding night.' When she only stared at him in bafflement, he laughed. 'I'm only saying that a man knows when a woman has been with another man.'

Jane merely stared at him. She could feel the heat flooding her face. 'Then I won't marry anyone.'

He looked at her as she raised her head and found it hard to drag his eyes away from her fascinating visage. 'It seems to me, Jane, that you made your denial in an emotional state which, though understandable, I would like you to reconsider.'

'I did not,' Jane declared, a trifle insulted at Christopher's judgement. 'I have made my decision.' Her voice caught for a moment. Now she wondered where the loveliness, the sweetness, the promise of half an hour ago had gone. She swallowed hard and continued. 'It was wonderful—what we did—the most wonderful thing that has ever happened to me. Please don't think I regret it because I don't, not for one minute. I am not ashamed. I will not marry you, because despite this attraction, this desire you seem to have for me now, you do not love me, nor care enough for me in any way that would make for a happy marriage. I will not live the rest of my life with any man in a loveless marriage made as a result of his temporary passion, to expunge his guilt. Now please excuse me. I should be getting back. I have much to do before Lady Octavia gets back.'

He captured her arm as she passed him. 'Wait.'

Her gaze flicked to his hand wrapped around her elbow and then up to his eyes. She glared at him. 'Please don't touch me again.'

'Do you have to leave Chalfont?'

'Yes. You are not my lord and master.' She wrenched her arm free.

He clamped his jaw shut and tore his frustrated gaze away. The haughty, wary look he gave her clashed with the desperation in his eyes. 'I won't accept your refusal, Jane. I know by your reaction to my lovemaking that you're by far from immune to me. I'm willing to overlook your refusal this time, but by God, I swear this is not the end of it.'

'As to that, we will have to see,' she bit out angrily. 'I think that now we understand each other.'

Picking up her riding crop, she walked out of the folly to where her horse waited. Keeping her face averted, she tried not to think of the intimacies they had just shared because it hurt too much to do so. Those moments together, when they had forgotten all else in the need to consummate their passion, had been some of the most exciting of her life. The wild behaviour was so out of character for her. It had been wonderful.

And then Christopher had spoiled it. He had asked her to marry him to clear his conscience.

She could not do it. She would not do it.

When he had blurted out the question, that in itself had been odd. He had spoken as though the words had been forced from his unwilling mouth. As though he had not wanted to ask them, but had felt obliged. Tears clogged her throat. He should have fallen in love with her. He should want to marry her for love. He didn't want her because he worshipped her.

Without a word he cupped his hands together in which she placed her foot. When he had hoisted her into the saddle she turned her horse for home.

It had turned into a soft, late summer's day. The

rain had washed the skies and tossed away the clouds, leaving the sun to shine where it would: gentle and warm and benign. On any other day Jane would have idled along, admiring the loveliness of the sparkling lake and Chalfont in the distance, the heady lilt of the skylark's song, but she neither saw nor heard any of it.

They rode back in silence. On reaching the stables, Jane dismounted and walked away.

Christopher watched her go and started to go after her, but then he remembered her words—*do not touch me again*. The words sank like a knife into his heart. He stopped himself, blind with bewilderment, loss and disbelief. In anger and frustration he slammed his fist into the stable door with a splintering thud.

Everything inside him raged to go after her and make her stay—to marry him, even if he had to force her to remain at Chalfont until she obeyed. But deep down he knew he would have to let her go. Self-disgust and burning fury coursed through him, reality crushing down on him as he suddenly found his life infuriating and complicated. Everything was in a state of utter confusion—and all because he had been unable to keep his hands off Jane Mortimer.

He had spent years of evasion, trying to avoid a situation such as this, and he had succeeded, believing himself immune, but it had only taken one look at Jane, one curve of her lovely lips, for him to fall into a trap of his own making.

Deep inside what Lily had done to him—her betrayal—still haunted him. He had deliberately put the memory away, not wanting to look too carefully, but now he found it rising to the fore like some awful spectre, so that he became caught up in its grip once more. To become deeply involved with a woman again, a woman who could seep into his mind, his body, his heart and his soul, was a situation he had always diligently avoided, but now, when he thought of Jane, he felt an uneasy surge of guilt.

Whatever it was Jane had done in refusing Christopher's proposal, it was too late to remedy it now. But she was unashamed of her feelings. God help her, but Christopher Chalfont had infatuated her from that first moment she had laid eyes on him—she loved him, but she had always known he wasn't for her, that she wasn't suitable to be his wife. She had had no illusions about that. Staying at Chalfont any longer was only a recipe for heartache and disaster. She would leave and he would forget all about her—and she would strive to recover from her experience.

The awful reality was that not only was she losing Christopher, she was also leaving Chalfont. For years she had lived within canvas walls, surrounded by rolled maps, battered leather travelling trunks, things that had comprised the elements of everything she had called home for most of her life.

And then she had come to Chalfont. She hadn't considered how it would be to say goodbye to the only place she'd ever lived that felt like home.

Two days later Jane was up and dressed at seven. After a small breakfast and after saying her goodbyes to Lady Lansbury in Lady Lansbury's room, she went down to the hall. It had been difficult parting from Octavia, but she got over it quickly when Lady Lansbury promised to take her to London to visit Jane.

Her trunk and cases stood near the door to be loaded on to the carriage that was to take her to the train. Jane kept looking around her, hoping to see Christopher, but there was no sign of him. When it was time to leave she walked outside to the waiting carriage. As she climbed inside and the carriage set off, she looked back at the house and felt a lump rise in her throat.

At the station she waited on the platform while the coachman dealt with her luggage. She half expected to see Christopher to come and say goodbye, but he didn't come. She boarded the train, looking out of the window in case he made a last-minute appearance, but as the guard blew his whistle and the train moved out, there was no sign of him.

Not that she had changed her mind about his proposal. So perhaps it was best that she didn't see him. Yes, she thought, it was best that he hadn't come.

From a window on the first floor of the house, Christopher watched Jane leave. The sky was a flawless blue fading into a pool of deep indigo on the horizon. Against its warm colours lay the silhouettes of nearby trees whose leaves dipped and turned like dancers on the morning breeze. For one agonising moment as she stepped up into the carriage, pausing for a moment before she took her seat, he thought she was going to turn and look up at him. Helplessly he reached out his hand, longing to touch her face, but all he touched was cold glass.

His gaze brushed the flush in her cheeks; the smooth, high line of her brow; the stubborn tilt of her chin. The manner in which her bodice clung to her breasts, outlining their round, firm shape until he swore he could feel their softness once more filling his palms. He just managed to stop himself from groaning out loud.

This was ridiculous. How was it he could want her so badly? He had made love to her once, and usually, for him, once was enough. Then why was this occasion so different? Why did it feel so different? He couldn't believe he was losing her.

He had known a lifetime of struggle to keep himself and his passions in check, a lifetime of suppressing all the hate, love and fear that had raged within him as a young man—a lifetime of swallowing his pride and looking away and pretending indifference when his own father had taken Lily. It was a lesson Christopher refused to forget, a mistake he would never repeat. He had sworn never to give one woman such power over him again.

Admittedly he'd got more than he'd bargained for when he'd kissed Jane Mortimer.

Coming on to the landing, Lady Lansbury went to stand beside her son, who was watching the departing carriage. Anxiously she studied the deeply etched lines of strain at his eyes and mouth. She had secretly harboured the hope that he might somehow persuade Jane to stay.

'We are all sorry to see Jane go, Christopher. We will miss her—especially Octavia.'

'I'm sure she will. Octavia has become dependent on her.'

'I know. I intend to spend more time with her. When the exhibition opens I have promised to take her to London. It is something for her to look forward to.' Lady Lansbury looked with loving eyes at her son. 'You look troubled, my dear,' she said quietly.

Christopher sighed heavily, unwilling to share his uneasy thoughts. 'I'm rather tired,' he confessed, having been up half the night working in his study, doing anything he could to blot out the thought of Jane's leaving.

'It's more than that, I suspect. Has something happened to distress you?'

He shrugged, turning to his mother when the carriage was no longer in sight. 'You concern yourself unnecessarily.'

'My dear Christopher. I have known and loved you since the moment you came into the world with your eyes wide open and making enough noise to bring the house down. Just two days ago you were happy. Now a shadow darkens your mood. Will you not tell me what it is?'

On impulse Christopher put his arms around her and hugged her warmly. 'There is nothing wrong, Mother, believe me.'

Lady Lansbury held him away from her. She could not bear to witness the pain she saw written on her son's face. 'Then why do you look so worried?'

Christopher tried to read his mother's face. Did she know? Was she aware of his relationship with Jane? He decided not to press the matter further, but his mother had other ideas.

'You have come to care for Jane a great deal. I would be blind if I did not see that. Is she the reason you decided against Lydia Spelling?' When he remained silent and turned from her she smiled. 'I, for one, am glad that you didn't marry her. It is my own bitter experience that impelled me to abhor your selection of Miss Spelling. I want you to be happy with your wife, happy enough that you do not need the companionship of women such as

Lydia Spelling—for all her money. You deserve better than that. I cannot help but believe that it is possible to be happy in marriage, despite my own poor choice.'

Something in the soft romanticism of her words stirred Christopher's ire, for they brought memories to the surface, memories both he and his mother had tried to banish. 'How you can remain such a romantic when the man you married caused us both such pain astonishes me.'

'Perhaps because my parents loved each other so passionately I know love within marriage is possible. What you need is someone like Jane.'

Christopher shot her a sharp look. 'Jane? What has she said?'

'About what?'

'Did she say anything to you before she left—confide in you?'

'We got on well, I know, but what confidences would she be imparting to me?' She cocked her head on one side and her lips curved in a knowing smile. 'Is there something you wish to say to me, Christopher?'

He was pleased by Jane's discretion, but his mother clearly thought there was something going on between them. All of his life he had always tried to be open and truthful where his mother was concerned and this time was no exception. So he told her about the proposal, watching the surprise appear in her eyes.

'You proposed to Jane?' A smile lit her face, lighting up her eyes. 'But—that's wonderful.'

'Not quite,' he replied drily. 'She turned me down.'

'Did she? I can't imagine why. Most women would give their right arm for the chance to be a countess.'

'Jane is not most women.'

Suddenly Lady Lansbury frowned as a thought occurred to her. 'Did you ask her, Christopher, or tell her? Knowing you, you were probably very autocratic and she told you to go to the devil.'

Christopher found it irritating that his mother might be right. 'She did.'

'And I cannot blame her. Not once have you given any indication that there was any kind of relationship between the two of you. I don't suppose it entered your head that she might expect to be courted before you ordered her to marry you. What are you going to do about it? Are you going after her?'

'Why? She made it perfectly clear that she has no wish to marry—me or anyone else for that matter. She likes her independence too much—and I quote—to sacrifice it on the altar of matrimony.'

'I see. Well, I do not believe that for one minute—and nor should you.'

'She has given me her answer. I will not go running after her.'

Lady Lansbury gave him a look of scepticism. 'You do want her, don't you?'

Of course he wanted her, his mind raged. He wanted her as desperately as a man dying of thirst wanted water. But Jane Mortimer's rejection had left him feeling bewildered, ill used and ill tempered. What did she expect of him? What had she expected him to do? Did she think him such a callous brute that he would abandon her, that she thought him capable of nothing more? His worry and confusion of the previous day had been replaced by a deeper, darker feeling of uncertainty. It was still a new emotion to him and one of which he was not particularly fond.

'I would not have asked her to be my wife if I didn't.'

'Then you must go to London and persuade her that marrying you is the only acceptable course. You cannot simply put her out of your heart.'

* * *

Lady Lansbury was disappointed that Jane had left Chalfont, but not defeated. She knew that her son could forget Jane if he made up his mind to it, but as his mother she would not allow that to happen.

She might just have the perfect solution, but it would mean enlisting the assistance of Jane's aunt, Caroline Standish.

Working on the exhibition was Jane's salvation. For a whole month she immersed herself in work in the spacious rooms Finn had acquired off the Strand to exhibit his private collection. She did not want to think about Christopher. She did not live in expectation of seeing him, but neither was she able to relax. She must try to forget that her dream was shattered and start again. In a way she was lucky, for this project which demanded her deeply involved attention would help her.

She was surrounded by crates and boxes containing all manner of artefacts to be displayed in glass cabinets and on plinths. The exhibition was to run for six weeks. Finn was negotiating for some of the exhibits—those not being returned to their countries of origin—to be taken over by the British Museum. Photographs and drawings of frescoes and mosaics, of archaeological sites in ancient Greece, Rome and Egypt, of temples in the Far East and India were to be displayed on the walls. Everything on display was listed in catalogues compiled by Finn to be sold at the door.

Jane had known Finn almost all of her life. He was in his midfifties with a shock of hair bleached white by spending years under the sun, fearless pale blue eyes, a firm jaw and a bright colour. Finn and her father had been good friends since their university days and had spent much of their time together ever since.

'It's good to be working with a lovely, talented young woman again,' Finn had said when she had arrived at the exhibition rooms more than ready to begin work. 'Your father would be pleased to know you're carrying on his work.'

'But I'm not, not really. What I'm doing is helping you with the exhibition. Although I'm glad you're going to exhibit some of his work, especially his photographs and writings. He would like that.'

Sorting through some photographs on the table, he paused and looked at her. 'What have you been doing with yourself since you arrived back in civilisation? I can't imagine you being idle.'

'I've been completing some of the work Father left unfinished. I've also been employed with work of a completely different kind.' She smiled when he gave her a quizzical look. 'Not the kind of work I am used to—in Oxfordshire.'

'I sent my letter to your aunt's house in London.'

'She posted it on to me. As a matter of fact I've been helping to look after a twelve-year-old girl.'

'Really? That's not like you. Who was she?'

'The sister of the Earl of Lansbury. She's a delightful child. Sadly she has—difficulties.'

'I'm sorry to hear that. And did you enjoy doing that—taking care of her?'

'Very much.'

'Then—why did you leave?'

'I—I had my reasons,' she said, averting her gaze in an attempt to hide the wretchedness of her parting from Christopher.

Finn's sharp eyes assessed the situation correctly. He perceived a struggle going on within her. 'Who is he?'

'Who?'

'The man you have fallen for. There is someone, I can tell, so don't try denying it.'

She blushed beneath his probing stare. 'You always could read my mind.'

'Precisely.'

She lifted her gaze solemnly to his. 'There—was someone, but it is over.'

Finn saw a painful sadness dulling her beautiful eyes. Anger at this unknown man for causing her distress weighted him down. 'And you are sure about that, are you, Jane?'

She nodded. 'I am not of his class. It could never have worked.'

'But you are a wealthy woman now. I know your father left you more than well provided for.'

'One thing I have learned, Finn, is that you cannot buy yourself that kind of thing. You have to be born into it. Yes, I have suddenly found myself in possession of a decent living, but I want nothing more than to live a quiet, modest, simple life and never need to depend on anyone.' She smiled. 'And to help you with your antiquities when you want me to.'

He chuckled. 'I will always need someone to do that. If I were younger, I would marry you myself just to keep you with me.'

'And if you were, I would accept. But to be perfectly honest with you, Finn,' she murmured, picking up a photograph depicting a desert scene, 'I couldn't resist the opportunity of being involved again. See this photograph. I remember my father taking it. What a splendid sight that was. Who else could understand what it is like to watch the glorious colours of a desert sunset as the sun drops gracefully, slowly, below the horizon, the heart-stopping glory of fiery brown, crimson and orange, spreading upwards as the orb of the sun sinks?'

She sighed wistfully. Finn understood. Dear, kind, lovable Finn.

'Besides,' she went on, 'I rather liked the idea of working with you—and I couldn't bear the thought of you being all alone and friendless in this great metropolis.'

He chuckled. 'I'm flattered, although you hit the right note. The people I know are mere acquaintances—not soulmates. I miss having a confidant—in truth, I miss your father,' he told her quietly. 'I don't feel I've had a proper conversation since I left Egypt.'

She smiled, empathising with him. 'I know what you mean. But you should get yourself a wife, Finn,' she teased in an attempt to lighten the moment.

Finn returned her smile. 'I'm too long in the tooth to change the habits of a lifetime.'

'No, you're not. I'm sure there are plenty of ladies out there willing to take you on.'

He stopped what he was doing and stared at her in theatrical outrage. 'Jane, how can you say such a thing? Do I look like a man who is in need of feminine company? A rake? A Lothario?'

Jane shook her head, laughing. From another man, Finn's declarations would be not just eccentric but alarming—however, there was something about the smooth fluency of his speech and the way that he was carefully examining a rather splendid statuette that he had just unpacked that made one realise that his word and gesture was just an affectation.

'What will you do when the exhibition closes?' she asked. 'Will you stay in London?'

He shook his head. 'A team of archaeologists are going out to Greece. I intend to join them later.' He suddenly looked at her, putting down the statuette. 'Why don't you come along? We can always do with someone to do the paperwork—cataloguing and such like. You're used to doing that kind of thing. You don't have to let it go now your father is no longer…' He faltered. After a moment he said, 'There are some on the team you will know and I will be there to take care of you—as if you were my own daughter. You know that, Jane.'

She smiled, deeply touched. 'I know that, Finn, and thank you. The appeal is still there. I will think about it.'

It had been four weeks since Christopher had last seen her. Four weeks since she had abandoned Chalfont and stormed out of his life. He had gone through the following days in a fog of desolation, going through each meaningless, dragging day by pretending to his mother that everything was just fine—that Jane Mortimer had ceased to exist. It was difficult when Chalfont echoed with images of her everywhere he turned. There was no escape from the memory of her, the scent of her, the taste of her. She was in his blood, under his skin, haunting him like a pitiless ghost.

He knew that he had hurt her. She had been an innocent, a virgin, and he had robbed her of that. He supposed it had been arrogant of him to assume she would accept his proposal of marriage, but that was what he had thought. Initially, his opinion of her as a woman had not been flattering, but he had not known her in any personal sense. But suddenly, in his sight she had become an alluring young woman, as desirable as any he had ever known.

He recalled her incredible passion when she had lain in his arms, her sweetness, how she had driven him mad with desire. She was like a drug to his senses that he could not name, but could not get enough of. She had fed his hunger and ever since she had left, a dull listlessness had followed him. There was something in Jane that calmed him, that moved him imperceptibly away from the misery which had caused him so much pain and desolation in the past.

Never had he been so vulnerable. He had not stopped wanting her with a torturous, aching want that seeped into the deepest parts of his body and soul. It was fatal to want her. But he did. He wanted to look upon her face, to touch her and to kiss her, to lose himself in her body and warmth. Yes, he wanted her, and until he had had her again he doubted he would get any peace at all.

For most of his life hate and anger had kept him going. He had fed on them for so long that they were the only emotions he recognised, the only ones he still knew how to feel. But Jane Mortimer had done the impossible. She had brought him peace.

When he thought of his life before she had entered it, he realised how empty it had been. Colourless. And then she had come and suddenly he felt feelings he had never believed existed and saw things he had never seen before. She had resurrected a part of him that had been dead for many years and given him a reason to look forward to the future rather than flounder in his past. She gave him friendship and the strength to face himself.

Without her he realised how much he missed her, how much she had come to mean to him. Did he love her? he asked himself. Was he suffering from that affliction he had decried since Lily?

Whatever it was, he knew he could not live without Jane. And so, driven by need and desperation and the desire to look upon her face again, he left for London.

Chapter Ten

Caroline was delighted to have Jane back in London, but she was surprised when Lord Lansbury paid her a visit when Jane was not at home. What he had to say concerning his proposal of marriage to Jane concerned her and she was curious as to why Jane had not mentioned it.

What he told her was confirmed when she received a letter from Lady Lansbury later on the same day. Lady Lansbury was involved in a charity event that Caroline was arranging and knew she was looking for a venue. Lady Lansbury wrote telling her that she would be happy to put Lansbury House at her disposal. It would be ideal for what Caroline was looking for and would generate a good deal of interest.

Caroline was indeed thrilled by Lady Lansbury's generosity, but troubled when Lady Lansbury went on to give her a brief account of what had transpired between her son and Jane before Jane had left Chalfont.

When Jane came home Caroline told her about Lady Lansbury's generous offer for the charity while withholding what she had divulged concerning Lord Lansbury's proposal of marriage. She didn't want Jane to think they had been gossiping behind her back and would like to hear Jane's account of what had taken place.

'Lord Lansbury told me that he has proposed marriage to you, Jane,' Caroline said when Jane returned home.

'He also told me how sudden his proposal had been and how he would like to court you in the proper way. I was very surprised, I don't mind telling you. You didn't say anything. Should I congratulate you? Are you unofficially engaged to Lord Lansbury?'

Jane was astonished. 'Certainly not. If that was indeed the case you would be the first person I would tell. But there is nothing to say. Yes, Lord Lansbury did propose marriage and my refusal was emphatic. Oh…' she gasped, anger rising up like flames licking inside her, spreading up her limbs

'…the arrogant, overbearing… How dare he come to you and speak of this? How humiliating.'

Caroline gave a wry smile. 'I take it that there is no romance, then, because if there is I will insist you tell me every single detail if I have to wring it out of you. But I can see by the look on your face that you do not want to marry him.'

'No, I do not, so please do not counsel me on the wisdom of my refusal and tell me how foolish I am to refuse an earl.'

'I wouldn't dream of doing any such thing. You are a grown woman with a mind of your own. Had you accepted his suit, then as your aunt I would have an obligation to you. I would be impelled to provide you with some counsel. But since there is to be no betrothal I wouldn't be so indelicate as to enquire about your reason for turning him down. Besides, being a countess would be a huge responsibility. I can understand your reluctance to take on such a role.'

'Exactly. My background is so significantly lower than his. My connections, though respectable, are hardly worthy of an earl. It all points to my complete lack of suitability to be a countess.'

'Lord Lansbury doesn't think so—otherwise he would not have proposed marriage to you. Have either of you mentioned this to Lady Lansbury?'

'I certainly haven't. As far as I am concerned the matter is no longer an issue.'

'I don't think Lord Lansbury thinks that,' Caroline said, watching her closely. 'He seems to care for you and he isn't the kind of man to take no for an answer. Do you truly think he will walk away and let you go?'

A worried frown puckered Jane's brow. 'I did. Now I'm not so sure.'

Caroline studied the violet eyes regarding her solemnly from beneath a heavy fringe of dark lashes and asked the question that had been plaguing her ever since Lord Lansbury had left the house, for she was not convinced by anything Jane had told her. 'You have feelings for him, don't you, Jane?'

Jane looked down at her hands resting in her lap, her throat aching with the tears she had refused to shed. She nodded, unable to deny it. 'Is it so very obvious, Aunt Caroline?'

She smiled. 'It's written all over your face.'

Jane gave her a wobbly smile. 'Oh, dear. I thought it might be.'

It was quiet and Jane was sorting through some drawings and photographs. Finn had gone to the British Museum to meet with the curator. Absorbed in her work, the sound of the door to the street opening made her look up. It couldn't be Finn back already. Getting off the stool, she removed the dust-grimed apron from about her waist and walked into the adjoining room, shocked out of her reverie when she saw Christopher. The bitterness of their parting sprang instantly to the fore.

She was wishing it had never happened. Or at least, she was wishing she could wish it had never happened. She had sworn to herself that she would put the matter from her mind, set it aside like a dying flower. She had believed she was managing so well, playing her part so well.

Until now.

And now her body was heating up because she could not forget what they had done in the folly that day. She wanted to think about it, linger on it, close her eyes and squirm with pleasure at the thought of those hot, blissful moments they had spent together. She wanted to dwell on each and every glorious detail.

Lightning seemed to scorch across the space between them, burning, eliminating everything in its path. Everything was obliterated but that invisible physical force searing through her body, so that she felt her flesh throb in agony as every nerve sprang to a trembling awareness of him—and instinctively she knew it was the same for him.

An unbidden flare of excitement rose up in the pit of her stomach, followed quickly by dread when she thought of their last bitter words and a stirring of anger when she thought of his visit to Aunt Caroline. Warily she watched him, looking at him nervously, wishing she could cool the waves of heat that mounted her cheeks—wishing she could run away.

Since his visit to Aunt Caroline she knew, of course, that he would come eventually. But why had he come? Had his feelings changed towards her? At least in her own environment she was better equipped to protect herself against him and his demands. Somehow she forced herself forward, her head held high.

'Christopher! You take me by surprise.'

Christopher stood with his back to the window through which the sun was shining, his face partly in shadow, the light gleaming on his dark hair. His mouth was a firm, grim line and there were shadows under his tumultuous eyes. He seemed taller than she remembered, bigger and more splendidly dressed, more magnificent. More intimidating even than on the first day they had met, more brooding, more remote. She dropped her stare, pained by the sight of him and a fleeting memory of the feel of his bare skin against hers.

'Yes, I can imagine,' he replied.

She stood utterly still, and with her dark eyes, which were so wide and solemn, she had an ethereal quality. Like a free spirit she confronted him, her head poised at a questioning angle, her hair tied back from her face with green ribbon. But there was a shadowed hollowness to her cheekbones. She was unaware that Christopher's heart took a savage and painful leap at the sight of her, that she seemed like someone he had never seen before, looking more at home here surrounded by antiquities than she had ever been at Chalfont. The aquamarine gown she wore was enticing and yet demure—the loose wisps of hair that framed her slightly flushed face set off her heavily fringed eyes and finely sculpted features, giving her a softly vulnerable appearance.

Suddenly he said, 'You look like a temple goddess about to be sacrificed to the bloodthirsty gods.'

'You mean I look terrified?'

'Panic-stricken.'

He crossed the room, his eyes never leaving hers, and Jane's heart leapt. She couldn't believe he had come. Had he missed her? Had he had a change of heart? Was that why he had called to see Aunt Caroline? Did he love her after all? She barely dared hope.

'What are you doing here?'

'I've come to see you. What else?' His tone was short, imperious, as though in reproach, and his eyes bore down into hers with cynicism. 'How are you?'

'I'm not with child, if that is what you have come to find out.'

'That is not why I am here. But thank you for telling me.'

'How are Lady Lansbury and Lady Octavia?'

'They are well, although I have to say that Octavia is missing you.'

Jane felt her heart wrench. 'I see. I'm sorry. When Lady Lansbury has the time she must bring her to see the exhibition. I know she would enjoy seeing the photographs.' Turning away from him, she walked back into the room where she was working, pausing by the table littered with photographs and the like. He followed her, glancing at objects on display around the room with interest.

'What is it you want, Christopher?' she asked, hoping he would tell her he couldn't bear being apart from her, the remembrance of the time they had spent in each other's arms being how he'd had the ability to render her defenceless, causing her to fling caution and reason to the four winds.

'I wanted to see you, but I had to come to London anyway. Attending Parliamentary sessions do take up a considerable amount of my time—and I have several business commitments that cannot be attended to at Chalfont. My mother is to come to London shortly. She is involved in some charity event being organised by your aunt. She has offered to put Lansbury House at her disposal.'

'So I understand. It is indeed generous of Lady Lansbury. Aunt Caroline raises funds in many ways for her charities and she makes it her business to know the names of wealthy people she can approach for monetary contributions. You must think her terribly mercenary to go around trying to extract money from people like that, but it's because she cares deeply for those less fortunate. Especially children. She is always hungry for money and is not afraid to say so.'

'Then we must make sure to invite those with deep pockets.'

Jane became still, facing him squarely. 'I know you called on her. She told me.'

'And I can see you are angry with me.'

She was angry. She was trying to harden herself against him, but how could she when her feelings for him were still so raw? 'I did not take kindly to you going to my aunt and telling her that you had proposed marriage to me when I refused you. It is clear to me that you hoped she would countenance your suit.'

'Yes, I went to her. As your closest relative I told her of my desire to marry you. I was hoping to get her on my side.'

'Aunt Caroline doesn't take sides, and if she did I would be the one she would support.'

'Naturally—being family. I know it is not necessary—you being of age, you understand—I was merely seeking her permission to court you in an honourable fashion. I did not tell her we were betrothed.'

'Because we are not. I have made my decision. Why will you not accept it?'

'Because I can't stop thinking of you. I've missed you—more than you realise. I remember the times we have talked—the time we made love,' he said, his voice low and fierce and wrenching to hear. 'I remember everything about you—the softness of your flesh, the way you responded to my touch, to my kiss, the way you filled my senses until I was unable to think. Yes, Jane, I remember everything. I swear I will make you remember.'

'Please stop it.' Her face was flushed under his watchful gaze. Despite his words, she had not forgotten their time together in the folly, not anything about him, and she could not believe he could think for a moment that she had. Memories of him were etched into her brain like carvings on a stone. 'You are trying to provoke me. It is cruel—saying such things to me when we both know it is only your determination to have your way that impels you to say them.'

'I take all the blame for what happened between us. I knew what the result would be, but I could not stop myself from making love to you anyway. Afterwards my whole concern was for you—that I do the honourable thing. I assumed that living at Chalfont as my wife would be enough. I see now that I should have chosen my words more carefully.'

'You were being honest. I would ask for nothing less. You may have meant well by speaking so plain, but somehow it seemed to me like the worst insult of all. I do not want to marry any man if it is all for duty and consideration.'

'I know I've hurt you and I'm sorry. It was certainly never my intention. You call me cruel when you are equally so when you will not allow me to make amends. I will not give up on you, Jane. I am determined.'

'You are persistent, I grant you that.'

Looking down at the table where she had been working, absently he picked up one of the drawings she had been assembling and scrutinised its content. After several moments his mouth slowly curved in a lopsided smile and one sleek black eyebrow lifted as he dragged his gaze from the drawing to her face.

'So, this is what you get up to when you are working. Shame on you, Jane.'

Too late she realised what it was. How careless of her not to have turned the drawing over, she realised, knowing there was no way to hide it now. It was of a Greek fresco with the image of men and women copulating, which was nothing out of the usual. Jane was used to seeing such things and after her initial curiosity they failed to affect her. But seeing them in Christopher's hands and the way he was carefully examining the drawing, remembering the time in the folly and their own lovemaking, she could feel the warmth spreading through her body, the warmth she felt every time she thought of what they had done.

She tried to take the drawing from his hands, but he held on to it.

'I would like to take a closer look.'

'Why would you?'

He chuckled. 'So that I can try to understand what it is that keeps you captivated by this kind of work. I think I'm beginning to understand. Are these figures Greek gods? Perhaps you could instruct me on the academic aspects because I confess to being bemused. What I see are men and woman making love. It is clear the artist had great skill, so is this fresco of purely historical interest or to do with the merit of the artist?' He raised his head, his eyes locking on hers, knowing precisely what he was doing and the effect his words were having on her. 'What is your opinion, Jane? Your intellectual opinion.'

She stared at him as hot colour flushed her cheeks. 'I—I don't have one—at least, not one that I can explain to you.'

'I don't believe that,' he said, looking down at other drawings on the table. 'These drawings are of an erotic nature. You must be moved when you look at them. The sensuality cannot be ignored—

but then, I expect you look at these pictures—and the real thing—with a purely academic interest.'

Jane's cheeks burned as he looked at her. 'I am not a qualified antiquarian,' she said quietly, turning away from him. All she could think about were the images on the table and the man standing next to her.

'Maybe not, but you are not without experience.'

'I deal with this sort of thing all the time. How can I not be moved? I am not as cold and unfeeling as you seem to think,' she retorted, unable to pretend an intellectual interest when there was this pulsating hunger in her body that made her skin burn and her knees go weak. Turning from him, she attempted to move away, but he put his hands on her shoulders to keep her there.

'I believe you, Jane,' he said quietly, lowering his head close to her face so that she could feel his warm breath on her neck. 'After all, having experienced the real thing, I imagine your work in matters such as this has taken on a whole new aspect.'

His words carelessly thrown on her already roiling emotions ignited like oil thrown on to a fire. As she spun round to face him he was forced to release his grip on her shoulders. 'I admit it. I am neither cold nor indifferent. And, yes, things have changed since—since I left you… What do you think I am? I am not made of stone. I am not without feeling.'

'You cannot blame me for wondering after the way you left Chalfont. You hide your feelings well, Jane.'

'That doesn't mean I don't have them,' she replied in a shaky, indignant voice. 'I have desires and needs just like any other woman. How could you think I do not?'

'Perhaps that's because you refused my offer of marriage. I did not expect it.'

'Clearly not. You have too high an opinion of yourself.'

'I'm entitled. I am an earl, after all,' he teased softly.

'I know. That's part of the trouble.'

'Sadly,' he went on, 'being a ladies' man cuts no ice with you, since you ruthlessly spurned me after I presented you with an offer I've never made to any other woman.'

'I'm flattered,' she retorted, 'but I'm sure you've had mistresses aplenty.'

'Several. Why? Is it important?'

'You never felt obliged to ask any one of them to marry you?'

'No.' He frowned, his eyes narrowed. 'What is this, Jane? Why the questions?'

'Because you are still something of a mystery to me. You revealed nothing of yourself. Ever since we met I have told you many things about me—about my life and my work. Yet you have told me little about yourself. I do not know you well enough to marry you.'

'What do you want to know? Ask away and I will tell you.'

She glanced around, biting her bottom lip, as if trying to think how to put what she wanted to say. 'There is something very wrong and you will not tell me what it is. That it is in the past, that it has something to do with a woman who let you down very badly, I know because you told me. She hurt you, I know it, but I feel there is something else—deep inside, I sense it.'

He smiled. 'And I always said you were a sensitive soul.'

'Please don't make light of it, Christopher. You asked me to be your wife—offered me your name. Why? Because you felt obligated and you were arrogant enough to think I would accept…'

He cocked an eyebrow, his smiled widening.

'And you say you do not know me well enough to marry me.'

She shook her head in vexation, turning from him and stepping away. 'Please do not jest with me. I think you know what I am saying.'

He moved to stand behind her and leaned close to her cheek. 'I know perfectly well what you are asking of me, Jane,' he said, his voice soft but with a hint of steel. 'I don't want to speak of it, to open up old wounds that have never completely heated and never will. That aside, I tell you that you know me better than you realise. No one knows me better. Not even my mother. Ever since you left Chalfont I have been resisting the urge to come to London, to tell you how much I desire you. You probably won't believe me, but I do not know what else I can do.' Gently placing his hands on her shoulders, he turned her round to face him, pushing his advantage. 'You desired me, too, Jane—not so long ago. I have not forgotten that and I am sure you haven't. Perhaps I could say what I feel with my body.'

Jane wanted to ask him again what was in his mind. Something had happened to him in the past, something more than the enormity of the debts his father had left behind and the woman he had referred to when he had proposed marriage to her.

Whatever it was, it was clear he did not want to share it with her.

She found him watching her with an expression she could not mistake. Desire was in the tense line of his jaw, in the burning depths of his eyes. Desire and lust. She knew it—read the signs. Because she felt it, too.

Forcing himself to remain calm, Christopher caught her glittering gaze and held it. 'I think we both know what we want, don't we?'

Jane scrutinised his expression warily. Her feelings were nebulous, chaotic, yet one stood out clearly—frustrated desire. Something softened in her, but she was determined she must stand firm.

'I haven't forgotten. How could I?' she whispered fiercely. 'I do want you,' she admitted. 'Very much, as it happens. Why do you want me? That is what I am interested in.'

'Why do I want you?' he repeated quietly, suddenly thoughtful. He took a moment to reflect on her strong will, a quality he admired. 'I cannot escape the fact that you have intrigued me for some considerable time. You have no artificial airs and graces and you possess a kind of courage that is unusual in a woman. You are also proud and independent, with bold, forthright ways which I admire.

Looking at you now, what I see in your eyes quickens my very soul, stirring my mind with imaginings of what life married to you would be like.'

Jane was deeply moved by what he said. It was more than she had ever dared to hope for. But was it enough? Could she live with that, knowing that she did not have his love? Now that she'd had a taste of sexual pleasure, as intoxicating as it was, she realised it was a completely separate thing from what she really wanted from him—an intimacy of the heart. As a lover he could take her to the heights of desire, but just like his title and the beauty and peace of Chalfont, this was no substitute for love.

'Don't you see? I don't want what I feel for you to be unrequited. I have to step back while I still have the strength. I don't want to consign myself to a miserable life, falling in love with someone I could never reach. When I fall in love I want that love to be returned in equal measure. '

Christopher stared at her, knowing exactly what she was saying, what she was asking. 'Neither of us know what will happen in the future, Jane. We can find a way that suits us best.'

She shook her head, holding his gaze. 'You are so hard to read. I never know what you are feeling. If I can't do that, how can I possibly trust myself to you the way a commitment like marriage will require me to? How can I give over the control of my life, let alone give you my heart, if I don't really know you? If I gave all of myself in marriage, I would want all of you in return. Without that our future together would be very dark indeed.'

'If that's how you think marriage to me would be, then no wonder you said no. My life has been—difficult,' he said very quietly, hesitantly. 'That is partly the reason why I am not so open. I suppose I thought it would not matter, that the less you knew of me, the better my chances of winning you.'

'You are so wrong, Christopher. Now, please, don't pressure me now. This is not the place and if you don't mind I have work to do.'

'You want me to go?'

'You must, if I am to get on.'

'I think the reason you want me to leave is because you are afraid of me,' he said, and there was a wicked note in his voice and a wicked gleam in his eyes.

Jane knew that look. Its power was not to be underestimated. Already she felt her blood warm inside her. 'This is nonsense,' she retorted. 'I don't fear you in the least. Why should I?' But, just in case, she took a step back.

'Because you know in your heart that I will eventually persuade you to do as I want. Because you can't resist me.'

'I can resist you perfectly well,' she retorted, trying not to sound breathless.

He smiled, that so-handsome smile. 'Can you resist me?' he said. 'Let me see.'

Taking her hand, he drew her to a tall screen conveniently placed across a corner of the room.

'Christopher…' She breathed in desperation, wanting to look away, wanting to stop listening, knowing that every word he spoke was drawing her deeper into love with him. She tried to pull away, but he had tight hold of her and would not let go. She wanted to present him with nothing but indifference, because then maybe he would let her go and leave her alone, but she found it difficult. He kept slipping past her defences. She wanted to be cold, but coldness was a hard thing to summon when he had only one thing on his mind.

Confined behind the screen, the limited space warm and dimly lit, Christopher took her face between his hands and they looked at each other for the length of several heartbeats. His features were less guarded than Jane had ever seen them and there was something so tender in his eyes that all she could do was stare.

'Please,' she whispered. 'We mustn't do this. Someone might come in.'

'I know,' he murmured, reluctant to let go of her face. He was content to let his eyes dwell on the softness of her lovely face, to gaze into the depths of her half-closed eyes, to glory in the gentle sweep of her long dark lashes which dusted her cheeks.

Almost unconscious of what he was doing, he lowered his head closer to hers, overcome by a strong desire to draw her mouth to his and taste the sweetness of her quivering lips, which he did, succumbing to the impulse that had been tormenting him for weeks. The moment he placed his mouth on hers Jane parted her lips to receive his longed-for kiss, her heart soaring with bliss. He kissed her slowly and deliberately, and Jane felt a melting sweetness flowing through her bones and her heart pouring into his, depriving her of strength.

With a deep sigh Christopher drew back and gave her a searching look, his gaze and his crooked smile drenching her in its sexuality.

'There are times, Jane Mortimer, when you confound me,' he murmured, placing his warm lips on her forehead.

Her cheeks aflame, Jane drew a long, shuddering breath, her whole being bent on recovery, until he lowered his head once more. His lips folded about hers in a way that drew the most wonderful feelings from the pit of her belly. His arms held her tight against him so that even through her petticoats she could feel his need of her.

Surfacing slowly from the mists of desire, she drew away from him and stared into his hypnotic eyes, dazedly watching their colour and mood change from the smoky darkness and passion to their usual enigmatic silver-grey, while she felt reality slowly return.

He kissed her lightly one more time before he drew away. 'If we don't stop now,' he murmured in an odd, strained voice, 'I'm going to repeat what happened between us in the folly—which I fully intend to do, but not here. Not today.'

They stepped from behind the screen. Jane kept her eyes lowered and smoothed down her skirt with shaking hands. Her heart did a somersault when the door suddenly opened and Finn came striding in. On seeing Christopher he stopped, looking from one to the other, assessing the situation correctly. He settled his gaze on the unknown gentleman with a combination of carefully concealed speculation and friendliness.

'Finn! I—I didn't expect you back so soon,' Jane said breathlessly, flustered, trying to compose her features.

'My meeting at the Museum didn't take long.' Finn studied her for a moment, thinking how delightful she looked with her face all flushed and her eyes bright, before shifting his gaze to her visitor. Finn regarded the gentleman curiously. He didn't need any explanation for what might have taken place in his absence or that this man was indeed familiar to Jane. 'Well, Jane, aren't you going to introduce me to your visitor?'

'Yes—of course. May I introduce Lord Christopher Chalfont, the Earl of Lansbury. Christopher, this is Phineas Waverley—Finn—an old and valued friend of my father—and me.'

'I am delighted to meet you,' Christopher said, extending his hand. 'I understand from Miss Mortimer that you are quite a traveller and that you have worked in some exotic places along with her father.'

'That is correct, but there is nothing exotic about it when you are actually there. In some places the heat and the dust leave a lot to be desired, I assure you. Since you—are here to see Jane I will leave you to talk.'

'Lord Lansbury was just leaving, Finn,' Jane was quick to say, 'so there is no need to go.'

Christopher glanced at her sharply, lifting his eyebrows with some amusement. 'I am?'

'Yes. I really don't think we have anything further to say to each other.'

He smiled infuriatingly. 'For now. Tomorrow is Saturday.' He looked at Finn. 'Can you spare your assistant for a few hours?'

Finn nodded. 'We don't normally work on Saturdays. Besides, we're almost ready to open.'

Christopher looked at Jane. All her life, of being shunted from one hot country to the next, living in heat and dust and desert sands, she had never had the opportunity to enjoy the luxuries of life. His mother was right. Jane had to be courted.

'We'll go for a drive tomorrow at two o'clock if the weather permits. I am looking forward to the exhibition when it opens,' he said to Finn. 'I'm sure I will find it most interesting.' Inclining his head politely, he strode across the room and went out.

It was with a heavy heart that Jane watched him go. It was a ridiculous situation. She had thought Christopher had more pride than to come after her, especially when she had refused him so finally. Maybe that was the reason he was persisting—his pride. She had dented it badly by turning him down—and now he meant to repair the damage by trying to get her to change her mind. Unbeknown to her, her face was unguarded. All her emotions and feelings were there for Finn to see.

'So,' he murmured, folding his arms across his chest and perching his hips against the stout table. 'Lord Lansbury is the gentleman who has got you into such a fix.'

'I'm not in a fix, Finn.'

'No, but it is plain to me that you have feelings for him. Am I correct?'

Jane nodded miserably. 'Yes. I can no longer fight or ignore what I feel.'

'Why would you want to—if you love him?'

She sank on to a stool and looked at him miserably. 'Yes, I suppose I do. Sadly I cannot choose who to love, Finn, for love Christopher Chalfont I surely do with all my heart and soul.'

'Well, then, what is the problem?'

'It's his inability to return my love that makes me hold back, because I will settle for nothing less. I love him and I want him to love me. Is it so very wrong of me to want what my mother and father had—that perfect love? Oh, Finn,' she cried, 'what am I going to do?'

As he heard the anguish in her voice, saw it in her eyes, Finn's heart went out to her. 'I truly have no idea, Jane, but the way I see it, the man's a fool not to love you. However, I'm not convinced that he doesn't. You could give him a chance and go driving with him tomorrow as he suggested. Some time away from this place will be good for you.' He smiled. 'Perhaps you might even enjoy yourself.'

The following afternoon at two o'clock precisely, Jane watched a shiny black carriage draw up in front of the house. Having dressed in good time, when Christopher was due to arrive she was ridiculously nervous and caught up in the heights of excitement. She had never been invited on an outing with a gentleman before, so this was all new to her—not that she could have refused, since Christopher had issued the invitation with his usual air of command and authority.

It was with some surprise that she watched him step down from the carriage holding a huge bouquet of red roses. He paused to speak to the driver, giving Jane a moment to observe him. He was casually dressed and bareheaded, the gentle breeze ruffling his thick dark hair. How handsome he was, how striking. Her heart wrenched with love as she allowed her eyes to dwell on his face, seeing the ruthless set of his jaw and his sculptured mouth.

It was never easy to remain composed when she was with him, for his face was so intense that she was affected by the force of passion that emanated from him, that seared her flesh and melted her bones. She wanted to tell him how much she loved him, how much he had come to mean to her, but until she knew he would reciprocate her love she would keep it locked in her heart.

When he walked towards the house she immediately ran into the hall and, without waiting for him to knock she opened the door.

'Christopher! What on earth have you got there?'

Raising a brow with some amusement, he gave the flowers a dubious look. 'They look very much like roses to me.'

'But—why—what for…?'

He held them out to her. 'They are for you, Jane.'

'Oh! Why—I—I thank you. How lovely. Somehow I didn't associate you with presenting ladies with flowers.'

'I'm not. You are the first. Red roses, I am told,

have a significant meaning. I believe the flower reigns as the ultimate symbol of passionate love.'

Jane stared at him, not having expected him to say that. 'It also began its symbolic history in Greece, in rose iconography—where it was associated with Aphrodite or Venus—the goddess of love.'

He grinned. 'There you are, then. I've got that right.' Handing them to her, he stood gazing down at her, holding her eyes in a wistful sheen of silver-grey.

'I've never been given flowers before,' she murmured, somewhat shyly. She glanced at him obliquely from behind the bouquet. 'Are you trying to gain my favour, by any chance?'

'Do I need to?' He looked at the flowers. 'In some countries I believe it is the custom for a woman to wear a flower on her dress to tell her husband of her desire.'

Jane laughed. 'Since I don't have a husband that does not apply. Perhaps I should put one behind my ear.'

He grinned, a wicked gleam in his eyes. 'I believe that means an unmarried lady is available.'

'In which case I shall put them in a vase and admire them.'

The maid, on hearing voices, burst into the hall, her eyes lighting up when she saw the roses. 'Ooh, how lovely,' she enthused. 'Shall I put them in water for you, Miss Mortimer, before I leave?'

'Yes, please,' Jane said, handing them to her and watching her disappear. Looking at Christopher, she realised he was watching her with a strange and tender smile on his lips. 'Why, Christopher! Do you court me?' she enquired in soft amusement. Her mouth curved into a tantalising smile as she moved towards him with almost sensuous grace.

Christopher caught and held her eyes. 'Would you mind if I did?'

'I don't know. I've never been courted before. If you do it would be the first time ever.'

'Would you welcome my attention?'

'It would be a challenge.'

'This whole situation is new for me—and my mother told me that if I am to court you then I have to do it properly—hence the flowers.'

Jane was aghast. 'You have told Lady Lansbury.'

He nodded. 'Don't look so worried. She approves absolutely.'

'But—she has nothing to approve of. I am flattered that you have decided to do things properly, but please don't imagine for one minute there will be any gain by it. I have not committed myself to anything and no matter how attentive you may be, I will not change my mind.'

'You will,' he told her with absolute confidence. 'I see you are ready for our drive,' he said, his eyes admiring of her light blue V-necked dress and darker blue short pelisse. Perched cheekily on her head she wore a small straw hat with a flat crown and long blue ribbons.

'I think I should be accompanied by a chaperone—that's the way it's done, isn't it? I know the rules of etiquette are necessary to protect young women entering society, but considering my background and the fact that I am not about to be launched into society, I do not think the rules apply to me. Aunt Caroline is visiting friends and her maid is going home so there is no one who can accompany me, which is unfortunate, but I am not going to forgo an outing to the park to appease society's narrow-minded sense of propriety.'

Taking her hand, Christopher escorted her out to the carriage and ordered the driver to head for St James's Park.

Jane sighed, relaxing into the upholstery and tingling with exuberance. Fresh, cool breezes floated across the park and the trees were changing to every shade of gold, bronze and brown. 'It's such a lovely day,' she said, looking about her. 'Autumn is such a glorious season in England, don't you agree?'

Seated across from her, quietly and without emphasis, he said, 'You have a lovely smile, Jane, one that could light up a room.'

The park was lovely and milling with people, some strolling whilst others gathered and sat in clusters to gossip. There were swarms of rosy-cheeked, excited children playing all manner of games. Flowers in beds and borders added a vivid splash of colour to the park and the grass was like soft green velvet.

Christopher suggested they leave the carriage to stroll along the paths, which they did, her arm in the crook of his elbow.

After a few minutes, acutely conscious of the attention they were attracting, Jane kept her eyes lowered.

'What's wrong?'

'I feel conspicuous. Everyone is staring at us,' she whispered apprehensively.

Completely impervious to the stir they were creating, Christopher flicked a glance around them, then shifted his gaze to Jane's flushed face.

'I see that,' he agreed. 'Don't let it worry you.'

It's a good thing I'm a nobody, otherwise my reputation would be destroyed.'

Christopher gave her a long, meaningful look. 'A countess may do as she pleases.'

'I am not a countess,' Jane returned.

'But you're going to be,' he said with absolutely finality.

Jane opened her mouth to argue, but he turned his head to acknowledge an acquaintance in a passing carriage. Sternly, Jane reminded herself of the arrogant, tyrannical and high-handed way he had negotiated this carriage drive, then she shrugged the thought aside. He was all those things and more, yet she cared deeply for him, too, and there was no point in denying it.

'Are you to return to Chalfont?' she asked.

'Eventually.' He looked at her and smiled. 'But not yet. I shall return to Oxfordshire before the charity ball—I think Mother can manage that without me. So while I am here I shall show you London.'

'I am no stranger to it.'

'I mean the real London. I can think of so much I want you to see.'

'But I have my work at the exhibition…'

'Look on this time as a holiday. Plenty of time for work later.'

Christopher was determined they were going to be married. He had decided that and his indomitable will was going to prevail as surely as the moon was going to rise in the east.

Chapter Eleven

As the days went by there were more carriage rides and strolls in the park, places of interest to see and explore. Jane particularly enjoyed the evenings Christopher escorted her and Aunt Caroline to the theatre.

He was always politely attentive and indefatigable in his attempts to please her and the days were a kaleidoscope of shifting emotions. He knew exactly how to treat a woman and to adjust his attitude to what he believed would please her best. In fact, he was patience and courtesy personified. He did not mention his marriage proposal nor did he kiss her or attempt to kiss her and Jane found herself wishing he would.

She was as happy and carefree as she had never been, aware of his moods, but always at the height of her pleasure she was aware of a warning voice telling her to have a care. She knew she was falling completely under his spell, but she need have no fear, she told herself firmly. She was not an innocent girl. She would always remember the sort of man she was dealing with—worldly and determined—and she would always pride herself on her common sense.

She learned a great deal about him. There was a serious side to his nature. He was extremely knowledgeable. He was something of a connoisseur of music and art and he was well versed in England's history. In London she was seeing much which she had seen before without noticing. He brought a new light to everything and that which had been insignificant had become of absorbing interest.

They were happy days. She would never forget them. But, she reminded herself many times a day, it was ephemeral. There had to be an ending. But she clung to each moment, savouring it to the full, although she had an uneasy feeling that she was becoming his victim as he had all the time intended that she should. She had lost sight of that fact in discovering this new side to his nature.

The day before Lady Lansbury was to arrive in London to prepare for the charity event, Jane sat on a park bench next to Christopher. 'These past days have been wonderful,' she said, watching a rather handsome peacock strut across the grass.

'It pleases me to know you have enjoyed yourself.'

'Very much, but I am afraid I have taken up a lot of your time.'

'The days have been spent in the way I wished them to be.' He looked at her. 'It need not end, Jane. You know that, don't you?'

'Be frank, Christopher. You have a motive.'

'My motive is to give you pleasure. Where would you like to go tomorrow?'

'Tomorrow I will help Finn. The exhibition opens next week. I have taken up enough of your time. I imagine you will find some other diversion.'

'Is that how you think of yourself? A diversion?'

'It is not what I intend to be.'

'But you have enjoyed our outings.'

'You know I have. I shall miss them.'

Christopher looked at her sharply. 'Are you going away?'

'There is a team of archaeologists going to Greece. Finn will be joining them when the exhibition closes. He—has asked me if I would like to go with them.'

'I see.' Christopher took her hand. 'What are you afraid of, Jane?'

'Afraid?'

'Afraid of letting me come too close.'

Jane sighed. 'Christopher, I'm different from most of the women you know.'

'You are. That is true. That is one of the things about you which I find so attractive.'

'I do not react as you are accustomed to.'

'And how do you know what I expect?'

'Because I have come to know a little of the life you have led. These past days I shall always treasure. You have taught me so much. I know you are passionate about English history, the kind of music you like, the books you like to read, but I know very little about your past—about your father and what has made you what you are. I wish you would open up to me about yourself.'

Christopher sat up straight and his eyes darkened. Suddenly agitated, he got to his feet. His expression became guarded, his eyes as brittle as glass. Casting his eyes skyward, he said, 'I think it's going to rain.'

Jane watched him, her heart aching. 'Why will you not talk about him? I do not care if he was a gambler, if that is the reason you keep silent—'

'We should go,' he interrupted. 'Your aunt will be wondering where we have got to.'

Jane remained where she was. 'Why will you not speak about him?' she persisted.

Christopher's face was impassive, but inside everything was shattering. "There are some things I don't want to talk about. You know absolutely nothing about me, Jane. Nothing.'

Jane got to her feet, smoothing down her skirts. 'No, I don't.'

Taking a moment to compose himself Christopher looked at her. 'What will you do about Greece? Have you decided?'

'No, not yet.'

'But you think you might go?'

'Yes,' she replied quietly. 'I think I might.'

'And if I asked you not to?'

Jane shook her head, nonplussed. What was he asking? Marriage? She was silent. She could hardly refuse him that which he had not asked for. But he hadn't asked her again. Why had she let this go so far? She hoped she didn't show her feelings. She was suddenly so wretched.

She watched the peacock arrogantly spread its bold blue feathers for a much less beautiful peahen. 'It's late. We should get back.'

* * *

For the next two weeks Jane's time was taken by the approach of the opening of the exhibition and Aunt Caroline's charity event. She had not intended to become involved in this, but she found herself being drawn in. She had not seen Christopher since the day she had asked him to tell her about his father. He had decided to return to Chalfont until the charity ball was over, leaving his mother to oversee matters.

Jane was invited to have lunch with Lady Lansbury and Octavia. It was clear to Jane that Christopher's mother had something on her mind she wanted to discuss with her, which was why she asked Maisie to take Octavia to the park.

'Walk with me in the garden, Jane. The weather is exceptionally warm for September. It's such a shame to be indoors on such a day.'

Jane followed her on to the terrace and fell into step beside her as they walked round the small rose garden.

'So, Christopher had proposed marriage to you, Jane. I can't tell you how disappointed I was when he told me you had turned him down.'

'You were?'

'Absolutely. It is my opinion that you would be

good for him—good for each other. Ever since he took over the reins of Chalfont—which, as you know, was almost bankrupt when my husband died—he has struggled to carry on. Work was always paramount to him, society and the major social events that are the life of many of his friends were of no interest.'

Walking slowly on, Lady Lansbury looked straight ahead. 'But that didn't stop people treating him with the deferential respect that his title commands—more so in America, where he abhorred the attention he drew, for he understood and despised the reasons why he was coveted. As a result his attitude towards any respectable female of his own class became cynical and jaded—which was the case with Lydia Spelling, I'm afraid. Those wealthy young women who trailed after him he treated with amused condescension—if one irritated him, he would deliver a crushing set down that was guaranteed to reduce the unfortunate young woman to tears.'

'Oh, dear. He is that bad? Well…' Jane sighed '… I am not intimidated by him, nor am I in awe of him, and I am certainly not dazzled by his rank or his power.'

'I know that, Jane. Would you mind if I ask why you turned him down?'

'No, of course I don't mind. It—it's just that—his proposal took me by surprise—and I do not know him well.'

'Has he told you anything about his early life?'

'A little.'

'So you know his father was a wastrel and a spendthrift,' Lady Lansbury said, unable to conceal the bitterness she felt whenever she thought of or mentioned her dead husband.

Jane nodded. 'Christopher always avoids speaking of his past.'

Sitting on a bench, Lady Lansbury drew Jane down beside her. The two sat facing each other.

'Christopher is a private person, Jane. He will not speak of his personal life—not even with me, even though we are close. He is a man of impeccable integrity, honour, dignity and respect. He is a clever man and true to what he believes. His family means everything to him.'

Jane smiled at her. 'That is something I do know.' On a more serious note, she said, 'I do know he was let down by someone—a woman—very badly.'

'Yes, yes, he was. He—he was quite young at the time. Nothing would have come of it, but he was deeply hurt by it. He has never spoken of it. In fact, when I look back, I can't imagine how he's survived everything that's happened to him—to this family—and remained sane. You know, Jane, if you marry Christopher you could not be marrying a finer man. There is no reason why things won't turn out for the best. You are a young lady of excellent character and breeding and excellent courage. There is also a gentle strength about you—a compassion and understanding that I believe will make you the perfect wife for my son. I know him very well. I have seen the way he looks at you. He cares for you a great deal and is in love with you—although he may not know it yet and may not even want to be.'

Jane's heart twisted. If only what Lady Lansbury said was true.

Lady Lansbury took one of Jane's hands and held it in her own. 'Perhaps if you were to understand him a little more, what drives him, it might help. Things have not always been easy for Christopher. As a boy he was bright, with a thirst for knowledge that put others to shame. He is not like his father—if that is what you are afraid of. When my husband died and left us almost destitute, Christopher drove himself with a blind, instinctive faith as his only survival. At first he seemed to take one step forward and two steps back and our situation did not improve—which was why he considered marrying a wealthy heiress. But, as you know, that did not last.

'Now his efforts are beginning to gain fruition. His newfound prosperity will bring him many luxuries, but little joy—not without the right woman by his side. That is something I would like you to remember, Jane, in the days ahead. Let yourself love him—I know you want to. And teach him how to love you. He has a great deal of love to give.'

Jane's eyes were cloudy with trepidation. 'I am deeply touched by your faith in me, Lady Lansbury, but what makes you so certain this can all work out the way you hope it will?'

'Because you are the person you are. You have warmth and courage and you can teach him how it feels to trust, to love and to be loved. Most men love easily and often, but Christopher will love only once. When he does it will be for ever.'

Jane's heart filled with warmth for the man who had asked her to be his wife. True, he was frequently distant and unapproachable, but the more she contemplated the matter, the more convinced she became that Lady Lansbury was right—he must care for her, or he would never have asked her to be his wife. He might not love her in the way she loved him, but the love she bore him would more than compensate.

'What are you thinking?' Lady Lansbury asked as she watched Jane's thoughtful expression. 'Are you going to reconsider his proposal?'

'I rather think I might—although the mere thought of taking on the role of countess is daunting for me to say the least—not to mention the many duties I would be taking on at Chalfont. I am far from qualified for such a role.'

Lady Lansbury laughed. 'You are, my dear, believe me, you are. You are more than capable—and you can begin by helping to put the final touches to this charity ball. If you can do that, then nothing is beyond you.'

Christopher returned from Chalfont unexpectedly. He was surprised to find Jane in the hall arranging flowers that had been delivered from Chalfont's greenhouses in large vases and urns, praying they would not wilt before the ball the next day. She was unaware of his presence so he took the liberty of allowing his eyes to dwell on her.

Their brief separation had given him time to consider what had to be done. One thing he was sure of was that he couldn't bear to lose her, because he'd realised that he wanted her more than he had ever wanted anything in his life. She had become a part of him which he could not deny. Her heart was the sweet centre in the headlong strength of her mind and body and, quite simply, now that he knew her and could see her for what she was, he loved her—for he did love her—and his heart swelled fit to burst as he admitted the truth to himself. He could not lose her. He loved everything about her.

Thinking of the woman he had so unwittingly fallen for, how could he not love her? Jane had drawn him from the darkness of his lonely world.

After much soul searching he had decided to tell her everything about his troubled life. There could not be any more secrets to tear him apart and ruin his future. No matter how painful the telling would be, it would be difficult, for he found it hard to expose his inner self, but Jane would understand—like no one else she would understand. Holding nothing back, he would tell her every sordid detail of what life had been like living in the shadow of a man who had made his life and that of his mother hell and the shameful manner of his death.

* * *

'Ah, I see you're busy, Jane,' said a deep, unperturbed voice behind her.

Jane whirled in surprise. The pleasure at seeing him again after days of not seeing him eclipsed everything else. He stood in the centre of the hall, a tall, slender-hipped, broad-shouldered man.

'I am—yes,' she said falteringly, walking towards him, holding a large spray of white chrysanthemums in her hand. 'I thought you intended remaining at Chalfont until after the ball.'

'I changed my mind.' Shoving his hands into his pockets, he regarded her with mild curiosity. 'I apologise for deserting you, Jane. I hope everything is progressing with satisfaction for the ball tomorrow night.'

'Yes—perfectly—at least it will be, when I have arranged the flowers.'

'And the exhibition?'

'Finn is managing without me. He has plenty of willing hands.' She turned her attention back to the flowers. 'I find it amazing that so many different blooms can be grown in your greenhouse, even in winter.' Casting a critical eye over her efforts, she sighed. 'I'm afraid I don't seem to have an eye for this sort of thing.'

Christopher cast an eye over the numerous vases filled with exotic blooms and didn't believe her. 'You underestimate yourself, Jane. They look wonderful.'

Jane sighed. 'I can't take all the credit. Maisie had a hand in deciding which flower should go with which. Lady Octavia was keen to do her bit, but I'm afraid she lost interest. Will you be attending the ball?'

He nodded. 'I shall insist on a dance, Jane. Perhaps two, if I find you are good at it.'

'I'm afraid you're going to be disappointed. I do dance a little, but on the whole it was one thing I never bothered to learn properly.'

Jane and her aunt arrived in good time for the charity ball. Entering Lansbury House, they climbed the curving staircase to the next story, where the ballroom was located. Footmen dressed in formal, dark blue velvet livery stood at attention beside tall silver stands of the exotic flowers Jane and Maisie had so carefully arranged the day before. The ballroom, with its tall windows and marble pillars, was not as large as the one at Chalfont, but it was every bit as grand. The butler stood on a balcony, his back ramrod straight, as he announced the arrival of the guests.

Clad in a rose-red gown of taffeta in simple lines yet full at the back, Jane wore a pearl choker round her neck and her bright chestnut hair was pinned in a sleek and elegant coif. It was a dramatic and sophisticated look.

With one shoulder nonchalantly propped against a pillar, from his vantage point Christopher idly watched her move serenely from group to group, untouched by the noise and bustle all around her. Suddenly he wanted her in a new and urgent way. He had thought her beautiful before, wholesome and innocent, with her sunshine hair, but she seemed different tonight. Her colouring was more vivid in this glamorous setting, he thought. She belonged in beautiful gowns and glittering jewels, he decided. They suited her far better than the sombre clothes she had worn when he had first met her. She was like a young woman fully coming into her own as she adjusted to her new place in his world.

Except that she was about to leave his world for the life she had known before. He would do everything within his power to prevent that.

Dancing was in progress, with some of society's

most influential and respected ladies and gentlemen dipping and swaying to the music. The room resounded with conversation and laughter and glowed with the brilliance of the immense chandeliers dripping with sparkling crystals reflecting the dazzling kaleidoscope of colour of gowns and jewels.

There was little opportunity for the ladies of the charity committee to relax and enjoy themselves. Full purses were plentiful. They never openly asked anyone for money—that would never do—but all of those who had been invited were aware of the occasion and were sympathetic to the causes and subscribed on a regular basis.

It was just before the supper break that Jane sensed Christopher's presence behind her. She even recognised the spicy tang of his cologne. Her throat went dry and a nervous quaking jarred through her as she waited for him to speak to her.

'Dance with me, Jane.'

She turned slowly to face him. He was watching her, his teeth showing in a lazy smile. 'I don't think that would be wise—at least, not if you value your feet.'

'I'll risk it if you will.'

Without waiting for her answer, taking her hand, he drew her on to the dance floor and into his embrace. It was a waltz, a swirling, exciting dance that brought couples into close contact as no other. He swung her into the rhythm with a sureness of step and she followed with a natural grace.

'You were not telling me the truth when you said you were a poor dancer, Jane. You dance as beautifully as you make love.'

Jane felt a sudden warmth infuse her body and she knew her cheeks had pinked. 'I must say, Christopher, that you do pick your moments.'

'I meant what I said.'

'Remind me. I have forgotten.'

'I will not accept your refusal to marry me.'

Leaning back in his arms the better to see his face, she met his gaze. 'I know.'

'And I never say anything I don't mean. At some point very soon I will have persuaded you to overlook your refusal and marry me.' The heat of his stare lent the weight of truth to his words.

'You are very sure of yourself, Christopher. Have I given you reason to believe my feelings have changed since you made your proposal?'

'It is something that I sense.'

'So you persist.'

'Because I cannot get you out of my thoughts.' His voice became soft and serious. 'I think of the times when we have been together—when we have talked, what it felt like when I held you, how soft your skin and how warm and willing your lips. I remember how you looked when we made love. In fact, I remember everything and were we alone I would swiftly prove the ardour you have stirred.'

'Christopher, please, stop this.' Blushing beneath his intimate, predatory gaze, she noticed the increasing interest of the gazes being directed at them. 'People are looking at us.'

'Let them look,' he murmured, his eyes shining softly, hungrily as he gazed down into hers. 'I am a man with a very beautiful and desirable woman in my arms. How else should I behave?'

'Like a gentleman would be a start.'

'Ah, my love. Am I really to believe that you care nothing for me at all? How can I believe that when you took such pleasure in my kisses—and I can pleasure you again? Do not deny yourself, Jane—or me.'

His gaze was now direct, challenging, raking her face upturned to his. The bold stare touched a quickness in Jane that made her feel as if she were on fire. She did want him. She wanted him more than she had ever wanted anything in her life.

And then the dance was over. Taking her hand, he led her off the floor and placed her beside his mother and her aunt, who had been watching the two of them with great interest and more than a little satisfaction.

When Christopher had walked away, Lady Lansbury leaned into her ear and with a little smile curving her lips quietly told her that she was to return to Chalfont the next day and that she was taking Octavia with her. When Jane turned to look at her and met her eyes, she knew what she was saying. Turning back to watch the dancers swirling by, her heart surged. She was shocked by the way her mind was working, but she had already decided that she would take the initiative.

The following day Lady Lansbury tactfully removed herself from Lansbury House and returned to Chalfont with the sole purpose of giving Christopher the opportunity to court Jane. She didn't say as much but Christopher knew what she was about. However, he was pleasantly surprised when Jane suddenly presented herself on his doorstep on her way home from the exhibition, which was to open in two days.

He opened the door himself. Night was descending.

'Jane.' His first word was spoken quietly. He smiled and reached for her hand to draw her inside. In the dim light his eyes shone softly as he gazed down into hers. 'May I say how lovely it is to see you—although I'm not entirely surprised.'

'You're not?' she said, slipping out of her coat and handing it to him.

'Not really, although I thought you would be too occupied with the exhibition's opening to visit me. We are quite alone here.' His eyes caressed her. 'Even the butler has the night off, but then,' he said, his eyes dancing wickedly as he draped her coat over a chair, 'I suspect you already know that.'

'I do?' Her gaze was one of wide-eyed innocence.

He nodded. 'You and my mother are not as devious as you think you are. I have a notion that the two of you have entered into some kind of—conspiracy.'

'You have?' He nodded. 'Would it worry you if we had?'

'No, not in the slightest, although your Aunt Caroline might have something to say about it—considering your reputation and all that.'

'It's a little late for that, when you and I have known each other as well as it is possible for a man and woman to do.'

The house was strangely silent as Jane followed him across the hall to a small sitting room. He went without a word to the sideboard and poured a glass of wine. Returning to her, he offered her the goblet, standing close before her, desiring yet not daring to touch her just yet.

Jane took the glass with both hands and sipped from it while her eyes softly searched his face. The goblet was lowered and Jane's gaze followed as confusion filled her mind. She could find no word to break the spell. Christopher's hand came up and gently caressed her cheek. Taking the goblet from her, he set it aside.

'Come and sit down. Before anything else I want to talk to you. I should have done so before now, but—it was difficult.'

Drawing her down on to a sofa at angles to the fireplace, they sat facing each other. He was tense.

Christopher couldn't know how Jane had waited for this moment. 'What is it you want to say to me? What are you thinking about?'

Gradually his shoulders relaxed and the tension left his face. 'My father and the long traditions that automatically make a man lord and master in his own house, regardless of his competence—or incompetence.'

'But is that not how it is in every house?'

'Sadly, yes. The law decrees that any greedy, self-seeking fool is entitled to chance the well-being of his family on the outcome of a horse race, or wager their safety on the turn of a card. It's madness.'

Jane looked lovingly into his eyes. 'Please tell me about him, Christopher. I realise that you are entitled to your privacy and if you choose not to talk about it, it is your decision. But until you face what happened to you, you will never be at peace. Tell me why he made you so unhappy.'

Thinking of his father darkened his mood. 'Not only was he a scoundrel, the aura of power and patriarchal control he exerted over others terrified me as a child. The lives of ordinary, decent people are subject to the whims of such men as long as they happen to be a husband or father. A man such as that is at liberty to exploit his dependants as he sees fit, even if his children go hungry and his wife, who might well come to him with a private fortune, ends her days in poverty.'

'That is what inequality of the sexes means, I suppose. It does seem most unfair.'

'I agree. It leaves a man free to take full advantage of the many privileges of his sex, the family he so casually abuses no more free to question his authority than the menials who clean his boots.'

'It must have been difficult for you when he died.'

'When I discovered the enormity of the problem, I racked my brains for some way to pay the bank and the creditors. I was determined not to fall into formal bankruptcy. The idea was almost too painful to contemplate. All my life I have lived beneath the shadow of my father's gambling and debauchery. My whole life has been an attempt to prove I was not tainted. All these years I've tried to forget. I put the past behind a door in my mind and tried to keep it shut fast. But it was always there.'

Jane looked at his proud, lean face, moved by the pain that edged his voice. 'And you are still tortured by what he did to you. I can see that.'

'There have been times when the pain was so deep I couldn't bear to look at myself in the mirror. He inspired me with nothing but disgust. On his death my mother found her peace.'

'And you?'

'I felt a thankfulness that eased my soul. But

when I remember the nature of his death, the…' He faltered and stared off into the distance.

'What?' Jane prompted. 'What do you remember, Christopher? Tell me. Lay your demons to rest once and for all.'

When he continued his voice was flat and drained of feeling, as if he were telling someone else's story and not his own. 'He was a brute—like an animal, a dirty, lustful animal.' He checked himself with a firm tightening of his lips against bitter comments so long unexpressed. A lengthy silence fell between them, during which Jane sat by his side, still and silent. 'He almost killed my mother with his indiscriminate infidelities,' he went on, his voice fierce with remembrance. 'Octavia was conceived in anguish. It was a terrible time for my mother. When she was into her seventh month of pregnancy he—forced himself on her. Two weeks later she went into labour. It was a difficult birth. She blames my father for Octavia being born the way she is.'

'And you? What do you think?'

'That she is right.'

'What happened then?' she asked softly, sensing his despair. Her warm fingers slipped around his and gripped hard, giving him strength.

'I had to go and find the man I loathed as effectively as death itself.'

'What do you mean?'

'I was in London when a note was brought to the house asking me to go to a certain address—a brothel, to be precise. It said a gentleman who was known to me was in trouble. I knew it was my father.'

'You went?'

He nodded. 'He was already dead—a seizure of some sort.'

He fell silent, but Jane said nothing. She simply waited, afraid that if she spoke he would retreat behind that wall of his again—afraid that he would make some glib comment to change the subject and never tell her the rest.

'He didn't live to see Octavia.'

Jane was deeply moved. Her heart filled with compassion, she pressed her hand over her mouth, listening in anguished silence, her heart breaking for him.

'You mother... Does she know how—he...?'

'I couldn't tell her. How can you tell your mother something like that?'

Jane knew that what had happened would be a part of Christopher for ever—it was burned in his brain, sunk deep in his heart. It would remain as clear in his memory as though it had just happened.

'But—that wasn't the end of it, was it?' She hated prolonging his pain, but better to tell everything and put it behind them. It was the only way they could move on. 'No more secrets, Christopher. Tell me about the woman who hurt you so badly.'

Closing his eyes, his lips compressed in a tight line, he shook his head. But after a moment his body relaxed and he opened his eyes, resigned. 'Lily. Her name was Lily. She worked at Chalfont.'

'She was a servant?' He nodded. 'And she betrayed you with someone else?'

'Yes. My own father. I was eighteen years old. Lily was my first love and I adored her. I suppose I always knew there was no future for us together—but for those few months we were together she was mine and for the first time in my life I knew a happiness I could never have imagined. My father was touring abroad at the time. When he came back and he saw Lily he—he lost no time in seducing her.'

'And Lily?'

'Went to him willingly.' His lips twisted bitterly and hatred burned in his eyes at the memory. 'Why would she want the boy when she could have the master?' he uttered fiercely.

'What happened to her?'

'Eventually she went her own way. As to what became of her I really have no idea. She became dead to me the moment she climbed into my father's bed.'

'And you still carry your hurt and bitterness around your neck like a millstone.'

Christopher's smile was one of cynicism. 'Does it show all that much?'

'Sometimes.'

'There are some things, Jane, that cannot easily be put aside. When I first met you, you reminded me of Lily.'

'How? Do I look like her?'

'No, but you have the same colour eyes. For a time I held it against you, which was stupid of me. But I was on my guard. You were unsullied, untouched by another man, and that suddenly posed a threat, a danger to my peace of mind. You were dangerous because never having belonged to another man made you different, gave you added appeal. I had no wish to become shackled in that way to another woman ever again. I'd been there once and had no mind to travel down the same road twice.'

'And yet you still asked me to marry you.'

He gazed at her, thinking how wonderful she looked. She positively glowed with health. Lifting his hand, he traced the outline of her jaw, unconsciously looking for some trace of the young woman he had met on the boat from France, the woman with the inviting smile and warm violet eyes, the woman he had fallen in love with, although he had not known it then.

'When Lily left me I persuaded myself that I would never fall in love again, that I would have the strength of character to withstand such a debilitating emotion, but then I had not met you.'

'And now?'

'Everything is changed.'

'It is? How?' she asked, awaiting his answer with baited breath.

'When I gave you the roses it was the truest way of expressing my feelings that I could give you. I have fallen in love with you, I know that now. I think I have loved you from the day of my mother's birthday party. When I saw you with Octavia—showing her the horses and telling her not to be afraid—that was the first time I really saw you. I want you more than I have ever wanted anything in my life.'

'Oh, Christopher!' She threw her arms around

his neck. 'I was so afraid I would never hear you say that to me—that you love me as I love you—a love that has grown stronger and deeper the more I got to know you.'

'Never doubt it, Jane,' he murmured, his lips caressing her throat.

Jane's lips parted in a low, wordless moan as his arms went about her, folding her into his embrace and bringing her against his hard muscled chest. His mouth touched hers and tested the softness of her lips, playing, warming, rousing. A soft sigh escaped her as he took her hand. Drawing her to her feet, without a word he led her from the room and up the stairs to his softly illuminated bedchamber, where, without pause, he drew her inside and closed the door. Pressing a kiss on her lips, he traced a molten path downward to her neck, before standing back and indicating the majestic bed.

Jane smiled a tantalising smile. 'Why, it's a bed fit for a queen.' Her smile widened. 'What are we waiting for?'

Slipping out of her skirt and blouse and loosening her hair, she shook her head until her hair formed a shimmering canopy about her face, leaving on the delicate chemise for modesty—not that she would be wearing it for much longer as she watched Christopher begin to undress.

Stripped to the waist, Christopher leaned against the heavy foot post of his bed, his eyes like burning brands as he watched Jane saunter toward him, moving her hips with an undulating grace. Her ripe breasts pressed wantonly against the gossamer confines, rousing his senses to full awakening. Her bare feet seemed to glide over the carpet and her lips were bent upward in a totally wicked smile.

'Now what?' she asked, halting several feet away from him.

His heated gaze seared her and he beckoned with his words. 'Come to bed, Jane, and I will show you.'

Jane gave a deep, throaty laugh and placed her hand son his hard, flat belly, sliding them upward over his ribs and chest, caressingly, tauntingly, feeling the heavy thud of his heart beneath her palm.

'I remember how manly you are, my lord,' she murmured as his hands came upon her waist. A low groan sounded deep in her. Slowly, deliberately, she leaned against him, first her lips and then the peaks of thinly clad breasts, rousing his hot blood to boiling as the heat of her touched him.

'Jane, Jane,' Christopher said and folded her in

his arms, crushing her to him and bending to cover her soft, reaching mouth with his. They stumbled and fell atop the bed. Jane rose above him slightly. Staring into those hungry silver eyes, she lowered her head to kiss him long and ardently. His hands moved to her waist, and the chemise fell loose. A tug at the ties of her bodice and it was off her shoulders. Jane crouched on her knees above him, tempting him with a kiss, an intimate touch, until Christopher rolled, pulling her beneath him. Then with fierce, naked abandon he possessed her, sweeping her with him to breathless spiralling heights.

Climbing out of the depths of sleep, Christopher woke as if from a trance, for one brief, haunting moment fearing that he had dreamed it all. But then he felt Jane's soft, warm body entwined with his, her slender thigh pressed against his, her lovely curving form nestled close, the fragrance of her perfume filling his brain, and he relaxed.

The memory of her passion fanned the fires in his mind. She tempted him with her arms, with her softness, with her lips, and had made love to him without shame. They had come together with a heat that melted them into one, each oblivious of everything but the other. All that had gone before was dimmed in the brilliance of the union. Her effect on him was total and complete—devastating when wanting her only led him to frustration and agony of mind and body, beautiful when they joined in love and she was his.

'Once is pardonable. Twice is a downright sin,' she whispered, placing soft kisses on his shoulder. 'Now I will have to marry you.'

Christopher's breath caught in his throat. 'You turned me down.'

'I've changed my mind.' Leaving off kissing him, she peered up at him. 'You do still want to marry me, don't you, Christopher?'

'Want you? Dear Lord, Jane, that is all I want.'

Holding her face away from his she smiled—a warm, tender smile that swelled and lifted Christopher's heart to see. 'Well then, now that has been said we'd better get on with it—just in case.'

'In case of what?'

'The result of this night is a child. We cannot risk a scandal. That would never do.'

Christopher laughed and gathered her naked form close, thinking what an absolute delight she was to him. 'I hope there is a child. Nothing would make me happier—except, of course, to have you as my adorable wife, lying beside me every night of our lives. Are you sure you want to marry me? You are going to a life which is different from anything you have known.'

'I know that, but I've never been more sure of anything in my whole life. I fell in love with you the first time we met. The hardest thing of all was trying not to show it.'

He laughed softly, but his look turned wistful. He wound a length of her hair around his finger. 'I cannot believe this is real—that you are real, that this is happening. Because if it's all a dream, I don't want to wake up.'

'It's real.' She searched his eyes. 'I love you, Christopher. Had you said you loved me when you asked me to marry you the first time, I would have accepted then. But I had told myself from a very young age that I would not marry a man who did not love me. I would settle for nothing less. But now you do, so that makes me happy, and—' she smiled '—we have a wedding to plan.'

'I agree. As soon as it can be arranged. Although I must warn you that my mother will suggest that it takes place at Chalfont.'

'I have no objections to that. In fact, I cannot think of any other place where I would rather be married.'

'When?'

'Christmas would be nice. It will give me the opportunity to help Finn with the exhibition. He intends to leave for Greece after that, but I am sure I can persuade him to stay a while longer. He's the closest I have to a father and I would like him to give me away. Do you have any objections to that?'

'If that is what you want, then it is all right with me, Jane.' He touched her lips with his own. 'A Christmas wedding it will be.'

The rest of the night was passed in slow and wordless love and exploration, finding again each other's body, and, towards dawn, had touched each other's soul. Lying together, Jane held him in her arms, a dreaming Adonis in all his pagan splendour. She touched his cheek, gently, and his hand rose to hers. Taking it, he placed a kiss in its palm.

'I love you,' he whispered, holding her in his arms, glorying at what was happening between them. He had never experienced anything like the tangible bond their lovemaking had wrought, so warm and tender yet strong between them.

He had not had a life before Jane. In coming together he felt reborn.

Epilogue

It was a time of excitement and great rejoicing at Chalfont. With a wedding to arrange for Boxing Day as well as to help Lady Lansbury and Octavia decorate the house for Christmas, Jane arrived one week before the festivities. Christopher was in London and was to travel to Chalfont with Aunt Caroline and Finn the day before Christmas Eve.

Winter spread across the countryside like ripples on a pond. Jane's airy laughter and light, ever-ready humour infected everyone at Chalfont. With her presence, it seemed the sun shone brighter. Hearts were lightened and everyone attacked the Christmas preparations with a zealous determination.

When Christopher finally arrived, snow had started to fall. Jane was outside the house when the carriage finally appeared in the drive. Christopher was the first to climb out and turned to help his guests before gathering Jane to him.

Lady Lansbury ushered Caroline and Finn into the house, but Jane and Christopher held back.

With his arm about her he tilted her chin. 'Happy?'

'I couldn't be more so.' The smile she gave him confirmed her statement. 'I love this house.'

'That's the effect it has on everyone.'

Taking her hand, he linked it through the crook of his arm and they entered the house through the large oak doors. There was a log fire blazing in the enormous fireplace, baskets of pine cones in the hearth and garlands of berried evergreens, mistletoe, holly and ivy decorated the hall.

Aunt Caroline gasped. 'Oh, how beautiful it looks. And just look at that tree,' she said, moving closer to the tall fir tree which was the centrepiece of the decorations. She stood next to Octavia, who was looking up at the fairy with wondrous awe.

Surrounded by a multitude of gifts, the tree was planted in a brightly decorated tub and secured at its pinnacle was a beautiful golden-haired fairy in a gold dress and wings and holding a wand. The tree was decorated with tinsel and beautiful ornaments, reflecting the light of a multitude of brilliantly lit little tapers, a servant on hand with a wet sponge to guard against fire.

'We usually have the tree in the drawing room,' Lady Lansbury explained. 'But Jane thought how nice it would be to have it in the hall where it can be seen by everyone who comes to the house. I have to agree it's an improvement. Now you must have a glass of hot punch to warm you up before going to your rooms to prepare for dinner.'

Christmas Eve was one of those winter days that lift the heart. The snow that had been falling throughout the night had stopped. The sky was a wide expanse of azure blue and the day so clear that one could see for miles. Serviceably attired in warm coats, colourful scarves and hats pulled down over their ears to combat the elements, dragging toboggans and floundering happily in the deep snow, Christopher and Jane took Octavia to a hill in the park.

With much hilarity they sledged for half an hour before abandoning the toboggans to build a snowman, which ended when Christopher engaged his rosy-cheeked companions in a snowball fight. Shrieking with laughter, Jane and Octavia managed to get Christopher on his back, where he begged for mercy as Jane stuffed snow down his collar before he pulled her down on top of him and kissed her soundly.

When all three were thoroughly wet, they returned to the house to change into dry clothes.

There were guests in the evening—neighbours and friends. The long gallery came alive and began to function. After many years of austerity it took on an air of being something more than an empty room hung with ancestral portraits. A fire had been lighted, a buffet supper was served and musicians played. Dancers swirled by, leaving scents of lavender and rose water in their wake.

Christopher drew Jane into the dancing, sliding his hand around her waist and drawing her possessively close. The soft music filled the gallery with long, warm cords that drifted around them, enfolding them in a bouquet of whispers and soft caresses.

'How are you enjoying your first Christmas in England?'

'I am so happy I can't believe it's true. I feel as if I am dreaming and any moment now I shall wake up. I can't believe that the day after tomorrow I will be your wife.'

'Believe it, my darling,' he murmured, staring down at the glorious temptress in his arms.

Along the length of the gallery the pair danced. Christopher swept his wife-to-be in a waltz that was sometimes rent with laughter as they made their own steps. They whispered sweet inanities, talked of dreams, hopes and other things, as lovers are wont to do.

The excitement of the evening was when a small group of strolling carollers arrived. They stood outside with their lanterns and rendered all the well-loved carols—'O Come All Ye Faithful' and 'Once in Royal David's City' and many more—with everyone joining in.

Afterwards Octavia helped Jane and Lady Lansbury hand round mulled wine and mince pies.

When the carollers and the guests had departed for their homes, everyone retired to the drawing room where gifts were unwrapped amid expressions of delight.

There was a moment when they sat roasting chestnuts, drinking port wine and laughing late into the evening, when the atmosphere was warm and welcoming, that Jane felt a moment of melancholy because her father wasn't with her. Gazing into the distance, she immersed herself in the nostalgic memories of Christmases past. She glanced at Finn, who, sensing her mood, raised his glass and said, 'To absent friends.'

Jane smiled. 'Yes, to absent friends.'

Christmas Day dawned and delicious smells of cinnamon, apple and roasting meats emanating from the kitchen filled the house. Unlike Christmas Eve it was a quiet day. Everyone went to church and afterwards there was the traditional Christmas dinner with turkey and all the trimmings followed by Christmas pudding brought ablaze to the table. It was a happy, relaxed time, with everyone's mind on the wedding of Christopher and Jane the next day.

Boxing Day came at last and Jane and Christopher were married in a private ceremony at the Chalfont village church. Octavia was Jane's sole bridesmaid, in a taffeta light-blue dress adorned with ruffles and ribbons, a white fur stole about her shoulders and carrying a small bouquet, a smile stretched from ear to ear. She was excited and so very happy that Jane was to live at Chalfont, that she would be her sister and never again would she leave. Lady Lansbury and Jane's Aunt

Caroline exchanged soft-hearted looks. They were both suffused with happiness at the way things had turned out.

When Christopher turned to look at Jane walking slowly towards him on Finn's arm, all coherent thought left his head. Her gown was cream satin and lace and she looked breathtakingly beautiful. She looked like a queen. The fabric clung like skin to her slender body. The neckline was square cut, outlining her breasts, following her trim waist to her hips, the train flaring out to heavy, shimmering folds to brush the stone flags as she walked. Her entire body seemed to gleam and then Christopher realised that the cloth had been sewn with hundreds of tiny glass beads.

Her hair was unbound, curling about her back and shoulders, her face aglow with happiness, and her beautiful violet eyes were fixed on Christopher. Loving him.

Christopher had not known it was possible to feel like this. Now that he did, he would never look at his friends with puzzlement and envy again. Jane was his life and he knew he would never regret leaving behind his lonely bachelorhood.

She had reached him, touched him in places he hadn't known existed. His gaze slid over her, lingering, wanting to undress her slowly, taking his time.

'Am I allowed to kiss my bride?' he asked Finn, who had taken time off from the exhibition, which was attracting a great deal of interest.

Taking Jane's hand, Finn handed it to Christopher, his eyes wrinkling with a broad smile, happy that his friend's daughter had found happiness with the man of her choice.

'Patience,' Finn told the younger man. 'In a moment you can kiss your wife.'

Christopher smiled at his bride, a wicked gleam in his eyes. 'Even better.'

Hiding his own smile, the priest began to say the words that would join them together. Afterwards he said, 'Now you may kiss the bride.'

With his thumb, Christopher tilted her chin and met her eyes, knowing there was nothing more beautiful in the world than what he saw in their warm, dark depths.

'My wife,' he whispered, lowering his mouth to hers.

* * * * *